The Candidate

Middle East Literature in Translation
Michael Beard and Adnan Haydar, *Series Editors*

SELECT TITLES FROM MIDDLE EAST LITERATURE IN TRANSLATION

All Faces but Mine: The Poetry of Samih Al-Qasim
Abdulwahid Lu'lu'a, trans.

Arabs and the Art of Storytelling: A Strange Familiarity
Abdelfattah Kilito; Mbarek Sryfi and Eric Sellin, trans.

The Desert: Or, The Life and Adventures of Jubair Wali al-Mammi
Albert Memmi; Judith Roumani, trans.

Felâtun Bey and Râkım Efendi: An Ottoman Novel
Ahmet Midhat Efendi; Melih Levi and Monica M. Ringer, trans.

Gilgamesh's Snake and Other Poems
Ghareeb Iskander; John Glenday and Ghareeb Iskander, trans.

My Torturess
Bensalem Himmich; Roger Allen, trans.

The Perception of Meaning
Hisham Bustani; Thoraya El-Rayyes, trans.

32
Sahar Mandour; Nicole Fares, trans.

The Candidate

A NOVEL

ZAREH VORPOUNI

Translated from the Western Armenian
by Jennifer Manoukian and Ishkhan Jinbashian

Syracuse University Press

The publication of this book was made possible in part by a grant from the Department of Middle Eastern, South Asian, and African Studies (MESAAS) and the Fesjian Fund at Columbia University.

Syracuse University Press
Syracuse, New York 13244-5290

First Edition 2016

16 17 18 19 20 21 6 5 4 3 2 1

Originally published in Western Armenian as Թեկնածուն (Beirut: Sevan, 1967).

∞ The paper used in this publication meets the minimum requirements of the American National Standard for Information Sciences—Permanence of Paper for Printed Library Materials, ANSI Z39.48-1992.

For a listing of books published and distributed by Syracuse University Press, visit www.SyracuseUniversityPress.syr.edu.

ISBN: 978-0-8156-3468-3 (paperback) 978-0-8156-5379-0 (e-book)

Library of Congress Cataloging-in-Publication Data

Names: Vorpouni, Zareh, author. | Manoukian, Jennifer, translator. | Chinpashean, Ishkhan, translator.
Title: The candidate : a novel / Zareh Vorpouni ; translated from the Western Armenian by Jennifer Manoukian and Ishkhan Jinbashian.
Other titles: Tegnatzun. English
Description: First edition. | Syracuse, New York : Syracuse University Press, 2016. | Series: Middle East literature in translation | Includes bibliographical references.
Identifiers: LCCN 2016028141 (print) | LCCN 2016028163 (ebook) | ISBN 9780815634683 (pbk. : alk. paper) | ISBN 9780815653790 (e-book)
Classification: LCC PK8549.V67 T4413 2016 (print) | LCC PK8549.V67 (ebook) | DDC 891/.99235—dc23
LC record available at https://lccn.loc.gov/2016028141

Manufactured in the United States of America

Contents

Acknowledgments

THIS TRANSLATION is the epitome of diasporic mobilization, drawing on the knowledge and know-how of experts and friends—some even of Vorpouni himself—throughout the Armenian diaspora. Many thanks to Carole Allamand, Lusiné Kerobyan, Christina Lalama, Kristyn Manoukian, Vartan Matiossian, Linda Ravul, and Asbed Vassilian on the East Coast; Talar Chahinian on the West Coast; Razmik Panossian of the Calouste Gulbenkian Foundation and Marc Nichanian in Portugal; Boris Adjemian of the AGBU Bibliothèque Nubar, Krikor Beledian, G. M. Goshgarian, Louise Lacroix, Andrew Stearns, and Houry Varjabédian in France; Haroutiun Kurkjian in Greece; Lilit Avagyan in Armenia; and Daniel Ohanian in Turkey.

A special thank you to Suzanne Guiod and Michael Beard at Syracuse University Press for welcoming a novel in Western Armenian into their Middle East Literature in Translation series for the very first time.

Translator's Introduction

To my Armenian professor, Asbed Vassilian

I FIRST CAME ACROSS Zareh Vorpouni's name in a footnote, where some of the most promising literary tidbits seem to languish. His name did not start flashing on the page, nor was I visited by the inexplicable sense of familiarity I often feel when I first read about a writer with whom I will come to spend more of my nights and weekends than any living, breathing human being. In fact, his name meant nothing to me—or to most anyone else, as I would soon learn—but the description of his defiant generation of French Armenian writers seemed as if it might end my search for the irreverent, experimental, and countercultural in Western Armenian literature, while at the same time satisfy the Francophilia that afflicts me.

In the 1930s, Zareh Vorpouni belonged to a group of writers that congregated in Paris, the center of Western Armenian intellectual life between the wars, around a literary journal called Մենք (Menk).[1] The group comprised young men who had fled Constantinople for Paris in the aftermath of the Armenian genocide and in advance of the founding of the Turkish Republic, and it led to a cultural revival that focused on the development of the novel, the examination of diasporic identities in literature, and the cultivation of Western Armenian as a literary language.

In the Ottoman Empire, Western Armenian was the standardized language used by the intellectual elite, many of whom were killed during the first phase of the genocide in 1915. The language, along with its speakers, fled into the diaspora, where it often came into fierce competition with the language of the host country.[2] Even in Constantinople, the cultural capital of Armenians in the Ottoman Empire, Western Armenian literature was teetering on the brink of death after the war. In an attempt at revitalization during the Allied occupation of the city, a surviving cadre of Ottoman-era writers worked to create a group of young men who had the linguistic dexterity and cultural consciousness needed to continue the Western Armenian literary tradition. Among these young men were Zareh Vorpouni, Nigoghos Sarafian, and Shahan Shahnour.[3]

Despite the expectation that they would bear the legacy of the old guard, Vorpouni and his contemporaries deliberately broke with their predecessors in theme and form, staging an outright rebellion against them. "We wanted to flatten them. That was our way of revolting. I think this sense of revolt was in the hearts of all of us and it was this revolt that created our literature against these honchos [*bonzes*]," said Vorpouni during an interview in 1978.[4] Their invention of new literary standards and their impulse to represent the new realities of the diaspora challenged the conservatism of the Armenian community, creating a fleeting period in which brazen interrogations of nationalism, clericalism, and sexuality became the norm in literature.

Whereas most of his peers lost their momentum after World War II, Vorpouni spent the second half of the twentieth century at the height of his creativity. His writing spurt in the 1960s and 1970s, however, coincided with the decline of Western Armenian. The diaspora was losing its ability, and its inclination, to read fiction in Western Armenian, especially experimental fiction that called into question accepted elements of diasporic Armenian culture. Consequently, Vorpouni's novels were read only by a dwindling number of literary-minded readers who were concentrated in the intellectual centers of Beirut, Istanbul, and Paris.

In the whole of the Armenian diaspora, Vorpouni's influence was marginal, but within his coterie of followers he was praised for his attempt to modernize the Western Armenian novel. Vorpouni integrated elements of French literary and theoretical currents, most notably the *nouveau roman* and theories of textuality, to produce a cultural melding unique in the history of Western Armenian literature. This is not to say that Vorpouni's work was a calque or derivative of his French contemporaries, but that he saw no use in aspiring to the cultural ideal within the Armenian diaspora that understood the acceptance of the "foreign" as culturally corrosive. Rather than pretend to work in a cultural vacuum in which only the "authentic" Armenian existed, thereby indulging the tendency to exalt the past, Vorpouni resisted tired tropes and nostalgia to affirm the constructiveness of the natural interplay of cultures in the diaspora. In other words, he wrote about the realities of diasporic life, rather than about a delusive ideal.

In *The Candidate*, published in 1967 in Beirut, Vorpouni's indirect apprenticeship with an eclectic collection of French avant-gardists (e.g., Georges Bataille, Maurice Blanchot, Marcel Proust, Paul Valéry, and Paul Verlaine) manifests itself structurally and thematically. The renegades of Western Armenian literature (e.g., Vahan Tekeyan and Taniel Varoujan) also make cameos in the novel, along with allusions to European intellectual giants, signaling not an aspirational yearning to be perceived as European, as it may come across in translation, but an assertion that the "foreign" can complement, rather than threaten, the Armenian.

Despite the rare depictions of diasporic Armenians in literature, readers should resist the urge to see *The Candidate* as "ethnic literature," designed to introduce them to a people and a culture. Vorpouni wrote the novel in a kind of secret language, an ethno-national language that few beyond those born into Armenian families take the pains to learn. The privacy of an ethno-national language like Western Armenian assumes a certain shared understanding of history and culture that sidesteps the need for explanation or didacticism in literature. Now, in translation, it is tempting to put Vorpouni's novel at the service of understanding the "Armenian psyche," but the original was not meant to *teach* its readers anything about the Armenian people. Above all, *The Candidate* should be seen as a work of fiction, a work of art that, like any other, seeks to muse on the anguishes, joys, and invisibilia of human existence. The novel is not a solutions manual for its intricacies, but an invitation to introspection and contemplation.

After the novel, readers will find Marc Nichanian's afterword, "Zareh Vorpouni's *The Candidate*: Testimony, Sacrifice, and Forgiveness," which reflects on three themes the work can offer to introspective and contemplative readers. Nichanian examines the singularity of the novel within the Western Armenian literary tradition and, through his analysis, exposes the range of academic disciplines to which it can add its insights, namely trauma studies, reconciliation studies, and narratology. He situates the book within its sociopolitical context and spurs readers to consider the contemporary lessons that can be gleaned from *The Candidate*.

This translation is the result of a transcontinental collaboration between me in New Jersey and Ishkhan Jinbashian in California. In 2000, Ishkhan translated *The Candidate* for Marc Nichanian's Armenian literature seminar at Columbia University. In an unexpected twist, I learned of Ishkhan's unpublished translation as I was working on my own draft in 2014. In the end, we decided to combine our versions and work together to overcome the complexities of translating Vorpouni.

Together, we fought to scale the novel's sharp changes in register. Because of the narrative's absence of linearity, in the span of one paragraph, Vorpouni can leap from metaphysical meanderings in a refined, almost lyrical, language to crass dialogue, complete with colloquial interjections, slurs, and idiomatic expressions.

Together, we strove to convey the levels of intimacy and formality between which the letters in the novel vacillate. We faced a particular challenge in the limited number of ways to open a formal letter in English compared to the variety in Western Armenian. This limitation was made all the more difficult by Vorpouni's explicit examination of these levels of formality in the text itself.

Together, we sought to be hypermeticulous about keeping our word choice consistent. In the novel, Vorpouni has a habit of doing away with narrative conventions to offer metacommentary on the process of writing. At times, he picks apart his own writing and returns to certain phrasing and ideas—sometimes even to mock their banality—at different points throughout the book, making consistency crucial.

Strokes of serendipity have led to each of my translation projects—one from a book poking out of a perfectly aligned row, another from a casual comment about a writer during an hours-long conversation, and now this one from a digressive footnote. From this footnote has emerged a translation that resists, much like in the spirit of the original. It resists the isolation and insularity of literature written in a minority language; it resists the idea that culture in diaspora is fossilized, stagnant, or in decline; and it resists the notion that Armenians have only their century-old plight to offer the world outside their national cocoon.

JENNIFER MANOUKIAN
February 2016

The Candidate

Malheur à qui scandalise les enfants!
—Matthew 18:6

C'est pourquoi il n'y a pas de crime
plus horrible que de souiller le cœur
des enfants.
—Paul Claudel,
L'oiseau noir sous le soleil levant

Dear Mademoiselle Arshalouys,

Vahakn is dead.

Yes, Vahakn is dead. Today, a police car took his body to the morgue. If no one comes to claim it after two days, the morgue will probably turn it over to a medical school. The Church didn't want anything to do with a suicide. I forgot to mention that Vahakn killed himself. Yesterday, when I came back to my room after work, I found Vahakn lying on the floor. At first, I thought he was just reading, since newspaper was laid out all around him. But then I noticed the pool of cold blood. He had slit the veins in his left wrist with a razor blade and rested his hand on a bed of newspaper. Then, if the peaceful expression frozen on his face is any indication, he waited calmly for death to come.

Here we are then, dear mademoiselle. I've done my duty. At least I think I have. These past few days Vahakn wouldn't stop talking about you. Now I know that he was subtly asking me to contact you.

Please accept my heartfelt condolences, dear mademoiselle.

Minas Yerazian
Paris
April 24, 1927

PS: *My address is on the envelope.*

He let out a sigh of relief as he dropped the letter into the mailbox and found that he felt lighter after ridding himself of that heavy burden. All night long he had tortured himself trying to find the right tone for the letter and now he was satisfied with the telegraphic form it had taken. The letter seemed more official that way, as if it were a war dispatch: *Private so-and-so has died for his country* or *private so-and-so is missing in action.* Yet he felt that he had ceded a bit too much to his emotions. Despite his hope that the letter would seem detached, he had only managed to stifle their intensity, not erase them entirely. Yes, compared to his earlier drafts, the letter was neater and quite a bit shorter. But it seemed to him that it was left in a way that required a response, despite the great effort he had taken to avoid just that. He had worked that whole night in a room where the memory of the dead was still fresh, still warm even. It was as though he were still there, alive, lying on the wood floor and giving orders from the dead, as though he were guiding the tip of the pen across the paper, composing the words just the way he wanted with an insistence unique only to the dead. Minas started the letter over and over again and the pile of crumpled paper he tossed onto the floor grew bigger and bigger. It was at that point that he decided to leave his room and come here to one of the cafés in Les Halles, where he felt that the commotion protected him from the meddling of the dead. The workday had already begun. The comings and goings of sellers and shoppers thundered through the streets, and in the flood of light, the antagonizing presence of the dead became impossible to sense, turning into a distant, and now somewhat enchanting, echo. Here he managed to finish the letter and immediately got up to drop it in the mailbox. It was only then that Minas could let out a sigh of relief, shed the burden, and shake free from the memory that oppressed him. He had barely taken a few steps from the mailbox when he stopped short. He wanted to go back and get the letter, but it was too late. It was too late to get the letter, but still too early to go to work. The clock on the façade of Saint Eustache had just chimed five o'clock, the sounds undulating and conjuring up the distress signals of a ship lost in the fog on a cold autumn morning, far out on the open sea. He had until six o'clock. It didn't take more than fifteen minutes to get to work near Grands Boulevards. He took a longer route than usual and passed through the heaps of produce that crowded the streets and square, breathing in the smell of fruits and vegetables that had mingled in the air. He changed his course once again near the Louvre and came to the wide, tree-lined path along the river, where carts as big as ships rumbled past, rushing to the capital the last fruits of the fall, dusty from their northern journey. From there, he walked to the Jardin des Tuileries, passed in front of the Comédie-Française, and took Avenue de l'Opéra until he reached the opera house itself. By then, the morning papers had already arrived. He picked up a copy and walked as he read under the streetlights, getting to work exactly at six. Walking distracted him from his thoughts, which filled the corridors of his mind like uninvited guests. Since finding Vahakn dead, it had been impossible to keep his thoughts at bay. His mind had not been able to function as it had before, but now that the letter was sent, he settled down and his brain allowed a tangle of thoughts to rush in. He stopped and leaned against the wall along the swollen waters of the Seine. A faint murmur passed through the air. The coolness rising off the water struck his face and he felt as though he had just been jolted awake. He hadn't slept at all that night and fatigue had numbed his brain. The sound of a motor caught his attention as it traveled through the lead-colored water. A barge had already arrived at the bridge and, lowering its smoke stack, it passed underneath like a man bowing his head to avoid low branches. A boyish exhilaration seemed to sprout in his chest as he watched the ship head toward Île de la Cité, following the right bank to Notre Dame, then to Asnières or Melun, and maybe even farther, crossing rivers and seas to foreign lands. The noise dissipated, and the water, which for a moment was cleaved in the barge's wake, healed to resume the secret whisperings that would soon blend into the uproar of the day. Minas continued on his way. If he wanted to keep surrendering to the early morning spell of the river, he would need to take a shortcut to make it to work on time.

He started to walk faster to make up for the lost time. And maybe to avoid feeling time pass, he started to go over the letter in his head. The whole night his brain had been so hazy, so scattered, yet the letter was somehow etched in his mind from beginning to end. But he couldn't get past the first line. How could he have written something so stupid? "Have I lost my mind?" he said to himself, smacking his forehead. "Have you gone crazy, Minas? Don't you know what you've done? How are you going to get out of this *now*?" He knew it was possible to get a letter back from the post office, but by the time he finished work, the letter would already be halfway there. Impatient and upset, Minas felt his heart tighten. He sensed that there was no fixing this big mistake of his. Just then he started to run after the train. There was no other way. The train whistled as it sped up, free and unencumbered, belching clouds of smoke and fumes into the open air. It charged forward into the distance, which it devoured inch by inch, neighing and whinnying like thousands upon thousands of horses. The earth trembled, terrified by its thrusts. Minas caught his breath for a moment and regained his sense of calm. The way the train cars were arranged on the Dijon-bound platform made them look like an army of hostages. The train panted slowly, as though forbidden from making a sound. Once Minas caught up to it and pulled himself onto the back of the train, it suddenly started moving again. The train was now speeding away on a rampage, laughing and taunting the crazy fellow who had the audacity to start racing it.

When Minas looked up and saw the Jardin des Tuileries around him, he felt as though he had just been pulled out of a dream. Shoulders hunched, he looked like a little boy who had just been beaten. It already seemed like he had walked into a trap. With the very first word of the letter, he had given that girl the chance to snare him. And why wouldn't she? What would she have to fear now that she had lost her lover? Now here she has his friend standing in front of her with his arms open wide, saying "Dear Mademoiselle Arshalouys," as if it were some kind of plea, some kind of invitation. Vahakn is gone; but don't worry, I'm here. "Dear madam," as he had written in the first draft, would have been just fine. Yes, that way would have been safer. So what point was there in using her name? "Dear Mademoiselle Arshalouys." The first version had a restrained, neutral air to it. It was cold and distant, like the instinctively self-conscious tone of the last paragraph, in which he had opted to write only "mademoiselle," since it was her name that disrupted everything. It was her name that corrupted the official tone of the "dear," appearing almost ingratiating and clinging to the name as if in an attempt to possess her. It might as well have read "My Arshalouys." Why hadn't he realized that the union of adjective and noun introduced into the sentence an emotional intimacy, despite the particular care he took to steer clear of just that?

As if this weren't enough, the envelope read "Mademoiselle Arshalouys Aghvorigian, Usine de Papier, Lancet, Isère." In an official letter, the recipient's first name would never be used. It would imply a certain closeness, which might even be read as off-putting. Isn't this why, in the top right-hand corner of a letter, under the date, we write the recipient's first name, last name, and address? As for the letter itself, we would start it with a simple "sir" or "madam." At most, we might throw in a "dear" or something more formal. He burst into laughter, but didn't understand why he was laughing; just that it put him in a good mood. He found some of his old cheerfulness and teased himself—in his own head, of course—about going over the nonsense he had written. No, the last thing he needed was to be seen talking to himself on the street, even if it was empty at that hour.

Now and then people would rush past, the sidewalk rumbling like an empty barrel under their feet. At that moment, the street—like a watchdog opening and closing its eyes—would wake up with a start, only to lazily fall back asleep. Most of the people on the street were busboys, waiters, or cleaners who worked in banks or government buildings. In their haste, none of them had time to care about Minas's mindless laughter. As they glided almost surreally like shadows through the shadows, his laughter boldly twisted into the sound of their footsteps and the sound of the trees along the boulevard that were beating the stone façades of the buildings, echoing and lingering in his ears. Her name—so undesirable, yet enlivened, nourished, and enriched by the association of ideas—had become an entire world in which he—Minas Yerazian—was being held prisoner. Of course, Arshalouys—Dawn—is a beautiful name. Yes, beautiful. He could admit to himself that it was in fact a beautiful name, undeniably beautiful, and no doubt it was because of its beauty that it had forced itself out of Minas's pen. Out of his pen, mind you, not out of him. There was a distinction to be made and in the distinction was the reason he didn't feel the need to chide himself. The pen was at fault, plain and simple. Be that as it may, the problem lay elsewhere. The problem was that her name and the halo that hovered over it worked its secret charms on him and drove him to defend himself against the laughter, which the passersby thought mindless, but which, through the underhanded and stubbornly persistent bidding of the name, was like a dagger cutting into its charm. The laughter swelled on its own and grew with a feverish desire to expel the name, but the word—stubborn and simple like the beauty of dawn itself—could barely stifle it in a powerless attempt at self-defense. And then, all of a sudden, he stopped. Why hadn't he thought of this earlier? True, in life, some law of irony dictates that things usually mean their opposite. The name Aghvorigian does not necessarily imply that the person bearing it is *aghvor* or *aghvorig*.[1] He once knew a French woman, Madame Lebœuf, who was as lovely as a doe and wore a bright smile across her thin, red lips, whereas Monsieur Lechat, the supervisor at a house where Minas once worked, barked like a dog all day.

What if it wasn't like that and Arshalouys turned out to be a dark-eyed or fiery-eyed Armenian girl? Who knows? Perhaps that principle doesn't apply to the Armenians as it does to the French. Vahakn had good taste. He couldn't bear ugliness. The proof was in his impossible coexistence with it in his own life. It was this thought that sent a jolt through Minas's heart. Nicole came to mind. Nicole, the object of his affection, was the dream that fed his thoughts and made him run through the streets of Paris in his free time. Minas couldn't imagine the streets without Nicole. They didn't dream without her and Minas passed through them feeling hollow, like a dry leaf that the slightest breeze could make sway back and forth, sad and lifeless.

He had already reached Opéra. He had left behind the long, wide boulevard, but it seemed to follow him, teasing him all throughout the walk. The kiosk in front of Café de la Paix was open. He bought a newspaper and kept walking. Without reading it, he tucked the newspaper under his arm and continued on with his head hung, sighing. Work hadn't even begun and fatigue was already weighing on him. More than fatigue, it was the burden that weighed on him—that small envelope with just a half-page letter inside felt so heavy. Thoughts must have their own weight to them, he mused, and in comparison, the idea of working seemed lighter. He picked up the pace, but soon stopped short again. He finally made his decision: "I'll write another letter tonight to let her know that obviously there would be no use in replying to the first one." With this, his steps grew lighter as he headed toward the corner of Rue du Faubourg-Montmartre, a few steps away from the hotel where he worked.

The hotel was on a dead-end street. At one time, it had probably been the home of an aristocrat. Bas-reliefs framed the windows and on both sides of the door rose pillars crowned with caryatids who took the entire weight of the hotel onto their shoulders, though their faces bore no trace of their burden. On the contrary, they seemed to take pleasure in their responsibility. It seemed that, at the time, maybe a century or so ago, the people who had had the door built valued work, or at least hoped it could be a source of satisfaction, like when people make a toast as they take a sip of wine. This was not an illusion, because you only needed to say the word and the caryatids would immediately start singing. Maybe they would even dance, too, or sing as they danced or danced as they sang. It didn't matter which. It was as if from morning till night for a century, all they had been doing was waiting for the order and pretending the wait didn't exhaust them in any way. Maybe the very right to feel exhaustion was denied to them from the start by the house's first owners. The temperament of the caryatids hadn't been enough; the owners sought and found a stirring kind of contentment in silence. It must be said that they couldn't have done a better job of creating that kind of environment. Whenever the four arms of the front door trembled and the silence, crouching in the foyer, fled up the stairs in terror, nobody knew where it went. But as soon as the door stopped trembling, the silence would return and carefully reclaim its place, guarding its surroundings like a dog stretched out and resting its snout on its paws, so that the next time it couldn't be tricked. The employees were also careful to speak in whispers, fearing the vengeance of the silence. Here silence was not an abstraction. It was palpable to the extreme, if not almost visible. Seen from the outside through the glass windowpanes on the front door, the interior of the hotel was an aquarium filled not with water, but with silence. Whatever it was, Minas owed his success to that silence. When he saw a woman coming down the stairs—inching step by step into the lake of silence and growing taller and more stately with each step—Minas, shy as he was, felt his tongue fall back into his throat and land in his stomach. In that moment, he couldn't have guessed that that slight woman—yes, slight, though she had seemed so tall as she was coming down the stairs—would become his teacher in love. At that time, Minas was still an inexperienced boy who blushed when he spoke to women, at best managing to mutter, "Your cheeks are the color of trout," like he had once told a girl selling fish in Marseille.

As the woman stood in front of him, barely reaching his chin, and stared up at him with olive-shaped pupils, he yearned to say, "Your eyes are like black lights," had his tongue not disappeared into his throat.

He realized that she was talking to him: "Are you the one Apkar told me about?"

He couldn't answer. He only managed a grimace, before the concierge came up and said: "Maybe he doesn't understand French, Madame. You know they're foreigners."

She shot the concierge a harsh look and puffed out her lips: "Shush, be quiet!"

Minas finally regained the power of speech. As the woman was reprimanding the concierge, Minas detected some concern for him. He told her that he didn't really know anything about the work.

"Don't worry," she said. "Apkar will show you. It's nothing, really. Tomorrow at six, then. Six on the dot."

For the first time, he was fifteen minutes late.

"'That bitch has already been in and out," Apkar told him, as he walked into the kitchen.

"Already?" Minas said, indifferently. Now it seemed that nothing could be more upsetting than what had happened in those past few hours.

"Be careful," Apkar warned him. "Don't be fooled by her kindness. One day, out of the blue, she could give you the slip and send you packing."

He was a strange guy, that Apkar. He was funny and lighthearted, but there was always something mocking in his laughter. It was as if words to him were like arrows that, once they had been shot into the air, sniffed around in search of a chest to pierce. He saw evil and filth in everything except his own laughter, which oozed bile every time he posited an opinion on humanity and raised his fist above his head to shriek obscenely: "Long live the Revolution!" After these incidents, Apkar would cool down and relax. He felt satisfaction in having taken revenge. Nobody knew on whom. His laughter bulged and widened, distorting the muscles in his craggy, hideous face, which lit up to almost become beautiful. On the street, Minas, pretending to be busy lighting a cigarette, would often let Apkar, always in motion, walk ahead of him. Through the flame of the match in the hollow of his two palms, he would watch Apkar's unsightly body move on his lame leg. Apkar didn't take kindly to those who let him walk ahead of them. He would feel their gaze like a knife splitting his spine open and would suddenly stop, turn around, and wait for them with his nose upturned. Then a flood of curses would spill from his lips. They were so powerful that it would be impossible to recall them here without feeling shame. That's how Apkar, born and raised in Smyrna, smeared his father and mother with all kinds of shit, not only without the slightest hesitation, but with a perverse kind of delight. Dark destitution ruled their home. His father was a drunk who had gone blind from his addiction. Every night he would come home with a single goal: to beat his wife, who would, in turn, beat Apkar all day long. The beatings would start when they were all fuming around the dinner table, where the scores would be settled. One of the issues that often came up had to do with the bread Apkar had eaten. The boy would swallow the crusts, still unchewed, as the blows rained down on him. One day, his father roughed him up and sent him tumbling down the stairs, where he caught his foot and was left with a crippled leg.

"Bastards!" Apkar would hiss. "They left me no choice but to turn to these whores."

True, seeing the state he was in, it was no wonder that only venom could flow out of him. Not a single kind word ever slipped from his lips. No woman would smile at him or glance in his direction and his indifference toward them found its expression in rude comments. "Come on! You reek—fuck off!" he would grumble. He often threw in his favorite word, "bitch," which he fired at everyone, including, for example, an unsuspecting woman who happened to have accidentally elbowed him in a crowd. His face reserved bitter disdain for beautiful women, whom he knew he could never have. But he showed the girls on the street a special kind of affection and friendship whenever they passed by. He loved wandering through the neighborhoods where prostitutes were lined up on the sidewalk, taking Minas along with him as though they were headed to some kind of carnival. He would stop, talk to the girls and laugh with them, displaying a kind of intimacy that made it look as if they were old friends who belonged to the same tribe, to the same family. Apkar felt at home with them. He would call them "my sweet" or "my love." For that man who wished with all his heart for the downfall of humanity and the destruction of the world, revolution was not a force that would save the world, as the song went, but one that would shatter everything with one decisive blow. But you should have seen him whenever they were short-staffed at work. He would run to Saint Michel, dragging his lame leg behind him, storm into the Billard, thrust his fist into the air, shout "Long live the Revolution!" like a soldier at full attention, and announce that the hotel needed someone.

Finding that someone and ordering him around made bliss fall like a cascade down his face and a smile bloom out of the dimples on his cheeks. It was in that exact moment that Minas realized that Apkar must have been handsome at one time. The coarseness of his face and form was the result of the sharp slopes that his handicap had imprinted on them. The shoulder on the side of his limping leg slanted downward, while the other shoulder was hiked up to his ear, creating an asymmetry in his features. Still, among the boils and depressions on his ravaged face, his eyes remained inextinguishable. Nothing could change them, even if they blazed and made their presence known when rebellion raged in him. This would happen when he yelled the most threatening line of a revolutionary song right in the face of a person passing on the street: "Les bourgeois, on les pendra . . ."[2]

During the catastrophe in Smyrna, he got on a ship and left the city.[3] What gave him the biggest thrill was not his escape, but the way he tricked his parents.

"Yes!" he sneered. "What, they thought I was going to go on feeding them until the end?"

He finished the story triumphantly, clapping his hands and punctuating it with yet another "yes!" One time, Minas asked him what exactly happened to his parents.

"The Turks must have slaughtered them like animals long ago," Apkar replied, gnawing at the inside of his cheek.

More than a year ago, Minas and Vahakn were sitting and having a cup of coffee outside at the Billard when Apkar stopped in front of them, laughing.

"Let me introduce you," Vahakn said. "Here's 'Long live the Revolution!' If you want work, he'll get you a job right away."

"That's right," Apkar told Vahakn. "This time, I've got one for you at the hotel."

"Since when do you take me for a slave?" Vahakn asked. "Work is for revolutionaries, isn't it?"

"I, Minas Yerazian, am a slave. I want to work and become a revolutionary one day, too," Minas said, inserting himself into the conversation.

Minas didn't understand why he was thinking about this now. Vahakn's death, Arshalouys's letter. Yes, since the moment he put that letter in the mailbox, everything had gone haywire and was now looking to return to normal. The past, the present, the future. The future being Nicole, whom his heart suddenly ached for like a mother who has just lost her child. He had buried Nicole's face in the tedium of the day. Someone tried to snatch her away from him, but he kept pulling her back. What was Nicole doing right now? It was early, so she'd probably be asleep, right? He tried imagining her in bed: her eyelids forming domes over her eyes, her mouth sealed, her chest rising and falling steadily in time with her breath. It was the peacefulness of a will disarmed by sleep, a serenity that kept her from seeming unattainable, crushed her resistance, and turned the assassin she became whenever she passed through the Jardin du Luxembourg into a victim. Now she was a wounded bird crouching in the shadows of a shrub. All he had to do was reach out and catch her. But how would he do it? Nicole, Nicole . . .

Suddenly he felt someone watching him. With a frying pan in one hand, he froze, keeping one eye on the golden omelet and the other on the woman leaning against the closed door, her hands clasped behind her back. The "bitch" had already become Hortense, not the widowed Hortense Bédier, just Hortense.

"Here we go," he told himself. "As if I needed this. Now *she's* going to come join the parade, too?" She was already clearing a path through the disorder in his mind, slipping out of the circuit to reach the very source of his pain. Who else is outside? Come in, come on in! Ziya, Sarkis, all of you, all of you persecuted people, come inside. It's a party and everyone's invited.

He nervously dabbed his forehead with his free hand, as if trying to blot away the anguish in his mind.

"Are you ok?" a woman's voice asked. "I know you lost a great friend. Did you already bury him?"

"No, Madame. They took him to the morgue. Students will have their fun cutting into him."

Now he heard Apkar's voice, roaring the song, "Oh, *Tashnagtsiou-tioun*! Let's go to Sassoun."[4] He was singing it, drawing out each syllable and making an obvious effort to show his contempt. Hortense quickly turned and glared at him. Did she think mockery was his way of dealing with grief? Her glare softened with compassion just as quickly and she shot Minas a sharp, inquisitive look as she turned her head toward him again. She was right. For the first time since he found Vahakn's body, his grief burst and caused a painful twinge deep in his heart. With his sleeves rolled up to his elbows, Apkar was bent over the sink, feverishly clanking plates under soapy water.

"Careful, the guests are sleeping," said Madame Bédier, tactfully hiding her fear of seeing a broken dish.

"Bitch!" Apkar growled, without stopping the noise he was making. "How the hell would *you* understand?"

How could Hortense know? How could she really know? Only an Armenian could understand his secret. The Armenian would be proud of the secret, proud of the disease. That's what Hortense couldn't quite understand. How *could* she know, when Armenians took such pains to guard their secret so carefully? He took refuge in the secret to the point of losing himself in it.

Once again, Apkar's gruff voice rose as unexpectedly as it had before against the peaceful morning silence of the hotel: "Oh, *Tashnagtsioutioun*! Let's go to Sassoun." But we hadn't gone to Sassoun. That was the problem. We came to Paris, Athens, Aleppo, Beirut, and even farther, to the Americas. Everywhere. Everywhere, that is, except Sassoun. But Armenians, down to the very last one, sleeves rolled up and arms elbow deep in soapy water, will still go on singing, "Let's go to Sassoun," until the skin on their hands is chapped and shriveled.

How could Hortense understand? People can only hope to know what they have lived themselves. We can't step into somebody else's skin. The skin. The skin is so tough and resilient that it frightens even surgeons and fills murderers with fear. Skin distinguishes human beings from other living things, from the world, from the universe. Skin alienates human beings from one another and imprisons them within themselves. It's like the thick walls of a fortified castle that easily collapse with the shock of a dirty look or a harsh word, but not with the sharp cut of a knife.

How could Hortense know? Dazed by Apkar's noise, she seemed to be trying to make herself even smaller to avoid a blow that would never come. Hortense—with her sallow complexion, sunken cheeks, tiny black eyes, and pointed chin—was looking all around her, eyes ablaze. Hidden beneath simple lingerie was the morning-fresh, almost childlike body that Minas knew well. Under his fingers, she had writhed in dark, damp soil like a worm enlivened by a caress of light after the stone covering it had been overturned. No, this wasn't the Hortense who once walked down the stairs like a bride, her body seeming to grow as tall as a poplar tree, her expression pensive and solemn, perhaps like the countess who had likely had the stairs built a century ago. She was the countess whom this bourgeoise of the Third Republic wished to imitate. That day, protected by the contented caryatids, Hortense approached him and, cleaving the sea of silence, asked: "Are *you* the one Apkar was talking about?"

Time passed quickly, but he seemed to be advancing very slowly, busy with the miserable task of sorting out his own thoughts.

The hotel guests woke up one after the other and he prepared their breakfast: one for the Englishman and another for the Frenchman, each one based on their individual tastes, whereas the German was quite at home with the local fare. Sometimes an image froze in his mind like a picture hanging on a wall. He began to ramble, but Hortense kept her eyes on him. She knew that that day a great friend of his had died. She was forgiving, even compassionate.

"Hurry," she said. "Send breakfast up to the man in room number twenty-three. He's in a rush. He needs to leave at nine."

Nine o'clock. It was nine o'clock already. Nicole must have been up by then. She would be squinting as her eyes tried to reconcile darkness with light. She would be pulling herself out of bed and stretching her long, delicate torso, yawning to recover the movements of waking hours, and with them, the will that had been led astray during the night. He imagined her standing at the edge of her bed, hesitant and unsure, not daring to take the first step into the day that had begun once again. Suddenly, she froze, tilted her head up, and screamed "Monique!" wildly, like a child calling out for her absent mother.

He would run to her the moment he finished work. He would wander the streets, the very same streets Nicole would walk through with Monique, who never left her side, arm in arm, shoulder to shoulder, in perfect step. Their bodies, as though fused together, swayed on their heels and convulsed in laughter, creating the rhythm of a song. Why did people, women especially, stare at them with tight smirks across their lips? It's true that they were a sight to be seen, those two, an extraordinary phenomenon in an ordinary street scene. They walked shoulder to shoulder, wobbling on their knees, their gazes never resting on anyone. It was as if they were alone, all alone, indifferent to the people and commotion around them. Deep in their own dream, they were asleep with their eyes wide open.

Being the fool he was, he used to go to the Jardin du Luxembourg in the evening. That's where they had met, right across from the statue of Verlaine. Sitting on a bench nearby, he and Vahakn were gazing at the poet's devilish head. Now he thought it would be enough to go back to that spot, as he had been doing for days, to find the girls again, as though they had turned into statues and would be waiting for him.

"Room number twenty-three. Twenty-three!" Madame Bédier snapped.

Hortense, why are you so patient and calm when we're together in your room, your lips parted tenderly and your only concern disturbing the silence? Your eyes, entirely mystified, seek mine as if to say, "Don't get upset. Just work." So in moments that should be as slow as the Divine Liturgy, why don't you tell me to hurry up? Instead, you tell me to slow down: "Undressing a woman should be a ritual. You undress a woman like you dress a bride. A woman should never feel it, but all of a sudden find herself naked, enrapt, as though she were dressed for a secret ritual. Love is a ritual, my son. Who taught you to undress a woman so quickly and impatiently as though you were peeling an onion? Is a woman an onion, Minas?"

"Now that room number twenty-three is taken care of, I am going to say everything I need to say, Hortense. Forgive me, but I can't help it. I can't get a hold on the images overrunning my mind. Look, it's like Niagara Falls in there, except the images aren't flowing calmly over the edge. They're gushing over it. Don't forget that Vahakn is dead."

But Vahakn isn't really dead. Isn't he, in fact, the one stirring up these frantic emotions in Minas? Vahakn was the one shaking his inner being as he tried to take up residence in it. From his stronghold in him, he launched countless rockets that burst in a thousand directions in the night sky, briefly illuminating the darkness with their fiery florets.

The room service orders had tapered off. He had time now. He started putting the kitchen back in order, just as he was trying to do in his own brain. The coffee pot was empty. He made a fresh pot. He arranged the teacups. Apkar didn't even have time to lift his head up from the sink. Trays filled with dirty plates arrived one after the other from the floors above. When Minas finally lifted his head and looked toward the doorway where the owner had stood, he was surprised to not see her there. "Vahakn's legacy," he muttered under his breath, as a faint smile bloomed and spread across his face. Like water trickling off a roof and freezing into icicles, the smile froze on his face and his gaze strayed, growing timid and distant. Sorrow lurched in his heart and regret rose to mingle with the frozen smile. He felt guilty. Hadn't he snatched away the job that Apkar had offered to Vahakn? He had interfered and put his nose where it didn't belong. He had even been afraid that he might have lost the job to Vahakn if he hadn't been fast enough. And yet back then, he had refused to give his aggression any thought. Only now did he feel the hostile urge that had consumed him so intensely. There he was. Minas saw his image looking back at him in the mirror, speaking to him, and saw the hand—his own—that had rushed to grab somebody else's things. "I, Minas Yerazian, am a slave. I want to work." This is how he became the heir to the poorest Armenian on Earth, who left him an immeasurable legacy. If he hadn't acted so imprudently that day, Vahakn would still be alive because of Hortense and her ways of preserving a man's dignity. He was the one responsible for Vahakn's death. The rest was just a story. Nothing more. Here he was, upstairs in the big hall on the first floor where Vahakn should have been. The curtains are drawn. They always are—heavy velvet curtains and dim light as weightless as a fairy on her feet. He is standing in the middle of the room, hesitant and shy. Hortense is on her knees, naked after quickly pulling off her slip, begging him to bite her breasts and pushing them out toward him. Minas, completely still, is struck by the way her eyes are shut and her nostrils are flared, quivering.

He covered his ears with his hands and tried not to listen, but the plea—stubborn and slick—resisted, coating his ears and skin and slipping into his heart.

"You know, Apkar, this was supposed to be Vahakn's job. He wouldn't have had a chance to think about death here."

"Please!" Apkar snapped, without lifting his head up from the dishes. "All of us go down the same path. Sooner or later, both of us will, too."

Apkar's perverse laughter exploded like the porcelain teacup that fell from his hand and shattered as it hit the floor.

Everything started the day they met Ziya. Thinking of Ziya was not a form of self-justification, but the escape route he was looking for. He didn't expect to feel a sense of responsibility and now it slowly, stubbornly seeped into the depths of his soul and settled there, spreading like a droplet of water falling onto the sand. He launched into a monologue of what-ifs. What if they hadn't met Ziya? What if he hadn't taken Vahakn's job? It kept Vahakn from meeting Hortense, and because only Hortense knew how to turn a boy into a man, Vahakn had remained a boy. Vahakn's life was a dangerous game that a little boy would play. He played with life like a boy plays with toys. Minas was also to blame for hitching his life to Vahakn's for two whole years. Of course, he hadn't planned on it, but in the end, knowingly or not, he had bound Vahakn's life to his own, diverting it from its course. He now understood why Vahakn was constantly on the move. He couldn't stay in one place for too long, because he needed to escape from himself. Every time he changed his address, he became a new man, leaving the old Vahakn behind: a new man wandering around new places, new cities, new streets, new houses, and a new existence that nurtured a new spirit in him. The only problem was that the one he left behind would catch up to him and seize him by the throat, forcing him to flee and face himself once again. Yes, now he understood. In the kitchen, his sense of time had shifted. The work had gradually lessened along with the chance that parasites would creep into his chain of thoughts. He noticed Apkar, who suddenly stood up straight in front of the sink, let out a sigh, and wiped the sweat from his forehead with his right arm. Minas instinctively tensed his body as though bracing himself for a slap, but Apkar, after taking a breath, leaned over the sink again and continued to work in silence.

He returned to his thoughts, his mental meanderings, and hastily caught hold of their thread, afraid that he hadn't yet finished the process of accusing, flagellating, and punishing himself. He resorted to talking to himself aloud in the silent kitchen, so he could jump and catch the breaking thread faster and more confidently. "Yes," he said. Yes, that's it, he understood perfectly. Everything seemed so simple now. His soul calmed as his guilt became clearer. He had held Vahakn hostage for two whole years, forcing him to gradually sink deeper and deeper into himself, because it was Minas who was blocking his escape route. He was guilty. He was guilty of crumbling weakness, which filled Vahakn with a meaningless sense of pity. The feeling would not have wavered even if he and Vahakn had refused Apkar's offer. This was his main issue. Why was he always in a state that inspired pity? He stopped at this thought, afraid of probing any further. It only lasted for a moment, because in that brief pause, he felt a sense of disgust that started in his throat and slid down toward his heart. He felt an uncontrollable urge to talk to someone, to share his concerns with someone, and he realized that he could only be open with Vahakn. And Vahakn was gone. The most unbearable part was that there was no possibility of talking to his dear departed friend. He was left with Apkar, whose scoffs he could already hear resounding off the kitchen walls, and Hortense, in whose melancholy eyes the thought was perched, as if at a supreme crossroads, and whose only concern was to endlessly clip the worm-eaten branches, so that the trunk could have a better chance of withstanding the four winds of life. That grimy feeling of disgust settled freely around his heart, besieging it and preparing it for the final onslaught.

Disgust is the kind of feeling that breaks ground, excavates, and destroys. It annihilates. Wasn't it the same feeling that led him to step in front of a train two years ago or wander away from the crowd to throw himself into the Seine? Undecided and hesitant, he had drifted along the deserted riverbank for quite some time, feeling the pull of both the flowing river and the city lights. If he had jumped into the water that evening, yes, if he had made a splash and brought about an extraordinary silence as powerful as nothingness itself . . . if that day he hadn't climbed up the stairs away from the riverbank and slipped into the crowd on Boulevard Saint-Michel that took him to the Billard and made him stop in front of it, he could have just as well gone in another direction, since he hadn't had anything in particular to do. He could have, for instance, wandered along the banks of the Seine—it certainly would have been better. The first decision is always the best one. Now that he saw himself in the same places, chasing the same obsession and bewildered by the same fear, he remembered that he had been afraid. But why had he been afraid of the river? It was spring and spring promises new life, but springtime in Paris is bitterly cold and the Seine sends chills through all those who throw themselves into it. There was no other explanation. It was fear. Everything scared him, so he failed at everything. It could also be said that hope was what held him back. It's hope that makes us grapple with danger and death. But Minas breathed out all his hope that day, while Vahakn—it's true, he had no hope—was still waiting for something. He was waiting and Arshalouys confirmed it: "He was waiting, but who knows what for. He said he was waiting and one time even said, 'Let's wait.'" So he went on waiting for something that didn't come and never would have, if Minas hadn't thrown Ziya at Vahakn's feet. Him. Always him. You see? It's not for nothing that a feeling of guilt is filling him, overflowing like the milk in the saucepan on the stove, catching him by surprise. Quick! He takes a sponge and wipes up the milk, releasing a sour smell into the air, while there, sitting outside the Billard on Saint Michel, Vahakn is overcome with sympathy. Poor boy, he looks like a lost dog.

A man pushes his way through the crowd on the street and stops right under the streetlight. At that instant, Minas—our curious lost soul—notices the face of a stranger, who calls to him from the entrance of the café: "Hey, compatriot!"

Minas stares at the man. Then he stares some more. He doesn't know him. Suddenly there's a flash of recognition, but he soon returns to that hazy place behind the dark curtain of his muddled memory. With his head raised and proud and his gaze distant, Minas has the air of a dreamer. The other man raises his eyebrows under a disheveled thicket of hair. The big eyes on his angular face reveal a mellifluent sweetness, glowing with the glimmer of irony. Sitting in the bistro chair, he seems agitated. And yet it's not his usual interest in solving mysteries that's preoccupying him at the moment. This time, his peculiar heartbeat tells of something entirely different.

He liked sitting outside the café for hours on end, lazily surrendering himself to the chair and watching and examining the feet that would approach.

It happened that a shadow came into his line of sight and caused his gaze to slowly retreat, only to appear again in the wake of the shadow, wholly transformed. He recorded the differences between the feet on the sidewalk, collecting points of comparison like posture, pant cuff, quality of socks, shoes, and finally something else, a breeze perhaps, that helped him solve the mystery. What he did next hinged on that initial calculation. He would gradually raise his eyes to check the subject's face and confirm his assumption. This bizarre pastime was not a sign of boredom in the least, nor was it a means of deception, as many supposed, even if he did rely on these games to make a living to a certain extent. Afterward he, like the others, was convinced that this way of life was a kind of obligation, dictated by some dark, internal forces that were suddenly revealed right after Ziya's murder, because at the very moment they were revealed, Vahakn retired from his pastime, despite the high cost of giving up his livelihood. In fact, he had already stopped thinking about living. He stopped caring altogether as soon as he escaped those dark, internal forces, as he called them, that mental state that he carried around—unpredictable, stubborn and obscure—until the moment that Vahakn vanished once and for all, surrendering his entire being to the anarchy of fate.

Now that Minas understood, now that these things had already come to pass, it was easy to have misgivings. And this was precisely what he couldn't forgive in himself, particularly the instructive hours he had spent with Hortense, while his friend, tense as a bow, willfully headed straight toward his own destruction. But the final blow was dealt the day he introduced Ziya to Vahakn. It was at one of the cafés on Boulevard Saint-Michel. That day, Vahakn, as though he were engrossed in his game and focused on taking it to the very end, asked Minas to leave: "Go take a walk. You're in my way."

After shooting a sharp look at the sidewalk, he waited patiently for a roaming, unsuspecting victim in the crowd, like a fisherman tossing his net into the water. As soon as he identified the person, he needed to concentrate on him with controlled focus. The person he chose would save him from having to pay for his coffee. As soon as the prey crossed into his territory, he would jump up from his seat to find a reason to strike up a conversation. It was inevitable. In those rare instances when the ruse failed, he would offer a stock apology. "I'm sorry, I made a bet with my friend to see who you were," he would say, gesturing toward the entrance of the café, where no one was waiting. Often Minas became an unwilling witness to Vahakn's modus operandi. Unwilling, because whenever Vahakn was at it, Minas usually made himself scarce. The mastermind preferred to work alone. He would approach his prospective victim with a cigarette dangling from the corner of his mouth. "Do you have a light?" he would ask. Accepting the light, he would inhale the smoke with gusto, pleasantly serious, while little by little a sunny smile would spread across his face. "What nice weather we're having," he would offer, and with a graceful nod of the head, would add, "Thank you." His lips burned with the desire to move to the next stage, but in the meantime, there wasn't much else he could do except fawn and simper like the wisps of cigarette smoke rising into the air. He winked and his face took on a certain harshness, like someone straining to hold a monocle in his eye socket, but it would pass soon enough and he would kindly and politely drop the bait. "I think I know you from somewhere," he would say. He understood the eloquence of silence. He kept quiet as if expecting an answer, even though he knew no answer was coming. The silence brought with it a chill that he tried to balance with never-ending, groveling "excuse me"s. It was at this point that his prey would often exit the scene, mumbling something under their breath.

Vahakn wasn't upset when he returned to his chair, rubbing his hands together in delight. Of course it was impossible to win every time, but he knew he had at least turned strangers into acquaintances, making them easy targets for his unsavory tricks. "Hey, hello there! Come, let's have a cup of coffee." This way, the city filled with infinite possibilities and day by day he added to his number of customers, which would one day grow to include the entire city.

On days that he would lose a prospect, Vahakn was careful not to show his frustration. He knew that it would surely invite the waiter's attention. As it was, the waiter always kept a watchful eye on him. Vahakn never gave up. There always came a moment when the waiter wasn't around. That was Vahakn's cue to slip away quietly. But the sidewalk was still teeming with feet. Evening had descended and the air had cooled. He started to feel cold. He really needed something warm, but it was more to earn the waiter's confidence that he ordered a cup of coffee.

"Very hot!" he yelled after the waiter, who was already inside the café.

Demanding customers always inspire trust and weaken the vigilance of waiters. It was the right time. He stood up. The waiter was out of his sight and Vahakn was out of the waiter's line of vision. But he had barely gotten up to leave when he muttered, "There he is," and sank back into his chair, almost dazed. Like a cat, he put his paws on his stomach and followed the circular movements of his prey with wide eyes. There was a pair of shoes that hesitated on the sidewalk among the throng of countless others, a pair that contradicted each other, as though each shoe belonged to a different person. The filthy, worn shoes must have been brown once. It was easy enough to imagine them without feet, just phantom shoes thrown onto the sidewalk, kicked around here and there by the stampeding crowd, like phantom ships tossed around by raging waves. "Here's an interesting case," he thought, like a doctor pondering an unusual illness. "A rare bird," he continued. In the same moment, the waiter brought his coffee, and as he was setting it down on the table, he blocked the curious scene unfolding on the street. Annoyed, Vahakn shoved the waiter aside and his hand hit the cup, spilling pungent black coffee onto the table. Fortunately, the filthy, worn shoes were still there, meaning that he would soon take his revenge on them for causing the accident. Meanwhile, the shoes paced the sidewalk for a moment, then returned to the lamppost and stopped, the tips pointed outward, forming an obtuse triangle that seemed to be yawning.

It was at that moment that, as noted above, Vahakn let out a heart-wrenching groan—"Poor boy, he looks like a dog who has lost his master"—and called out, "Hey, compatriot!" Their eyes met. They kept looking at each other in bewilderment, without a glint of recognition, just an image etched into his mind from the past that made its way into the present. He jumped up from his chair mechanically. He was standing, his brow knit and lips drawn tight, thinking. He waited for the other man to say something. He made some swift motions with his head, so as to wrench the gleam of recollection away from the stranger. His sharp chin, perpetually drooping from too much sneering and mocking, now sunk even lower in his effort to search for a memory. The exertion left his mouth agape.

"I remember you from somewhere," Vahakn said, as he approached him. "From Constantinople, maybe? Were you in an orphanage?"

"No."

"From around here, then. How long have you been here?"

"I've just arrived."

"From Lyon?"

"No."

"Damn it," Vahakn said, while in the memory of the other man, an invisible director was starting to set the stage. It was a long street, loud and lively, a cross between a southern city and an eastern city, with sidewalks overrun with Armenian refugees, Africans, and cheap whores. Children's shrieks echoed in the horns of the cars. It was here that he was now surprised to see himself, staring at his surroundings as though in a dream. There was a thin ray of light in his eyes that illuminated the images in his mind. The city opened like a book, page by page, as the anxious face of the man in front of him melted into the swarming crowd. But he wasn't the same man who once walked, restless and miserable, the one who went to his friend Ghevont in hopes of finding a job. Despite the doubt he felt, he now saw himself happier in those times, because tucked between his eyelashes was also the scene that would follow soon afterward at home, where he would proudly announce the good news he had received from Ghevont. He would bring relief to his mother's pained expression. His heart rejoiced, mingling with old sorrow, walking with his soul in perfect harmony as he made his way home to restore a share of his lost pride. It was on this street, as the invisible director made perfectly clear in his imagination, that Ghevont lived with his wife and two children in a seedy hotel called The Ararat. The building's large façade towered over the street, sheltering countless refugee families between its musty walls. A group of children at the entrance let out cheerful cries, which led him to conclude that their parents had not yet come home from work. Same for Ghevont, so there was no need to rush. He began walking up and down the street, seeing Armenian grocers, barbers, shoe shiners, and throngs of people on either side of him, before stopping, baffled, in front of a shop window. It was a watchmaker's shop, but the watches were not what drew him to it. It was the book on display in the window. Beside it, a cardboard tag read: "Rare copy. Five francs." The title was embossed in big silver letters on the cover: *Pagan Songs*.[5] Even now his heart jumps thinking about it. The anguish that rose and spread through his chest swelled in front of the stranger before him, who had given him the chance to revisit his pain. When the soul has been emptied entirely, an insignificant pain can bring it back to life. This was what happened at that moment in Minas Yerazian's soul.

He had walked all day, roaming along the banks of the Seine where the temptation of death often visited him. He was worn out and had no sense of time. It was an old story, lost either in time or in a haze. He remembered that his mother was dead and that he was so estranged from grief that it was now overshadowed by his outrage over a stolen book. At last, he returned from his mental travels through the recent past, which didn't seem to belong to him. Choosing a curt tone, he hastened to put an end to the stranger's suspense, and especially to his gaze, which kept stubbornly probing his inner sanctum.

He lifted his eyes serenely, more out of exhaustion than out of inner calm.

He looked the stranger in the eye and said, "Marseille."

"Could be," the other conceded, as he extended his hand, trembling like someone caught stealing, immediately adding, "Sit down, let's have some coffee."

And so he sat. As he surrendered his body to the back of the chair, he felt his mind shatter bit by bit and his conscious world collapse. Suddenly his body began to shake and he sprang out of a deepening sleep that was about to swallow him. "He'd better pay," Vahakn thought. He was surprised that he could still think. He even went on thinking, "He's the one inviting me, right?" It was the first time he had talked to someone since he had arrived. He had turned his monologues, which in the end created nothing but a feeling of emptiness and nonexistence, into an abstraction. Look, he could even extend his hand. He didn't need much courage for that. And when he did extend his hand, he noticed a pleasant tremor reverberating in the other person's heart.

"My name is Minas," he said, reinvigorated. "Minas Yerazian, Minas of the Yerazian clan, whichever you like."

"They call me Vahakn, no last name. Well, Vahaken, officially. The French insist on spelling it that way."

"It's better that way," Minas replied with sudden excitement.

From this moment on, he would feel a kind of sad delight. "It's better that way," he repeated. "It's like a Finnish name, like Kekkonen, Varjalainen, Vahaken, right? Nobody would take you for an Armenian. It's hard to get a job with an Armenian name."

Vahakn smiled quizzically. But then his gaze hung on the edge of his thoughts and his expression darkened.

"No, brother. It's impossible to separate ourselves from being Armenian. Even if we try, it won't let go of our collar. Being Armenian is a sickness, a sickness rooted in revenge, and the horrible thing is that it's revenge without hatred. We Armenians genuinely don't know how to hate."

Minas suddenly discovered the secret of Vahakn's demise in the words he had said that night. In those words from two years earlier was the weapon—the one that would someday kill him—that was already waiting to ambush him, like a worm gnawing its way out of a piece of fruit. After exacting revenge, only hatred would protect the resilience of the soul, nurturing it with its formidable being. It was as if Vahakn knew, or at least had an inkling, when he said, "And the horrible thing is . . ." "Poor Vahakn," Minas shuddered. Who knows what monstrous mask the horror wore when it introduced itself to Vahakn at the moment his sinewy fingers gripped Ziya's throat before slowly letting his corpse slide into the Seine. He lived with that shudder for an entire month. His hands trembled. He couldn't eat. He couldn't drink. His eyes were swollen, drained of their vitality after seeing horror up close, face to face. Vahakn died because he couldn't hate. He couldn't hate Ziya. On the contrary, he loved him and killed him out of love. Often Minas was jealous of their friendship.

"Brother," Vahakn would say. "We Armenians are a sad people. It's always possible to be happy with Ziya."

At that time, Vahakn didn't know that he would kill Ziya.

It was a cool, spring evening, as cool as evenings can be in Paris. Winter was still lingering. During the day, it surrendered to the sun, but in the evening it slowly reclaimed its losses. This is the moment when people can breathe in the fragrance of new budding tree branches. Spring is alive in the smell of the plants. The crowd had already doubled on the boulevards. It was spring. People were outside, walking and taking in the fresh air. Among them were Vahakn and Ziya. They were walking down Boulevard Saint-Michel, laughing and having a great time. Ziya was tall and slim, and as they walked, his handsome face tilted slightly toward Vahakn. As always, his face bore a charming expression. He listened carefully to the silence following a sentence, waiting for the next one, which always lagged because Vahakn took special, excessive care in preparing his words. Ziya filled the pause with the gentle expression in his eyes. Usually his mouth would be half-open, not suggesting naïveté but rather an almost unhealthy sensitivity. Ziya was afraid of hurting other people. He usually suffered even more than the person he offended and thought he was to blame when somebody hurt him—if he hadn't been there, there wouldn't have been the chance for it to happen. He was at fault because he happened to be right there at that exact moment. And what if he was the reason for the pain? My God, what did he do? Quick, he has to ask for forgiveness! He had a pathological obsession with being forgiven. His sensitivity would grow heavier and more complicated still, reaching absurd proportions when an inadvertent offense was directed at one of their friends. He had written Vahakn quite a few letters of impassioned regret to beg for forgiveness. Once, in a rush, he had passed him on the street and didn't say hello. The following day he wrote him an apology: ". . . I realized it was you only after I had passed you." If he invited Vahakn and Minas to the movies and one of them complained that the movie was a waste of time, a letter would certainly follow. "I couldn't sleep all night. Forgive me for wasting your valuable time. Forgive me, my *pasha*. I know you will, because I know your compassionate Armenian soul, but still I feel the need to ask for your forgiveness" or something to that effect.

So Ziya was like that, always apologizing for mistakes he didn't make and always haunted by the fear of an old mistake. To spare the Armenian's feelings, he developed his sensitivity, cultivating and nurturing it like an exquisite flower. Ziya had cleared the air on the very first day they met. They were sitting outside at the Billard. Having noticed Minas, Ziya let out a loud cry and came to sit next to him. Leaning forward in anticipation, his chin tilted down and his mouth open, he was ready to exchange pleasantries, which could already be seen in the glimmer in his eyes. Vahakn and Minas, both deep in thought, were busy tallying the day's expenses, counting the money that was left. That night, they had to pay for the room they were renting and couldn't figure out where the money had gone. Vahakn was horrified by the idea of sleeping on the street. For a while now, ever since he had started looking after Minas, he too had grown accustomed to a warm bed. Losing or spending money could deprive him of this new luxury and it began to alarm him. But when Minas turned to Ziya and introduced him to Vahakn, he instantly forgot his concerns about the bed and the money. Ziya extended his hand, which trembled from the effort it took to formulate the words he was trying to say. Suddenly, with surprising ease, he said, "Nice to meet you, effendi. Very nice to meet you. Minas effendi couldn't say enough nice things about you. Isn't that right, Minas effendi?" During the conversation, he lowered his voice and pleaded, "Please, let's forget the past. What am I guilty of? It's too bad. I love the Armenians. All my friends in Istanbul were Armenian." They *did* forget the past. They were young and life was inviting them to enjoy beautiful things, beautiful sensations. Life was a constant standing invitation. It was that kind of an evening. Outside at the Billard, the cheapest café on the street, Armenian workers would gather every evening in the back hall where they could scream and fight without disturbing the conversations of the other customers. Vahakn loved sitting outside the café. Even in the winter, he would sit by the brazier, his eyes fixed on the glowing flames that showed through the holes. He loved stretching his legs out in front of its warmth and leaning against the back of his chair. Sitting across from him, Ziya spoke excitedly about his university lectures, especially one on French literature, which he talked about with a certain reverence. "I envy that you're staying in this country," Ziya said abruptly after a long pause, measuring his words in a trembling voice that was anxious not to be misunderstood. It seemed to him that their minds constantly wandered beyond his words, beyond their meaning, walking across muddy fields in search of a secret thought. It was for this reason that Ziya lived with unrelenting torment. Sometimes signs of his turmoil would spark in his eyes, making his shoulders sway and letting him escape, forgetting himself. Ziya seemed uncomfortable when he spoke, like someone who, afraid of falling, uses a cane to walk, even though its necessity is scarcely clear to the outside observer. In the end, he saw that his friends weren't suspicious and this made him uneasy. His unease came from the fact that Armenians were incapable of leaving the past behind. They lived clung to it like a drowning man clutching a blade of grass. He always forced himself to stay alert. Vahakn would listen to him enrapt, without blinking, encouraging Ziya to keep talking. And he would, but would stop suddenly, bewildered, at exactly the moment his two friends would heave a long, admiring "Oh." After that, he would pick up his train of thought as though nothing had happened to stop him. Once Vahakn interrupted: "He's learned quite a bit, our Ziya. It's too bad that he'll forget everything once he goes back." Ziya felt genuinely betrayed by this. What did Vahakn mean? His enthusiasm depleted, mouth agape, an endearing smile across his face, Ziya looked at Vahakn inquisitively, examining the unspoken words in his eyes. Since Ziya's face wore a curious expression, with light and shadow intermingling to form a contradictory image—his mouth telling of stupidity and the sparkle in his eyes showing profound intelligence—Vahakn burst into laughter and Ziya was infected by it too, but Minas, breaking the silence that had fallen, asked, "And then what?" Ziya took a deep breath and continued his story.

It was on that evening, during that lively conversation with Ziya, that Vahakn was plunged into a peculiar state of mind for the first time. It can't be said that his mind was elsewhere, although he did look absent. He didn't seem to be following what Ziya was saying, even though he was transfixed by his enthusiasm. The truth was that in his state of near self-abandon, his attention was drawn to Ziya's neck. The intensity of his stare made his eyes grow so narrow that they couldn't see anything beyond his neck. Even if he had found the strength to pull his gaze away, it would have returned once again to settle on that dark spot, which was nothing more than the tint of his skin.

It was there that Ziya's protruding Adam's apple undulated with the rhythm of his enthusiasm. The darkness of his skin had a charm of its own, but this wasn't what made him so tense. What he saw couldn't be seen. It was the part of the neck that was right under the knot of his tie. It was what couldn't be seen that stirred murky turmoil in him. Vahakn's face expressed such amazement that Ziya couldn't possibly have sensed the hidden, stubborn, insidious chase inside him that would cost him his life. But there was a moment when Ziya felt an involuntary shock from Vahakn's fierce, prying gaze. This was the moment after Ziya said, "I envy that you're staying in this country." Vahakn's hand rose slowly and hesitantly. His index finger—extended as he clasped his other fingers into his palm—landed on the smooth skin of Ziya's neck. "It's nothing," he said. "Just some cigarette ash."

Suddenly there was a sound of something shattering. It was Apkar, who had broken yet another glass. Minas realized that, like him, Apkar was also in an agitated state. Everything had been turned upside down.

"You know," Minas said. "I wrote to his fiancée. She lives in Lancet and works at the paper factory."

"What fiancée?" Apkar said, surprised. "She's his wife. They were married. Didn't you know? He left on their wedding day."

"Damn it," said Minas, thinking of the letter. "I wrote 'mademoiselle' on the envelope."

He had barely finished his thought when a sense of delight came over him.

Here was his chance to write a new letter and change the familiar tone of the last one. Fortunately, life always comes to the rescue, though we rarely know how to make use of its goodness. He wasted no time. He drafted the letter in his head, so he would be ready to entrust it to paper once he left work.

"Dear Madame Arshalouys."

Here he was making the same mistake again. Yes, *that* was the mistake. It wasn't the content of the letter. The mistake slipped out in the salutation. It was the salutation that contained the familiar tone that brings two heads close together and makes a pair of hearts beat in time, their sounds mingling until they become indistinguishable. Wasn't this his goal? His goal was just to do his duty. And so he wrote without wasting any time. Of course, it was all in his imagination, but even there, he heard the rustling of the paper under his fingers. On this imaginary sheet of paper, he wrote:

Dear Madame,

Please excuse the ignorance of my mistake. Today, by chance, I heard from a friend that you are, in fact, Vahakn's wife. Believe me, when I learned this, my sorrow grew even deeper. I am sure you will not deny forgiveness to someone who has made an honest mistake.

So, dear Madame, etcetera, etcetera . . .

He left work. On the metro, despite the crowd, or perhaps because of it, the wheels of his mind kept turning like the blades of a windmill. He sealed, opened, and rewrote the letter several times with a stubborn fastidiousness that ruthlessly tried to drive away any hidden emotion that might sneak into his words and end up becoming an endless source of trouble in the future. He figured it out as he got off at Odéon. For a moment, his inner voice was forced to give in and fall silent, only because he was busy searching for a place for his feet in the dense crowd leaving the metro. An old man staggered up the steps in front of him. He grew irritated by his useless attempts to get around him—stepping to the right and then to the left—but when he finally got out of the metro station near the statue of Danton, he regained his train of thought. Truthfully, it must be said that his train of thought regained him. Like a hailstorm, thoughts pelted his mind, where a sense of confusion took hold. Fortunately, at that moment, his imagination came to the rescue, scattering the onslaught of thoughts. He took a deep breath and with it a certain joy crept into his heart as he ruminated on the fragility of thought. Seeing the bustling crowd coming out of the metro was enough to make him remember that boy who one day told Vahakn why he had quit his job. He used to wash dishes at a restaurant. On his way to and from work, the metro was at its busiest and it was a nightmare for him. He was desperate to find a job that would let him take the metro when it wasn't as crowded. "Do you understand, Vahakn?"

he would say. "The metro is packed. There's not even room to drop a needle. You're surrounded by women on all sides. It's horrible. Horrible. You feel so lecherous. It's as if you're holding the women in your arms as you're riding."

"I have a friend who's a poet," Vahakn said, glancing at Minas out of the corner of his eye. "He says that if you want to relive the feeling of life in utero, take the metro. It's like being in your mother's womb all over again. It's a safe place with no responsibilities. My God, how pathetic people are."

Then, as now, Minas felt intense heat at his temples and his forehead grew moist as sweat tried to burst out of his pores. At that point, he almost returned to his old concerns in a frenzy and mechanically erased the "etcetera, etcetera," replacing it with "please accept my deepest condolences." Of course, this formality did not have a particular goal. "Please then, dear Madame, accept my sincerest condolences." "No," he said, silently, of course, since he had not yet reached his room. There he could speak to himself out loud, even to his reflection in the mirror. But on the street? Now he was walking up Rue Monsieur-le-Prince, which leads directly to the Jardin du Luxembourg and rises slightly before reaching the park. "My condolences," he muttered and stopped. He stopped and his train of thought, quite literally, did too. When he started walking again, his thoughts followed. What link was there between walking and thinking? He didn't know. All he knew was that every time he stopped, his thoughts would flee, chased by an unfamiliar force. It reminded him of how shadows would suddenly scatter, pushing one another and cowering behind furniture when light suddenly illuminated a dark room. This is why he would stop after taking only a few steps whenever his thoughts were bothering him. As soon as he stopped, the view of the street would fill his eyes and create a kind of barrier between him and his thoughts. When he walked, the street seemed to flow and slide past his eyes. The street became unreal and dreamlike. Thoughts stormed in, occupied abandoned territory, and did their bidding freely and boldly, like kids racing out of school to play, causing chaos in the empty town square. When Minas stopped walking, the street became ordinary in its familiar details. There was the British restaurant, with its low balcony, and the Armenian tailor. The tailor would raise his head and lift his needle whenever anyone passed. The Viennese pastry shop, which looked half-buried in the ground, always had dark Linzer tortes behind a glass display case. Then the bookstore with its green façade, the Romanian restaurant, and here, stretching lengthwise, the immense mansion that housed Lycée Saint-Louis. Everything else, all of it, was so mundane and commonplace that he preferred to walk. It allowed him to create a dream world where he could clear a path through the images in his mind and walk all the way to the entrance of the hotel. That day, Minas stopped often. He still hadn't gotten very far from the metro. Usually, it was the exact opposite. Usually, the thoughts locked in a dance inside his head would be sweet. They would be about Nicole. But not today.

In the end, why did he insist on seeing a hidden agenda in his letter? The words meant exactly what was written. It was as simple as, say, the street sign that he had stopped in front of, which read Rue Monsieur-le-Prince. At that, his fear receded. "My condolences"—even "my sincerest condolences"—seemed conventional and formal, something that would be in all letters like this. But when he started walking again, an inner voice got the better of him. "Don't fool yourself," it said. "What convention was it that told you to add the word 'sincere?'" The inner voice was right about the word "sincere." Where did it come from? Why did it want to disturb him? What were its intentions? He also had an issue with the word "sorrow." "My sorrow grew even deeper." The letter should clarify, not show emotion, which, like all displays of emotion, was just an invitation. And so the sincere transformed into the hypocritical. It seemed that he had set a trap for Arshalouys and it was the fear of her falling into it that tormented him the most about his letter to her, though, as you will see, the torment came from elsewhere. The truth was that he was the one who had set the trap near that poor, lonely, grief-stricken, bewildered woman by stubbornly forcing her to express her emotions, whether they were "sincere" or not. Feeling disarmed, he decided to surrender everything to chance with the hope that once he was in his room, in front of the desk, he would be able to approach the issue with composure.

His room was on the first floor. They felt proud when they decided to rent it—proud to be living on the first floor. Only later did they realize that they were able to rent that particular room because no one else had wanted it. The first day they walked in, elated, and immediately opened the window. A stench rushed inside. "It smells like shit," Vahakn grumbled, quickly pulling his head back inside and scrunching up his nose and mouth. Minas stuck his own head out the window, looked up, pinched his nose, and looked down. There was a space as long and narrow as a pipe, which the agency referred to as *sur la cour.* That was it. Above them, far above them, beyond the fifth floor, a dark sky looked about the size of a sheet of paper. Minas closed the window and they never opened it again. "It's a food smell," he said. "It must be coming from the kitchen at The Ani." He thought for a while about The Ani, the restaurant downstairs. Even in that putrid smell, he found something pleasant. Whenever he gave his address, he would say he was "right above The Ani" and would be surprised if the person didn't look at him with wonder. The Ani had a certain charm for him, but seemingly not for anyone else. The restaurant was one of the most ordinary in the neighborhood. For Minas, its charm stemmed from the fact that it was where Armenian artists and writers met. Even Tekeyan would sometimes go there for lunch.[6] Once he bumped into an old classmate as they were both walking into the restaurant.

"Vanadour!" Minas called out.

"Oh," Vanadour sighed from atop his tall, thin frame. "You're here, too?"

And that was it. Vanadour went inside and the door slammed shut behind him. Minas stayed outside on the sidewalk. He forgot what he was doing. Why had he gone out? Was he going somewhere? He suddenly felt wounded. The chance encounter with Vanadour had been an intense thrill, but now, as he stood in front of the closed door to the restaurant, he was like a bird with its wings clipped. Vanadour's words refused to leave his ear. They were grating and sticky, and though he couldn't tell why, they had a repellent quality to them at the same time. It was the tone that had hurt him. He had expected an invitation. He had imagined that Vanadour would have turned to him and said, "Well, what are you waiting for? Come on in!" In these words, he had wanted to see the compassion of someone who shared his fate, when in fact, to his ear, Vanadour's surprise in seeing him and his tone of voice contained something accusatory, raising a barrier between them. "You're here, too?" meant "You don't belong here." As he walked into the restaurant, Vanadour didn't look back. Minas, standing dazed on the sidewalk, stared at the back of his old friend as he disappeared behind the closing door. Between the opening and closing of the door, a voice reached Minas that scattered his unpleasant thoughts.

"Antranig, quick! Some *fasouliayi pilaki*."[7]

They all knew that *fasoulia* just meant beans, but they preferred to trick themselves with words. How comforting it must be to call a dish by its old name and feel that they had never been separated from their mothers, that life had continued with their families, as if nothing had changed, as if nothing had happened in their lives. But Minas remembered his mother and forgot the rest. Thank God she was still alive. A heart attack—that was it. Stupid! Why had he gotten scared and left, leaving his mother, sister, and brother alone? Now he trembled at the thought of going back. It was as though a permanent barrier had been built between them after one grave, irreparable misdeed. His mother would write to him, "Be careful, son. Don't catch a cold. They say Paris is a very cold city." He kept her letters like relics there in his bag. She would also write, "Don't go catching any kind of disease." Of course, he knew what she meant. But he wasn't like Apkar. If he ever went to those neighborhoods, it was just to keep Apkar company.

He stretched out on the iron-framed bed. From his vantage point, the room felt narrower, like a long intestine. He had a hard time figuring out the color of the wallpaper. The flowers must have been blue at one time. Now they had no color at all. The dampness had turned the walls a pale yellow with open wounds here and there. Leprous walls. An armoire that had lost one of its legs, which was replaced by a piece of wood. A desk so worn that it looked filthy. A crippled chair. They had lived in that room for more than a year.

Now and then, he glanced over at the spot where Vahakn still seemed to be sprawled, his eyes wide open and a profound sense of calm on his face. The envelope from the office was still in his hand—a summons from the police station. Minas had no energy to get up from where he was. Fatigue came over him, pulling his body down and making it feel heavier.

This is why his thoughts were disobeying him. They were like retreating soldiers who would no longer take orders from above. Perfect anarchy. His mind couldn't concentrate on one thought and let it run its course. He tried to stand up, but he couldn't. He had to get up. He had to write the letter. He had left the door ajar to let in fresh air from the hallway. He got up and closed it carefully, afraid that the past might wake up and charge into the present. With the door closed, the present slipped into the room, and little by little, the shadow on the other side of the bed gradually became a desk. He approached it, sat on the crippled chair, and didn't move again. He took out a piece of paper and an envelope from the drawer. Suddenly, his gaze fell on the alarm clock. It was past seven. It was too late. The post office would be closed. He decided he could write the letter later and drop it in a mailbox on his way to work in the morning. With that idea, he felt lighter, as if a piece of rope binding his arms had loosened and come undone. He let out a sigh of relief as he did every time something saved him from an unpleasant obligation. He was almost content. There was plenty of time to work on the letter with his mind at rest. He already saw it finished exactly the way he wanted, freed from the fictional nightmare he had woven around Arshalouys. He noticed a book on the desk. It was Tristan Corbière's *Les Amours jaunes*, which he hadn't touched in two days. The loves of a kindred spirit. "My God," he exclaimed, holding the book and caressing it with trembling fingers. Perhaps not realizing what he was saying or why, he continued, "What is this disease you've infected this poor heart with?" No, his exclamation was not without reason. Something had dawned on him the moment he saw the book that made him stare in awe. He understood why his mother loved him with a kind of painful anguish, as though she were always at the bedside of someone gravely ill. The secret of her consoling words, her advice, was kept hidden: it was because he was the lost son, fallen into obscurity, whose penchant for drifting crushed her. He stood up and paced the narrow room. Once again, he had found a means of escape: reading to ignore life's imperatives. He hesitated for a moment before picking up the book. If he started reading, the whole night would rush past like a river and he would sail into the distance, always far away from life. But it was intoxicating, my God, so intoxicating. And as he passed the desk, he couldn't resist. He was like an alcoholic grabbing a bottle of exquisite wine and finishing it in one gulp. He opened the book. He was taken aback, and for a moment, looked at it, still and entranced. Tucked into the pages of the book was an envelope. On it was Vahakn's handwriting. He tore open the envelope, his hands shaking, and started to read:

Dear Minas,

Don't think that I'm writing out of a burning desire to write. It's common practice among those who die before their time to leave a note. I see a kind of vanity in this. People who voluntarily enter the infinity of the great beyond also try to secure for themselves some kind of immortality on this side. I would have liked to leave quietly on my tiptoes, but that's not why I'm writing to you. The idea first came to me in front of Ziya's body. You know, when they pulled his body out of the water two days later and called us both in, I figured there must have been people who had seen us together almost every day. So I decided to write this while I was standing in front of his body. If they hadn't called us in, I wouldn't have written anything, because I'd already decided to kill myself that day. For a month now, I've been struggling to decide whether or not to write. But I'll do it. Not for my sake, Minas, but for yours. Pay close attention to the words of this dead man. Yes, these are the words of a dead man, words from the dead. I was already dead when I stood in front of Ziya's body.

I wrote every day and tore it all up, until I became entirely convinced that I had to write. I'll give you an account of my experiences over this past month as well as of our friendship over these past two years, which has brought me to this point, to this bliss. No, this is not an accusation. On the contrary, I'm grateful to you for showing me what friendship can be and for living with me for a month after I was already dead inside. I'm that lucky one who could survive among the living for an entire month. Only I realized what life was like on this side and what it looked like from here. No, don't torture yourself with that nonsense we call remorse. This is about something else. Of course, this wouldn't have happened if you hadn't introduced me to Ziya. But would that have been better? No, absolutely not! I would have just carried on with my miserable life. I would have always remained a candidate. Can someone be a candidate for candidacy for his whole life? At a certain point, you have to become the professor. So I became the professor, Minas. This is why I'm letting myself lecture you, the poet. Yes, don't argue. Poetry is too sacred a thing for me to let you make a game out of it with ridiculous excuses. Living as a dead man for a month, I know what poetry means. Poets are the ones who inhabit death and see life laid bare. I want you to be proud, just as I was proud of you. Everyone needs a certain measure of pride to be able to live. Did you really think I would have stayed with you? It's me we're talking about. I never knew how to stay in one place. Something grabbed me by the hand and flung me every which way. Hurry! How did you expect me not to be a thief and a cheat, eating the hard-earned bread of others? There's something I have to tell you. My friendship with you was not entirely out of self-interest. If I had left you, I'm sure you would have fallen into the clutches of the people who frequent those upstairs cafés on Boulevard Saint-Michel. The literary types, I mean. Nothing is deadlier to a poet than an environment like that. Our place was fine, the Billard, the cafés of people like Apkar. Never mind that their brawls used to embarrass the ones upstairs. Note that I'm already talking in the past tense. When I say that this is a dead man talking to you . . .

At any rate, promise me, Minas, that you will never go to those cafés. Do you think I didn't notice your anguish whenever you would walk past and glance over at them? Your eyes would be glued to the door of The Ani whenever we came out of the hotel. Keep to yourself, Minas, alone. Go ahead and burn in your own blaze, but escape the flames like a bluebird. Be one of the accursed. The accursed are God's spoiled children. I understand why you read Corbière and Lautréamont. Those spurned poets are your brothers in spirit, but you must read in Armenian, in particular. Hate what isn't written in Armenian. Hate even what is written in French with its astounding beauty. We need to hate, otherwise we will be lost. You can't imagine the sorrow I felt whenever you would go up to listen to them, especially to the men at La Source.[8] *Do you know what they were discussing? They were talking about Bergson, Keyserling, and Spengler, as if they were professors, as if nothing irreparable had happened to us. Be careful not to turn into one of those men. One day, all the air will be let out of them. As I said, you have to be alone, alone like a saint before God, alone like a man in love before a woman. I know your life will be filled with bitterness, but you will measure it from within against the bitterness of our people.*

Fine, I suppose that all of this sounds like a lecture. This is not why I sat down to write. This came once I started writing and took precedence, because I loved you the most.

Do you remember what you said to me outside the Billard on our way back from seeing Ziya's bloated corpse?

"Bravo, Vahakn," you said in amazement. "How did you manage not to give yourself away? Your body language didn't betray you at all."

There was nothing clever or masterful about it. If I had been like everybody else, I would have surely given myself away, because the living live in fear of losing their lives. Fear is the enemy. But you're forgetting that I was already dead and death is a place where fear is afraid to set foot.

Now listen to me. What I'm about to say should not be ignored. The fate of an entire people hangs in the balance. That people is us, a thing called the Armenians. We can all give speeches on Bergson, Keyserling, and Spengler in cafés, we can all—as fathers sitting in our homes in front of our wives and children—work to make a place for ourselves in life and be buried in that place, unaware of the fact that a Turcocidal impulse has been planted in each one of us. A killer plotting in the dungeon of our souls is waiting for the chance to leap out of his hiding place. The Turks didn't know what they were doing to us when they slaughtered us like chickens, embedding in us their future sentence. Don't laugh. If someone told me the same thing a month ago, I would have laughed, too. Now we are done laughing. Fini de rire. Finita la commedia. *Would you understand if I told you that Ziya's killer is not the one writing this note? The one writing this note is himself the victim of the other, the one who, the night that Ziya and I were walking along the river, suddenly stepped out of me and started walking alongside me, his arm slung through mine, our bodies almost one. Sometimes I felt that I was looking him right in the face. Even when I took Ziya's neck between my fingers and pressed, it seemed as though I were a witness to a crime being committed by someone else.*

All Armenians nurture a Turcocidal impulse in the darkest crevice of their heart. A part of every single piece of bread eaten goes to feed the killer inside, nourishing it continuously with such instinctive force that it will survive for generations to come.

One Sunday, I went to church. As usual, there were crowds inside and outside. Inside were the ones praying; outside were the ones mingling. I went inside, not to pray, but to hear the music of the liturgy. I often go into the churches I come across. Nothing soothes me more than the music of the divine. My whole being coils into my soul. At no other time do I feel anything so powerfully, almost to the point of seeing my own being within me. The liturgy went on and the faithful prayed passionately on their knees, sometimes standing up and making the sign of the cross. The word "God" could be heard through the wisps of incense. I was standing motionless in a corner. I took in the scene through half-closed eyes and my soul filled with the feeling of being surrounded by a congregation that had surrendered itself to an unknown, omnipotent power. Suddenly, I can't say how, the feeling of that presence began to blur, as if it were being transformed by suspicion. Little by little, it seemed that the liturgy was just preparation for a conspiracy, that from one moment to the next, the will of the congregation would be unleashed by an omnipotent power from above and turn this pious gathering into a mob. Already the clank of the swords resounded in my ears, even though I saw it was just the sound of the dzndzgha *ringing.*[9] *The priest, leaning against the holy table at the altar, turned around, raised his paternal hand, and said, "May peace be upon you." It was in that instant that my mind played a trick on me, making me believe that the priest was in fact about to signal the start of a bloody battle. I jumped up from my seat with both hands clasped over my mouth, stopping myself from yelling into the crowd: "Murderers! Murderers!"*

I ran to the park on the Champs Elysées. I felt like a wild beast, but a surprising calm came over me as soon as I sat down on a bench. It was so peaceful underneath the trees. It was a kind of serenity that only a Sunday could bring. I started to think. I thought about my plans. I started to organize my life in my mind. After my breakdown in the church, the quintessentially human practice of organizing a life seemed like a miraculous feat. Go ahead, laugh! If they put a knife in your hand right now and threw a Turk at your feet, you probably wouldn't have time to laugh. Just as I didn't with Ziya. And look, this is what happens. Murder, then suicide. Something to be avoided at all costs. That shouldn't happen. Let's suppose for a moment that three million Armenians kill three million Turks, causing three million suicides. Who wins? The Turk again, of course, because there would still be fifteen million left. So we must always make sure that the three million Armenians are, wherever they may be, still capable of killing three million more Turks and can do it again and again until the very end—the natural end.

Now I've come to the point of my letter. By the time this note reaches you, I'll have ceased to exist. Why? Who is forcing me? My crime will not have left a single trace behind. A clean crime. And yet tomorrow, after I finish writing, I will kill myself. If the same opportunity arises one day, I don't want you to go the way I have. Don't argue. Listen. You're Armenian like me and you have a heart. Having a heart is our biggest danger. Experience has taught me that the resilience of the heart depends on how much hatred we fill it with. Let's fill it with hatred. Let's make it swell with hatred. Despite the practical education Hortense gives you, despite her efforts to help you become a man, you're still a boy, a naïve boy who chases after Nicole, after a shadow. Now that I'm thinking about this, I don't regret the lesson Fatma taught me. Thanks to her, I was able to carry out my duty as an Armenian. Of course, you don't understand what I'm talking about. I've never talked to you about Fatma. What use was there in telling each other our stories, right? Each one of us has inherited a similar one.

Fatma is the Turkish woman who adopted me. She freed me, so that I could come here. She didn't know what she was doing either.

We had been walking for days. Our feet were raw. We were hungry and lightheaded and could barely keep ourselves upright. I was so exhausted that I constantly lagged behind. Standing in the middle of the deserted road and raising my arms into the air, I cried and screamed until the corners of my mouth began to tear. I always lagged behind. I was struck with terror whenever I saw the caravan slowly disappear down the road ahead. My mother had to run back to drag me along, begging and pleading, "Son, don't fall behind. Walk, for God's sake, walk! The gendarmes will kill you."

It's true that those who lagged behind went down with one stroke of the sword. There was no time. The caravan had to keep moving. I couldn't walk. There were others who couldn't walk either, old women and children like me. From time to time, commotion swept through the caravan as mothers ran back to collect their children. Lashes of a whip brought the caravan to order and it continued to advance slowly and sorrowfully.

One afternoon, we reached a village. Seeing houses drained me of energy even more. The will to walk had left me. I didn't want to take one more step, though my terrified mother was pulling me by the hand. The Turkish villagers had gathered to watch the miserable procession. My mother didn't stop screaming. Falling to the ground, I resisted her tugging and asked for water. I couldn't understand why she refused to give me the water that was so indifferently following its course down the river a few steps away. Suddenly, one of the gendarmes grabbed me by the hand and threw me toward the villagers. My mother, losing her mind, shrieked and screamed, but I didn't budge. The gendarme tried to kick her toward the rest of the caravan, but she continued to shout weakly, "my son, my son," choking on her tears. Then the gendarme drove his sword into my mother's chest. The caravan kept going for better or worse. Worse rather than better. My mother stayed where she was, painting the earth with her blood.

To this day, I still haven't been able to resign myself to the idea that I was the cause of my mother's death. But how can I explain the terrifying tyranny of thirst? As I walked, the road suddenly turned into a rushing river. The water swelled, wave after wave, and I threw myself into them with the force of my entire body, only to find myself on the dry, dusty road, clutching dirt in my arms and feeling thirst as heavy as rocks in my mouth.

Fatma took me to her house. She took care of me for days. She soothed and caressed me, pressing me to her chest with all her might. "Oghloum, oghloum," *she used to say, as my mother's voice still rang in my ears.*[10] *It was only her voice within me. The skin on my body was like a thick hide that nothing could penetrate. Within me was a world where terrible loneliness reigned, where my mother's screams were drowned out by my sobs, the unfettered lament of a night storm.*

Then I started going to the fields with Fatma, but I couldn't work. I couldn't have worked, even if I had wanted to. My head was as heavy as a boulder. I couldn't do anything at all. Every one of her pleas to work encountered resistance in me. Out of the corner of my eye, I would watch Fatma, who, encouraged by my glance, would smile at me and mutter something, her words suddenly stiffening my whole being with an inexplicable inner recalcitrance. Only when I was alone in the summer would my spirit lighten for a moment as I watched larks soar into the sky. But when they pulled their wings in and dipped into the plowed fields, I would suddenly start throwing rocks at them, moved by a fierce rage. And I would cry. I would cry with my whole body. I don't know what would have happened to me if I hadn't cried. Maybe my shriveled heart would have split open and emptied out. One day, when I had surrendered to uncontrollable, insatiable sobbing, I started to choke, unable to stop my sobs, until Fatma, startled, ran over to me and took me in her arms.

"Oghloum, oghloum," *she said. "Don't cry. This is just how the world is."*

But I kept shaking and grinding my teeth.

That was when something terrible happened. Hugging me tightly to her chest, Fatma kissed my cheeks. As she kissed me, I could hear a strange irregularity in her breathing. I remembered my mother's kiss and Fatma's kiss frightened me. When my mother kissed me, quickly and anxiously, her *kiss moistened my cheeks, calmed my soul, and made me feel as happy as a soldier returning triumphantly from battle. There was something else in Fatma's kiss. It had such an impatience in it that it reminded me of a fox that I'd seen devour a chicken in our garden early one morning. All of a sudden, I don't quite know how, fear awakened my numbed heart. I was scared and so I ran. Fatma ran after me. My twelve-year-old legs carried me far from her. I spent the whole day in the forest—confused, shaken, and weak. As it started to get dark, I returned to the house with my head hung and my feet unsteady, like a dog with its tail between its legs. That day, without warning, I resigned myself to my fate. I became a yielding slave.*

Fatma was waiting for me at the door. She brought me inside and we sat together at the table. We were silent. We didn't speak. After dinner, I went to bed, curled up and trembling, my head buried in my arms, as though to protect it from an impending blow. That night, Fatma sowed in me the seeds of a murderer. For me, the bed was the very edge of the world, beyond which there was nowhere to retreat. This is how resignation settled in me. I had surrendered, but I felt that my resignation was a hidden, puzzling, grinning, unrecognizable kind of determination, which, mingling with my resignation and acting as its support, was like a force condensing in the core of my soul.

Of course, I wasn't aware of this back then. It would be years before I realized it, until Ziya nurtured those seeds and helped them sprout under his warm, misty gaze.

But let's not get ahead of ourselves.

Sometime later, Fatma came into my room. Time suddenly stood still. A sense of looming danger overcame me. I was still and petrified. Fear squeezed my throat again and, burrowing my neck into my shoulders, I summoned all my strength to forget my own existence. I was trying to ignore the danger that mounted as the cautious sound of Fatma's bare feet padded across the wooden floor toward my bed. My ears were so finely tuned to her footsteps that even when they stopped, their echo resonated in me, carrying with it the shudder of fear. At last, silence settled, spreading and encompassing the entire world, and I felt alone, vulnerable, and helpless. It seemed as if it were my last day, as if suddenly everything were about to come to an end. I kept hugging myself tightly, so tightly that even the force of a knife would be powerless against my strength. The silence grew more threatening, more disturbing. It was a disintegrating silence that wore out even the most determined sense of patience. I threw off my blanket, wanting to put up a final fight and confront the danger face to face. Fatma was standing by my bed with a kerosene lamp in her hand, and . . . how should I put this, Minas? She was naked, completely naked, her head resting lightly on one side of the lamp. In the dim light, her lips offered a sweet, pleading smile. Her eyes greedily searched my gaze, looking for the promise of consent and reminding me of the way she drove her shovel into the ground for the next day's harvest.

Do you know what? Even today I still don't understand why the infinite sweetness in her eyes—a supplication—terrified me so much that I took my head in my arms in order not to see it, unable to scream and stifling the cry in my throat.

"My son," Fatma said. "Don't be scared. Fatma doesn't want to hurt you."

Then she got down on her knees and brought her face close to mine. Once again that breathing—driven by a fast, irregular heartbeat, bringing to mind leaves blown here and there in an autumn breeze—came to furrow my face with evil, as I sought refuge on the mattress spread across the floor, clawing at it, clutching it with all of my might. Suddenly, I lost my resistance. This is what sent Fatma into a rage. In her anger, she tried to grab me—begging and coaxing as she tried to hug me, press me against her naked body, and undress me at the same time. She finally succeeded. I had no strength left and just lay there, silent and lifeless. She started to knead me with her body like dough. Closing my eyes to what she was doing, I thought of my mother's blood, which was still outside on the road. It hadn't yet been washed away by the rain. Neither my agitation nor my submission could disarm Fatma. The more I tried to avoid her touch, the more violently her passion burned. Do you know what the result of this struggle was? Fatma began beating me with tightly clenched fists, abandoning herself to unbounded rage. I don't know where her wrath would have ended if I hadn't suddenly taken her in my arms to neutralize the blows. At the same time, she seized the chance to press me against her chest with such force, such vehemence, that my body began to tremble from a terrifying cramp in my thighs, and I hugged her even more desperately to stop it, to lose myself in her. The silent shudder through my heart and thighs became the last tremors of death. The tremors gave way to a boundless feeling of lethargy as they slowed and disappeared one by one. I felt something warm and wet on my thighs and then right after . . . I don't remember anymore. What I do *remember is that the next morning, to my surprise, I found myself in my bed. I looked around. Everything was peacefully in its place. It seemed that I had spent a long time in the grips of death. I had found a way to make life bearable, to forget life by living in death. This led to my quest to find the moment that opened the door to nothingness, the door that I would pass through. Can you understand that state of mind in which you can no longer feel anything, where all thought is absent? A vegetative state. What am I saying? At least a vegetable has a drive to live. It knows how to veer its course to avoid an obstacle and mount quiet, stubborn resistance against all hindrances, until at last it emerges into the light. Let's say that I was like an object that was always subdued and never showed the slightest sign of life. You throw it, it lands where you want it to land. If you throw it into a corner, it stays there. If you throw it into water, it sinks slowly to the bottom. If you toss it into the air, it falls back down. Never does it ever resist. Fatma did all of these things to me and I gave in to them. If someone had told me that I was a living being and not an object, it would have surprised me to hear, despite the fact that, as an inanimate object, I would have been incapable of feeling surprise. I used to wait impatiently, yet passively, for those moments when she would come to me, sniffing around like a dog finding a spot to shit. With that hoarse voice of hers she would purr* "oghloum, oghloum" *as she kissed my cheeks. I was like a piece of timber. On the inside, I was like a wooden plank, but on the outside my arms and legs shook to perform the movements I had been trained to make mechanically. Then we clung to each other like crazy people about to throw ourselves into nothingness. I would end up convulsing, which brought me a dark awareness of something happening outside of me faraway, but which was in fact deeply rooted in me. From deep within, I felt my arms wrap tightly around her body and my teeth and buttocks tighten, shaken by the anguish that people likely feel when they find themselves face to face with death.*

I'm sure you haven't forgotten the day that Apkar, with a dirty snicker, played that game with us outside the Billard. The three of us were sitting silently, sullenly. Apkar had grown bored and kept yawning. Suddenly he got up and, with a smirk that told of the wicked deed to come, took out a piece of paper, folded it a few times, and made it into a little man. He put it on the table and dripped some of his coffee onto it. The paper man started to writhe, squirm, and soften, giving Apkar some childish joy. The writhing of the paper man reminded me of the movements of someone during particularly depraved sex. I couldn't control myself and unjustly slapped Apkar, because in his paper man, I saw the image of Fatma and me as we sank into nothingness.

But I also remember the day—I remember it as if it were yesterday. How could I forget?—the orphan collectors came to our village with two Allied soldiers.[11] *Yes, I remember it as if it were yesterday. Together with a few other orphans, we waited as the collectors went from house to house. I didn't understand what was happening. I stood there sadly with my head bowed along with the other orphans who were just as quiet and scared as I was. We didn't talk to one other. There was absolutely no exchange among us. Sometimes we lifted our heads and glanced at one other, quickly looking away if our eyes met. All the kids were younger than I was and had forgotten their language, their past, their identity. There was a small, chubby boy who managed to hold my gaze and had a big, sad smile on his naïve face. It was in that moment, raising my head to avert my eyes from the boy's heartrending stare, that for the first time I noticed the landscape that I had lived in for years, oblivious. In the distance was a wide horizon. The spring sun had cast a misty veil on the hills that stretched from north to south, a milky haze—still and ethereal—that hadn't been able to rise higher than the damp earth. Above, the sun had dulled the blue of the sky. Beyond it was the dense forest where I had fled one day, frightened by Fatma. Along the edge, a stream swelled with melting snow and rushed through the visibly calm air. Our house was on the other side of the stream—that's what Fatma used to call it: our house. In the garden, the plum trees and cherry trees had bloomed, looking wildly happy, like a colorful postcard. In that instant, I had forgotten the filth and ugliness of the shack, the hungry dog and Fatma's husband, a soldier who hadn't yet returned from the war. From afar, our house looked so pretty beneath the blooming trees. My heart grew fuller and my vision blurred. Here and there were the other houses in the village, spaced far apart from one another and hiding behind a curtain of fruit trees. My God, how big the world seemed! I understood then that I was coming out of a narrow, dark cave, thrust into the bright world like a butterfly springing from its cocoon, flapping its new wings in the sunlight after a short period of sadness. I, too, was a butterfly, who now flew and fluttered, intoxicated by the sun and air. I started to cry, to sob. Huge teardrops streamed down my cheeks and filled my mouth, and I licked their saltiness with delight. Fatma was watching from a distance. Encouraged by my tears, she probably attributed them to our separation and took a few steps toward me with her arms extended, but a soldier raised his hand to stop her. From a distance, Fatma smiled at me, a melancholy smile that still wanted to hope. A ray of sunlight shimmered over one of her eyes and I could see a teardrop. Yes, Fatma thought I was crying for her. But really, whom was I crying for? For the memory of my mother, who now painfully returned to my mind? No, I didn't know why I was crying. I only knew that as I was crying, a mass of emotion was dislodged in my heart, and at times my crying became the ecstasy of a bird soaring into the sky. I cried like a newborn just entering the world, distressed and choking on his tears.*

"Why are you crying?" asked one of the orphan collectors, assuming that it was because I was being separated from my mother, Fatma. That was how

it was for many of the children who had forgotten their real mothers. They were crying and wanted to run away from the orphan collectors and—who knows?—maybe they were scared of the unknown, of an uncertain future, and their tiny souls clung anxiously to the present.

When we finally left the village and rode away in a military car, clouds of dust rising to obscure the village behind me, I sensed why I was crying. I was sitting in the back of the car brooding and daydreaming, my gaze fixed on the distance, on the village fading into the landscape, from which rose muddled and unwelcome images. The most vivid image was that of my mother—my mother who had lost her mind and, with pleading hands, was still calling after me, and there I was, laying on the road, stubborn and deaf to her pleas. This was the boy I was leaving behind. The farther away the car got from the village, the more he sunk into the shortening horizon, which closed in on him like a lid until, totally cut off from me, I no longer had any connection to him. Then big teardrops started falling from my eyes, slowly, involuntarily, and strangely peacefully. I cried for my childhood, for my tarnished, violated childhood, which had been snatched from me cruelly, just as I had been taken from my distraught mother years ago. Now the car drove away with a twice-orphaned boy of fifteen, jostling him as it jumped over the bumps and depressions in the road.

In reality, Minas, it's hard to pinpoint in our dark, inner abyss the decisions that eventually drive us to commit the fateful acts that shape our lives. This is not a novel that you can construct any way you please. A novel is a reality unto itself, a self-contained reality, which renders acceptable the truth-like, even arbitrary, elements that go into composing it. We're dealing with life here, the reality of life, so obviously it's critical to understand the exact motives behind our actions, isolate the moment of their genesis, identify their basis, accept and digest, if you like, the special task of their classification, recall the instant of their manifestation in our consciousness and, even more, the organization of that manifestation in the realization of the act. Like I said, this is not about aesthetic pleasure or construction, but rather about a life lesson. This is a study. For this very reason, we are forced to record events with the utmost precision, then research and investigate whatever has collected in the subconscious. Like bubbles rising sporadically in water only to burst once they reach the surface and evaporate into the air, our inner impulses are neutralized on the surface of life by the daily demands that make up the struggle of existence.

Everything seems easy when it's over and done with. At first glance, it would seem that just taking a closer look would clarify everything. But it's not like that. The reality is much more complicated. When I sat down, what I had planned to write seemed plain and simple. Now, the more I think about it, everything seems more elusive, more unexplainable. Everything is turning into a puzzle. The issue is knowing the limits that compose and shape the danger. What was the moment that passed through his senses and was recorded and captured on film? It was the one that would eventually turn Vahakn into an inept stepson of life. In other words, what would turn him into the candidate of his Turcocidal impulse? Which one of the restless waves stirring in the ocean's deep dungeon would sink the distressed ship trapped in the storm above?

That one and not any other.

This whole story, as you will see if we were to look closely, is just the tale of a handful of filthy sediment. No, I'm not talking about the ash on Ziya's tie. That was just where the eye needed to rest for a moment to notice the filth everywhere else, the filth that my life has made a constant effort to flee from. You know, there's no need to list the times that I've fled. As soon as I'd settled down, I would steal or cheat, and leave. I had just gotten married—I hadn't even slept with my wife—the last time I fled. It would take too long to go into them one by one. In any case, the filth was what I always tried to escape. Wherever I was, the filthy feeling would engulf me. I fled convinced that I would be freed of it, that I could leave it behind. At least that's what I thought. I saw everything as pure, because I needed to see everything as pure. It was a need to lead an upstanding life. Soon enough, though, the filth collected around me. On my wedding night, it seemed that once again I was about to get into bed with Fatma and enter a world devoid of thought and feeling, a negation of my life. Back then, as a boy searching for death, nothing was more desirable than that sense of nothingness, and I gave in to Fatma like someone willingly stepping into his own grave. Then I learned to like life thanks to the orphan collectors, who gave me the intoxicating freedom to think and feel, which reminded me of the soaring larks, but like them, I fell to the ground and into a muddy field. I tried to avoid this fall whenever

I fled, but that impossible escape was really anything but an escape, because what I didn't know was that what I was trying to flee from would always be there. It was rooted in me, clinging to me, attached to me like a Siamese twin. It was in my soul. I've carried it everywhere, from country to country, city to city, fooling myself into believing that I had run away from it.

Maybe I'm not explaining myself clearly. Now I'm afraid that I won't even be able to go through with killing myself. My days are numbered. I'm already dead, right? Otherwise, how would I be able to see things so clearly? If I return to life, everything will be filthy again. Minas, when you write, do it in such a way that you can't sense your own mortality. Only the dead have the power of discernment and fearlessness. Suddenly time has stopped. Past, present, and future no longer exist. Everything is in the present. Everything. But it's not the present as we know it. It hasn't been given a place in the dictionary. We have to create a new word. This is your job; some thinkers have called it eternity. But this word is suspicious, or if you prefer, it has a suspicious ring to it. For me, it's an image. I leave it to you to confine it to a word. For example, let me take a math problem we were given in school. A few cubic meters of water run out of a faucet and into a bathtub in the span of a minute; a lesser amount runs into the drain at the bottom of the bathtub at the same rate. How long will it take for the bathtub to be filled to capacity? The tub will fill up, but the amount of water won't be enough for a bath. This word "enough" corresponds to the idea of the present. We see the same image in mythology with the tub of the Danaides. The Danaides were continuously trying to fill a tub that was continuously emptying, but the tub would also fill by retaining its contents. The words "contents" and "enough" have the same meaning here and that meaning can be summed up with one word: reality.

That other kind of present that we use in daily conversation is a deceptive, slippery thing. How can anything be in the present when, as soon as it has broken from the future, it has already turned into the past? That present is an illusion. It's past and future at the same time. A state outside time that the eye can perceive in its entirety, as though everything were at your disposal, strewn around your table, and you only needed to give shape to it and organize it as you pleased, moving an object here, another there, like a theater director in charge of all the elements of a play: the script, the actors, the set design, the stage—not the tiny wooden stage the size of a box, mind you, but the whole of the universe. After all, isn't life a play that has been thrown into the universe?

You might be wondering if there is a point to this long digression. You might even be thinking that I'm trying to justify myself for all the evil things I've done, especially to you, the one who has enjoyed their bitter fruit. No, my dear boy, what is the importance of criticism to someone who will cease to exist tomorrow? What interests me is the search for truth. It's truth that forces us to walk through life with our eyes wide open. But, alas, it's always at the eleventh hour that truth appears, once we have our eyes fixed not on life, but on death.

Before, I wrote about how we left "our" village in a military car, raising into the air lazy, calm dust from the road as I carried with me my violated childhood.

Can I tell you something? These are all just words. Obviously they have a weight and an emotional charge that can easily bring listeners to tears, but they're still nothing more than words. We must explain, convey a concrete meaning, even if it weakens the emotional resonance, and be truthful first and foremost. As I've said already, only the truth counts. What does a violated childhood mean? Explaining it would require a detailed description of a four-year story of how filth had settled little by little in the soul of a boy, like coffee grounds settling at the bottom of a cup. My soul was like that cup. How? You can't be serious, Minas. Why wouldn't a soul look like a coffee cup? You have a strange understanding of the soul. People have always loved abstract concepts. But the abstract doesn't exist. The only abstraction is God. You can be sure that one day we will hold Him in our hands like a Mickey Mouse doll. You don't believe it? But you do realize that they wash coffee cups after the coffee is gone. Now let's suppose that a coffee cup had been left unwashed for four years. You would agree that the cup would be harder to wash than one that had just been used that day. It's the same with the soul. Don't be troubled by that word. I know that you're a year older than I am, but don't forget that I'm dead, so I have already grown old and can slip into your father's role. It was the feeling of being forced to scrub away four years' worth of crusty sediment and filth that suddenly made me cry with all my heart that day. We know what to use to wash a cup. Water, obviously. The soul isn't a cup that we can wash with water. I didn't say the soul is a cup. I said it is like *a cup. You could assume then that the soul can be washed with tears. No, tears only streak our faces and tire the heart with the startling emotions that pass through it. You could assume this because I did cry when the time came to wash my soul. Yes, when the time came. But it wasn't the time that had come, it was the unexpected awareness that it was coming. How would I do it and what would I do it with? This was what brought about a long, constant string of searches and escapes, and in the tears I shed that day, connected to my newfound awareness, were also hidden many trials and tribulations. I haven't cried since that day. Not once. Not even in the most desperate of situations, because tears wouldn't be what would wash my soul. And I waited. I waited for the idea to come on its own, just like everything else that arrives just at the right time for those who know how to wait, for those who allow themselves to wait, always open, like a poet to inspiration. Later becomes too late. All things deferred are subject to loss. It's not for nothing that they say not to leave till tomorrow what you can do today.*

Here are all the different parts of the machine and each one has its function. We can't say that one part is better than another. Take away any part and the machine will stop working. There is also a driving force that brings all the parts together to form a whole for the sake of its function and power. I prefer another word: existence. But existence is blind, dark, devoid of consciousness, a kind of elemental force whose roots lay within the filth of the soul. Hence the tragedy in which we swim. We swim in filth. Yes, we're filthy. That's why they call us "filthy Armenians." We've become so filthy that we look like those people who don't dare enter a party and instead stay outside by the door under the sun and the rain. Every Armenian, you and I, the men at La Source, all of us, all of us live with the anxiety of being washed. One day a terrible storm splattered all the mud in our land, expelled us, and settled in the depths of our souls. We want to be cleansed, Minas. We want to be cleansed, so we can live.

The ancients used to spill the blood of a rooster, a lamb, or a slave, and fathers used to sacrifice their own sons to cleanse their souls, to please God. What heathens, Minas, heathens! But then again, how true! And then Jesus came and said, "Live in peace. Love each other. I shed my blood once and for all, for all of humanity." In other words, he civilized humanity. I think it was Pascal whose soul rejoiced at the drop of blood that Jesus shed in the name of salvation. But Jesus's blood has been watered down for a long time now, blended with the earth and rendered powerless and unrecognizable. What the Armenian needs is Turkish blood: red, fresh, warm, and fragrant.

Do you remember that day outside the Billard when I brought my index finger to Ziya's neck to brush off the imaginary cigarette ash on the knot of his tie? Ziya—the ever-happy Ziya—kept on talking. I don't know what he was talking about. His hands were dancing in the air. His sharp chin had weakened and seemed to hang. As he spoke, the tension in his small mouth tried to keep his chin from falling. That part of his body was so ugly, but so childlike that it was not lacking a certain charm. What am I saying? This was his charm, the innocence of his expression, which made him endearing. His tiny black eyes would gleam and twinkle whenever he became animated. He was calm, like a summer afternoon, but within, something was raging in the bubbles that swarmed his heart. His dark, matte complexion concealed their existence, but you could sense a hidden, helpless restlessness, a kind of mysterious effect. The expression in his features seemed lifeless. This was the result of the mixture of the Mongolian paleness and the darkness of his skin, but the intensity of his eyes—their sparkling, mischievous darting, which snapped back and forth between you to me—revealed an extraordinary vitality. His gaze traveled back and forth, each time tearing a strip of his smile off his face and tossing it onto your face, where it stayed stuck like gum. In that moment, did you also feel a sense of defiance finding a place for itself inside you, as though leading you to take that stifling mask off your face? Sometimes his gaze would wander and linger on the commotion on the street, his chin low and protruding into the air and his eyes squinting. Was he thinking? No, he wasn't. Whether he was or not, his pensiveness gave the impression that something had been lost and evoked the sorrow stirred by that loss. I consoled myself by thinking that maybe he had noticed an acquaintance or a girl passing by on the street, and that the reason for his sorrow was that he was with us, that he had fallen victim to our friendship, and was being deprived of a chance to have some fun. One day the strings of this game unexpectedly came undone in front of my eyes, when Ziya once again cocked his head in the air and assumed what had become a familiar position to us. All of a sudden, I realized that he simply chose to be absent from us. Mentally absent, he also imagined himself physically absent from us, too: invisible, an attempt to flee from us like an ostrich burying its head in the desert sand after realizing its enemy is coming.

Once, when his gaze was floating back and forth between us, it rested on mine for longer than usual. No, not longer, but that's how it seemed, because his gaze focused on me as it passed; he studied me and went deep into my penetrating gaze for a unit of time that—how should I put this?—can't even be called an instant. It was precisely the amount of time needed for curiosity to be born and immediately die, during which quite a number of things happened. For instance, his chin suddenly relaxed; his mouth hung open, suspending his words in his voice; his cheeks grew round with the blooming of a fake smile; and his right eye twitched slightly, as if to say, "I know. I know what you want, Vahakn. But I forgive you," when he sensed the heaviness of the moment in my gaze, embarrassed. Carried away, I turned my gaze to the cigarette ash that my imagination had invented.

After that, I stopped listening to Ziya's stories. My eyes were busy constantly searching for specks of ash on the knot of his tie, behind which was the concave part of the throat that yields so easily to the slightest pressure of the thumb.

An inaccurate inference could be made from what I just wrote. When I say that I stopped listening to him from that day on, it makes it sound like it was a conscious decision on my part. In reality, I should have said that I wasn't able to listen to him. Indeed, I couldn't even have done it if I'd wanted to. Whenever I found myself in front of Ziya, my mind became entirely absorbed by the strange shaking in my hands. It was an unease that I couldn't calm. On either side of me, no matter where I was, my two hands—even though they were part of me—formed a self-governing reality at my sides, independent of me, with demands and a will that evaded my own. I was like two people in one—one in constant conflict with the other. The more my will worked to prevent their free and independent functioning, the more irritated they became and the more they argued, remaining unmoved by the limits of their self-determination. My hands had a mind of their own, and I did too. The two were at odds, in true competition to suppress and surpass each other. Often I caught myself conversing with them.

Yes, I talked to them, tried to reason with them. What did I try to reason with them about? I didn't know. I reasoned, that's all, and with fierce resolve. Sometimes I would suddenly change directions on a walk, run to the café, sit down at a table, and immediately the argument would begin between me and my hands. I looked at them with the pitiful look of the defeated. They refused to be reprimanded. On the contrary, they were ready to break the table and chair in two. The one thing I managed to do—of course not deliberately, simply automatically, like a person does instinctually in the grips of a headache—was to put my hands on my forehead. With this, the defiance in my hands subsided, but my headache did not. Yet when Ziya approached with a smile on his face and rushed to extend his hand, that calm was different. Both my hands lunged to meet his and clasped them with unusual joy, like friends reuniting after a long period apart.

The day after his "I know, I know," he left me a note at the hotel. "Please forgive me for my inconsiderate behavior last night," he wrote. "Love is so blind that it makes me forget how sensitive you are. Once again, I ask for your forgiveness and beg you not to see any ulterior motives in my words. Until tonight, Ziya."

You went to work. Left alone, I couldn't go out as usual. I was afraid. I'd had a premonition. When I did go out, it felt as though someone else was in my place, roaming the forest of the Parisian crowd. Hands in my pockets, I let my fingers graze Ziya's note now and again, letting its shock pass through my fingers. No, this particular letter did not resemble any of the ones from before. Gone was the spirit of forgiveness. Suddenly, I encountered a different Ziya. But what was it exactly? My mind couldn't rest. I couldn't stop seeing his gaze in front of me, hidden within the folds of my eyes. Anywhere I went, it would follow. If I turned right, it did too. If I turned left, it followed suit. It was calm only when I walked straight ahead, but the gaze remained fixed on me, not letting me go. It stopped feeling that panic that seized it whenever I turned back—a panic for which I no longer have an explanation—but it threw itself into imminent danger. It was terrified when I accidentally put my hand in my pocket. I didn't need to see the words in the letter. They were already recorded onto my tongue and I repeated them like a broken record. Sometimes I had an uncontrollable urge to open the letter in my hands and look straight into the eye that was hidden there, the one that played an evil game with my fingers when I had my hand in my pocket. It was one thing to know that the eye was there through the simple, trembling touch of my fingers; it was quite another to suddenly have it in your open palm, under your nose, and to look at it face to face—of course, not without trembling. I didn't have to look at it to start trembling. Thinking about it was enough and realizing that I was the one who put Ziya's eye in my mind, retrieving it from my memory. Afterward it became very hard to purge my mind of such a scheming image, like a fly that comes back to the same spot to rest on the same wound after being shooed away.

Then I pushed myself to go to the Jardin du Luxembourg. I circled the park. After the morning's gusty rainstorm, the sun had come out and lounged like a houseguest. The park, of course, was filled with people, but when Nicole and Monique passed by the Grand Bassin, laughing arm in arm, shoulder to shoulder—perhaps they had been telling each other funny stories—they seemed to be lost in a daydream. Their laughter sounded like a pizzicato and rose like bubbles, not only making them oblivious to their surroundings, but also making the whole park seem deserted. It was as though as they passed, the park offered itself to them and became theirs. They sauntered through it freely as if it were a dream. The park was a dream. They were not. They had long disappeared. The lace of the dream hung over the eyes of the park's visitors and estranged them as much from themselves as from their surroundings.

I don't know where I went after that. I forced myself onto the street. All that's stayed with me is walking out of an open gate onto Rue de Vaugirard. After that, my brain didn't record anything else. Suddenly I found myself sitting on a bench in the park behind Notre Dame at the sharp corner of the island that juts out into the water and splits the river in two. A feeling of hunger twisted my stomach, but I couldn't eat. I was hungry and unable to eat. It was probably something else that gave me that sensation—something that tricked me into turning my attention toward my stomach. Everything had become unreal since we had seen Ziya's body together. I knew you had gone home a while ago. The cold had set in. That end of the island is always chilly in the evening because of the raging waters of that part of the river. There was an added chill, which slowly descended from the sky as the evening approached. I made an effort to stand up, mustering up strength by thinking of the food you must have brought home with you. I sat back down. Eating was out of the question as long as that eye was in my pocket, folded into the note, wound into the letters and eating me up little by little, chewing and ruminating. Suddenly my hand flew out of my pocket with the piece of paper. Under my gaze, there was only one sentence. The first lines were completely smeared or had become illegible because of who knows what. So the letter had become: " . . . beg you not to see any ulterior motives."

It was like on a stormy night, when lightning strikes and you see, standing right in front of you, the stump of a tree, which moments before had been cloaked in black—how sharp, how clear its dark, dense mass becomes when it's isolated from the surroundings to which it belongs, how it penetrates your eye and illuminates your consciousness like a thunderbolt. Minas, I understood the hidden meaning in those words through the light that had flooded my mind.

That day, as he spoke like an old lady with his chin hanging low, not a single word reached my ear. If it did, it flew out as soon as it arrived, because of the roadblock in my mind, which was entirely preoccupied by the ash on his tie. My gaze immediately drifted upward to rest on that spot, so close to his tanned neck, and especially considering the strange feeling I had about the blood circulating beneath his skin, I thought Ziya had guessed that I had been sniffing for his blood, inspiring a dark thought in him. But then my lingering gaze prompted him to give a mischievous wink and puff out his lips as if to say, "I know . . . I know." The idiot that I was, I turned my eyes away from his accusatory stare and bowed my head in shame like a boy caught red-handed. And yet, do you see how clever he was? Convinced that we hadn't been able to break through the hidden meaning in his words, he came to us with an apology the following day, as usual, intent on directing our attention to that which he thought had escaped us, to the essential word. The other words had been written to fill space, as decoration, so that he could write the other one, both hidden and obvious, the "ulterior motives," which could not have been more "ulterior." He could not have been more provocative in his sly, fake, and meandering manner.

Now I understand. There is a word that rings in my ear, and then another one and another one still. I don't know how they stayed there and why now they are waking from their slumber. Their ringing is so loud! Since you weren't as obsessed as I was, how come you didn't understand? You're to blame. Do you know why? Because you think it's natural: since you can be in love with a French woman, Ziya can be in love with an Armenian woman. It all seems so natural to you. Perhaps it is natural, but tell me, is there anything natural in our lives? In the life of an Armenian? No, don't you think he told us so tenderly about the love he had for an Armenian woman to convince us of his sympathy for the Armenians? And to go on talking of ulterior motives, when it was his goal to make us feel that motive in the right way, so that—even though we may be far from them and released from them—we will continue to suffer on these distant shores. Oh, Ziya. Ziya. I've searched for that gaze of yours ever since, but it never rested on the blacks of my eyes again. It slid over them like oil. I wished for it to return once more and perch on the corner of my eyes like a bird sitting daintily on a tree branch.

Oh, Ziya's gaze.

It was what I sought for days and what led my eyes to rest on the knot of his tie near the spot where the ash had landed, so that when it appeared again, it would be easy to capture right away. Yet, my eyes came to my aid unsummoned and willed it, so that my pursuit didn't flounder, but burgeoned and ripened, making room for the ash and putting it on the knot of his tie. It was there whenever I looked sharply and intently, whenever it was supposed to be there, because the fluttering of his gaze suddenly seemed close and similar—not similar but identical—to Fatma's gaze, whenever we used to quietly sit cross-legged around the low, round, wooden table to eat. Fatma's eyes would be staring at me and watching me, transfixed. Then her stare would flitter, attacking my nerves with a shudder brought about by her hideous fantasies. From her thoughts that thing would happen again and I would contract and tighten to become smaller and more distant. Fatma would stand up and come closer, her maniacal eyes looking into mine as I tried to keep my gaze down on my palms like a boy waiting for a beating. But Fatma, transformed into an uncontainable vortex, would jump on top of me and turn me around with a whack of the arm. In those moments, I felt as if I were a lamb about to be slaughtered, as I had seen her do, holding the animal's snout in her left hand and slitting its throat with her right.

Now do you understand why I tried to strangle Ziya to death that day outside the Billard? But my restless fingers were suddenly relieved of their tension and I only ended up taking my index finger to the knot of his tie to say with absolute calm, "It's nothing. Just some cigarette ash."

That day I knew how I would kill Ziya. I would strangle him. Did I know? Someone in me did. I hadn't thought about killing him until that last day, until I reached the Square du Vert-Galant. It hadn't even crossed my mind, even when we got up to take a walk and wander the streets, over the Pont Neuf and down into the Square du Vert-Galant. We sat in the park on the tip of the island under the trees. As always, it was Ziya who did the talking. I couldn't talk anyway. We had barely come down the steps before I started to feel empty. I felt infinite pressure, tense and petrified, through which passed not a flicker of thought. Ziya continued his endless stories while his eyes played and his hands danced in the air, his face as pensive as ever. Then we came close to the edge of the water. I had turned my back to the bridge, while Ziya stood tall like a statue against the water in the background. For a moment, he turned his gaze toward the river, dreamy and melancholy. When he turned back to me, he started telling his story again in a soft, low voice, as if someone could have overheard us. There wasn't anyone in sight. It was freezing along the river on that March night. It was late already—close to midnight. I had forgotten that it was time to go to Les Halles. Ziya spoke so sweetly that it seemed as if he could have gone on talking like that forever, right there underneath the lovely trees of the Square du Vert-Galant on the banks of the Seine, to which he had turned his back. As he gestured, a ray of light from above, from one of the lights on the bridge, suddenly shined into his eyes and illuminated his pupil. He blinked as he uttered a word heaving with meaning, then lifted his head and broke into laughter. Yes, Minas, Fatma was there, on the knot of his tie. Then I realized, at last, that I was going to kill Ziya. I understood this with a sense of complete composure, like a programmed machine that knows exactly where to put its thumb and press, on the very spot where harsh, vigorous pressure can make death instantaneous.

He could only say one thing—nothing more.

"What are you doing, Vahakn? Hey . . ."

Ziya's lifeless body began to fall and was about to collapse as I slowly laid him down on the ground, his neck still in my hands, which continued to squeeze fiercely. I couldn't move from where I was. My knees grew weak and I sat down next to his corpse. At the moment I laid his body on the ground, gently but calling on all my strength and making complete use of the terrible tension in my hands to prevent him from suddenly collapsing, a shiver passed through my thighs and gradually grew more intense before dying down little by little. Once I was sitting by his corpse, I realized that what had just happened within me was the very same clenched force that I once used to resist Fatma, a struggle followed by a complacent weakness that had kept me unconscious back then in a kind of agony. I must have sat there for a long time before coming out of that moment. First my head awoke, then my senses, and finally my muscles, which I could move very slowly, but without too much effort. I saw the river. Along its shores, the lights from above, lined up like worry beads, flickered and watched over the night's calm. It was because of that calm that I realized so much time had passed. The city takes on a pensive look after midnight. Then, before I stood up, I knelt down, gently gave his lifeless body a push, and silently surrendered him to the water. He stayed clung to the riverbank for a while, as though he didn't want to be separated from me, until the current carried him away, calmly and peacefully, at times wavering but always moving, and the farther he went, the deeper the sky became above my head. The distance grew and the corpse became smaller before my eyes. It wasn't yet morning. Then I climbed up to the bridge and came home. You were sleeping.

When I came home from the park behind Notre Dame, you were in the room, nervous, trembling, and lost. Poor Minas. You were pacing back and forth along the long intestine that was our room. You didn't know where to put your hands.

"Come on," you said at last, seething with impatience. "Hurry up already!"

For me, there was no need to rush anymore. Ziya's note had thrown my mind into chaos. I don't know how long it took me to get back to the room. No, I didn't need to rush anymore, but you didn't know that. I had a fever. I stretched out on the bed, speechless and mute, while your agitation grew, feeding on itself. Soon darkness would fall and it would be impossible to chase after the illusion. I had seen Nicole in the morning, but I hadn't told you. For one thing, I didn't have the strength to open my mouth, and then I was surprised to see you in that state. An ocean separated us. We were so far from each other. What tone should I have used to make you understand if I had dared to say, "Minas, don't run. It's pointless. You'll end up feeling deceived." If you had only heard their laughter that morning, their soul-wrenching, contemptuous laughter. From the silence of my window, I watched you in your haste. Your very being was dangling by a thread that a mean comment, an unkind word, or a throaty snicker would have been enough to snip. The ache of a man in love is truly a thing of beauty. Indeed, to fall in love is to fall ill. As I watched you, I thought of Ziya—the Ziya whom I was about to kill. The Ziya who, sitting with us outside the Billard that evening, was reliving, for our sake, the ache the Armenian woman had caused him.

Suddenly, noticing the dulled glow in my eyes, you asked me if I was sick and put your hand on my forehead. "It's hot," you said. "You're burning up."

You ran out into the street and came back with a box of aspirin, and when my fever went down much later, you were convinced of the good those aspirin of yours had done. But in reality, it was something else. It was something else entirely, my dear Minas.

With his note, Ziya had raised unnerving suspicion in my mind, set my head on fire, and put out the flames. Your ache, that admirable ache that I would never feel myself, undulated in front of me and got me thinking: here I am, then. I'll be dead and Minas will one day find peace in Nicole's arms, in Nicole's embrace, like Ziya so tenderly embraced the Armenian woman. Can you believe that the one who would soon strangle Ziya had, at that moment, come around to the idea of Ziya's love by seeing your own love for Nicole?

They say that a man who is about to die sits down to reckon with his life. My reckoning didn't take long. It didn't take long because my awareness of time had come to an end. I reckoned with life as I stood to face death, already feeling its peace, whereas I know for you the minutes sometimes seemed like centuries, like on that day. I reckoned with life and it was the reckoning that cured my fever.

So I started evaluating everything. Crowns of light fell over my eyes. Was my life only a lie, a delusion, which I've recorded here in all of its phases? What if all of this was nothing but the ravings of a madman? How is it, then, that next to both your lover and Ziya's lover stood Fatma's shadow? There she was, constantly lusting after that old sadism and offering me her nipples to twist once more like a booger between my thumb and index finger.

Fatma was a villager. She was not urbane like Ziya or a poet like you who suffers pain in silence. So all of this is a lie. I have constructed a story for myself to justify my unnecessary, disgraceful life.

We all think our lives are novels filled with hardship. Many times people have told me their life story, after which they stop, let out a long sigh, and say, "Ah, my whole life is a novel."

It's a novel not by virtue of what we have lived, but by virtue of how we narrate it. I've noticed that at least half of each story is a lie. Since every life is incomplete, the imagination completes the incomplete with fiction. So life is a tragedy. Life is like dough thrown onto the world. We complete nature's unfinished work by kneading, shaping, and molding our own piece of dough.

I'm afraid that I too have fallen prey to my own imagination, so here I end the rough draft of my novel and sign it in blood.

Vahakn

Usually he didn't feel the cold. So why did he feel the chill of that March morning so much? True, he was tired. He had spent the whole night stretched out in bed, reading Vahakn's papers. The rustle of the papers falling from his hand to the floor, one after the other, seemed like a whisper in deepening silence. Attuned to the sound, he listened to the fading, then dying, of the whisper of the night's stillness as he gently dropped a sheet of paper onto the pile on the floor. No, fatigue couldn't be the reason for the cold gnawing at his skin. How many nights had he been out on the street, even in the winter, and had met with courage the cold that found refuge and condensed in the heart of the morning—a cold that, transformed into ice, grated and cracked under his feet. He wasn't alone. Next to his feet were Vahakn's feet, which stomped on the frozen ground in anger, causing shrapnel of white ice to fly into the air and fall to the ground like shooting stars. No, he wasn't alone. So it was the solitude that made him feel the chill, not unlike that spring evening two years ago, when, cold and dejected, he met Vahakn outside the Billard. Only then did his teeth stop chattering, as though Vahakn had suddenly entered his chest and warmed his heart, taking it in his hands. And now they were happy around the table. They were still laughing well past midnight.

They turned the passersby into objects of their pleasure, noticing things to make fun of about them. Life boiled in their blood. Their good moods, their convulsive exuberance could only feed their lively warmth. Now and then, though, Minas's face darkened. The empty coffee cups shattered his cheerful disposition. Vahakn was immediately affected. A shadow fell over his face, making him look pensive, like when passing clouds cast their gloom on the mirrored surface of a lake.

"What's wrong?" Vahakn asked.

"Nothing," said Minas. "I'm doing really well, actually. In fact, I've never felt better."

And suddenly he unburdened his mind:

"You see, I had been so defeated when I came to Paris. I didn't leave my room for two days. Last night I was out until late. Let me be honest: I left the room because I wanted to put an end to my life in the Seine. But I couldn't. What can I say? I just couldn't. On my way back from the river, I couldn't find the hotel. I have a friend who used to live on Rue Saint-Jacques. I had gone straight to his apartment from the train station only to find out that he had moved. It's tough to live in Paris when you don't know anyone. Last night I stayed out on the street. I combed through every street in the neighborhood. I couldn't find the hotel, even though its image was etched in my mind: the moldy façade pocked by crevices formed by moisture. The entrance was through the café. You have to order something to drink every time you pass through, otherwise they will give you a dirty look. Even if I had found the place, I wouldn't have dared to go in.

He couldn't finish his thought. He fell silent, but soon continued the hotel story to avoid giving himself time to think about what he wasn't saying.

"I only remember a name around there. And it's only because it has to do with history—Danton. I think it should be the next street over. Do you know that street?"

"No, no, this is the last night," he replied hastily after Vahakn asked about how many days he still had left to pay. "I spent everything I had to pay for the past four days. I thought it would be wiser to keep the room until I met someone or found something. Paris is such a big city. It's terrible without a room—terrible."

"Forget it. I came out of the winter palace today," said Vahakn with a disgusted expression in which the pain of a lost opportunity was clear and understood by everyone except Minas. "I have no intention of suffocating between those four walls," he added, feigning indifference. "We'll walk together all night. You'll see that Paris is very interesting at night. You'll learn about the city, too. That's how you should learn about it: street by street as if you were turning a book page by page."

Minas's mind was already elsewhere. Vahakn was talking to himself. Minas didn't even hear his voice. His brain was separated from the world by a dense fog into which he sank slowly, but with an overpowering weight that pulled him, pulled him down into his inner darkness.

The outdoor part of the Billard was so nice with its fireplace and lights along the boulevard, which warmed his heart as they watched them.

"Did you say 'winter palace?' What is that?" he asked Vahakn, suddenly coming out of his thoughts.

Vahakn burst into laughter. Minas's innocence had disarmed him.

"Prison, my dear. Prison. Didn't you know?" he replied cheerfully.

He shrugged his shoulders slightly, looked into the distance, and focused in on Minas's face, squinting. He didn't find what he was looking for. Vahakn had leaned back in his chair to enjoy Minas's surprise from afar and with relish, but there was no surprise on Minas's face. To Minas, Vahakn was not a hero. He only saw a bored look in Vahakn's eyes, in which thoughts sank like a stone falling to the bottom of the ocean.

Vahakn was about to take his earlier position, a bit disappointed for not having impressed Minas, when Minas asked him, "No beatings?"

"Oh, no," Vahakn answered, enlivened, certain that this time he could educate his interlocutor. "Eat, drink, sleep. That's palace life."

"No beatings?" Minas repeated, as though he hadn't heard Vahakn's quip.

"Well, they beat you up at the police station the day you're arrested."

"I know that," Minas said, curt and dreamy.

He stopped at the corner of Boulevard Saint-Denis. He gathered it was five minutes to six, because just at that moment, the mouth of the metro spewed out the day's first wave of human vomit. It would continue until one in the morning on the dot, vomiting onto the streets, spilling, swelling, and colliding with a human mass that would slowly lessen in the morning, only to immediately resume, assailing the city with an endless current. The people leaving the metro threw themselves onto the sidewalk as though they were being chased by invisible demons—elbowing one another and looking like they had just evaded death—and started running like ghosts in a frenzy, sleep still lingering in their eyes and the fear of being late for work churning in their minds. Suddenly someone stood on the steps amid that useless jostling and yelled, "Are you crazy?"

Raising his elbows to make a path through the crowd, Minas immediately recognized Apkar, who was pushing his body forward as he spit out bitter curses. At this, Minas jumped almost mechanically to hide on the corner of Boulevard Strasbourg and instantly regretted it. He knew it was bad. Deeply upset, he wanted to hide his face and, always giving in to impulse, turned his head toward the window of a clothing store. He pretended to window-shop, but all he saw was his own image, which, having grown sullen, was complaining to its bearer. It scolded him. His eyes fell on the blue dress a mannequin was wearing. For a moment, he felt calm, but only for a moment, because although he couldn't see his reflection on that dress, he knew it was waiting for him in the space between the mannequins. However hard he pretended to take an interest in the dress, he chased out of the corner of his eye the phantom, which stubbornly kept a look of dissatisfaction on its face. He was caught in the trap and couldn't turn back. Why did he hide? Why did he leave Apkar alone? Of course it was out of shame, so that he wouldn't be seen as the friend of the surly cripple, his compatriot. Especially his compatriot, a foreigner. Isn't it in these situations that we are naturally driven to use our own language, so as not to be understood by others? "What is it, Apkar? What happened?" It was precisely in those words that Minas would have found his justification. Yes, he did well to hide. If he had spoken, the others would have discovered his own foreignness and felt emboldened to heap abuses on Apkar. So he had indirectly stood in Apkar's defense. He was relieved by this realization. He was even proud of having carried out his duty and kept going, but immediately stopped in his tracks. In the shop window, the image hadn't changed any of its sullenness. It looked straight at him. This time he really was embarrassed. There was warmth in his cheeks. What he had done with that initial impulse had not ceased to be a bad thing. However you looked at it, bad was bad. He could barely recall how he ended up leaving the window. Now that he was alone, no longer surrounded by others, he would show his bravery by forgetting the incident in front of the shop window and his memory lapse, but when he tried to catch up to Apkar, Minas saw that he was already on the other side of the street. He hesitated and, terrified by a new wave streaming out of the metro, was forced to tense his muscles to withstand the brutal force colliding with him on the sidewalk, just as Apkar had done immediately before. Then he remembered Vahakn's words from that evening outside the Billard, when Apkar had announced his good news. "What?" Vahakn had shot back in contempt. "Do you take me for a slave?" At the time, Minas had interpreted those words differently, but now, yes. Yes, slaves, slaves, look how they're running, ruthlessly trampling a cripple without even looking down—a vulgar swarm of faceless, nameless waves.

He caught up to Apkar on the opposite side of the street, but he preferred to follow him from a distance without letting him out of his sight. As Minas walked, synchronizing his steps with Apkar's, he noticed that his limping was a peculiar sight to be seen. His left foot trailed behind with each step and he pulled it with great effort, dragging it on the ground behind him and then all of a sudden propelling it forward. His body followed a moment later once his left foot was behind him. Then he threw the same foot back to position the bad foot ahead of him. But it was at this point that the worst thing happened. Once his left foot was ahead, suddenly and with all its might, his right foot would take a long step to situate itself a bit farther than the other one, creating an odd balance for the body to follow. To someone watching from behind, the process left the impression of a stormy sea. But there was more than a storm in the movements of a man constantly trying to find his balance; in particular, there was Apkar's perfect torment, which manifested itself in his heart and on his face in those deep, craggy furrows. Seeing that Apkar was in fact moving, Minas tried in vain to convince himself that his limp was common, or at least commonly seen, a matter of getting used to it, and that the suffering he imagined in Apkar did not correspond to reality. And yet his own attempt at persuasion did not take hold. The cripple's pain was undeniable. If it wasn't a physical kind of pain, then it was certainly a moral one that must have opened in Apkar a deep hole that kept him away from his own kind and, whatever the sort of pain, did not allow him to feed his most basic human emotions.

Like someone waking up from a bad dream, Minas sprang out of his thoughts. The wide boulevard stretched into the distance on that calm, deserted morning. The Maison Saint-Denis and Rue Hauteville were already behind him. The boulevard had started to slope downward slightly and the edge of Faubourg Montmartre had come into view. Apkar was quite far ahead of him near the kiosk that sold newspapers on the corner. Apkar stopped, bought a newspaper, and continued walking. Stopping again to open the paper, he scanned the headlines. Minas stopped too, and as he did, something startled him. He looked around. Fortunately, there was no one there. It was just as he stopped that he realized that he was limping in exactly the same way as Apkar. He quickly brought his hand to his mouth and was about to bite his pinkie. He stood there terrified. If Apkar had turned around and seen him, he would have certainly thought that Minas was making fun of him. Would Minas be able to tell Apkar that it was an attempt to share his pain? But Apkar would still think it was out of malice, and with no chance of being forgiven, he punished himself by continuing to live out the fate of the damned.

He wistfully remembered those mornings when Apkar would come out of the metro in that same spot. Often under the pretext of celebrating their chance meeting, they would go to Tout Va Bien, have a quick cup of coffee, and then walk side by side. Apkar came by metro from a distance. Minas would go from Luxembourg to Châtelet, walk down Boulevard Saint-Michel, and cross the two bridges over the island where he sometimes stopped, leaning over the edge of the bridge to take in the sleeping river of the early morning, quietly awakening underneath its blanket of mist. The massive golden clock on the courthouse rang and its heavy sound lazily released into the air, searching for its way. With this, Minas pulled himself out of the daydream that, once started, did not relent. It was five thirty. Boulevard de Sébastopol was still long, its nose in the air, breathing in the biting aroma of coffee wafting out of the cafés that had just opened for the day. In nice weather, he never went underground. With all his senses, he relished in the unusual scenery on the streets as the night brightened—the virginity of the day. It's true that he felt both the pain and pleasure of defiling a virgin. The heavy footsteps of the masses on their way to work changed with each season. They were a torrent in the summer, bold and fast, and reluctant in spring, because after a harsh winter, the footsteps gently fell from stiff muscles to linger in the caress of the sweetening weather. But above all, those footsteps were invitations to kindness, which made him enjoy the presence of people. He delighted in watching them fade into the panorama. By then, he was used to the seasons. He recognized them in the air, in the smell and touch of the air, which, to the person heading to work in those early hours of the morning, was different and always new in each season. And when he set foot in the doorway of the kitchen with great satisfaction, he was already sated by life before starting work. That's why he'd said it. That's why he'd said, "I want to be a slave." But that day he hadn't gone into the kitchen with the same sense of contentment. That day was a lost day. In front of the throng coming out of the metro that had jostled Apkar, he had felt a sense of loss, an awareness that something had been ripped out of him. Someone had stolen something from him while he was walking in Apkar's heaving footsteps. Strangely, Minas was at ease despite the pangs he felt at the painful sight of his friend, and having achieved a kind of equilibrium by making Apkar's pain his own, he didn't know what to make of that unfamiliar feeling rising from below and mingling with the entangled goings-on above, flittering about, nibbling in the dark, gnawing like mice invisible to the eye despite the keen sense of their presence. It would be impossible to figure out where they were and where they were going, because when we prick up our ears to consider the surrounding silence, the chased cease to move, like buzzing insects that suddenly stop when they sense danger, thinking that stillness makes them invisible, quieting down only to start again once we have lost interest. He found himself playing a game of cat and mouse in which the cat did not have an imaginary toy to play with, like Minas, who in that moment, felt within himself the presence of the unknown, both rousing and disturbing, like when we find our house has been ransacked while we were out. It's the rage that overwhelms us, not so much because of the stolen or lost belongings, but because of the mystery that comes to us from the unknown, putting a face and a name on our own powerlessness. He stopped here. He stopped and his gaze fell inward, where it sought something soothing, just a word even. The word. He suddenly felt the power of the word. "*Passez-moi le mot, passez-moi le mot*," a frustrated man says when the right word escapes him in conversation. If Minas had found the word and said it, even the mouse working in the darkness of his deepest layers would be unmasked and be forced to face him. Minas also knew that he couldn't punish the culprit, demand restitution, or even stroke its back in gratitude.

He lifted his head to take a breath. Apkar wasn't in his field of vision anymore, but his image remained underneath his eyelids, reminding Minas of a ship caught in a stormy sea, struggling against the waves. But of course, Apkar had disappeared like someone turning into the woods before reaching the café on the corner—nothing surprising about this. After all, this part of the city used to be woodlands, and Faubourg Montmartre, Rue Drouot, and others were nothing but paths that opened into valleys. In fact, what difference is there between the woods and the city? Perhaps it's easier to get lost in the city than in the woods, as he had seen with Apkar earlier. The unending rows of trees and giant buildings. . . . Within a few minutes, human forms sprout like moving trees, people and city once again. The woods grow so much deeper, and the number of people running—always running—grows so much that it confuses the general mass with its stillness and turns the city not into woods, but into a real jungle. The proof? Look how Minas has gotten lost. When he looked around in bewilderment, springing out of his thoughts, he realized he had gone quite a distance past work. He hadn't turned right at the corner café. He walked faster. He ran. He ran like everyone else. It suddenly seemed that hours had passed since he had come across Apkar in the metro, but now he was already in the doorway of the kitchen, having unknowingly gone through the revolving door like a breeze and seeing that he was the one who pushed the door. He saw that he had pushed it. There was no doubt about it: he was the one who had pushed the door and it was about to turn when he felt his lips moving. They moved to speak. Why else would lips move? Indeed, Minas mumbled something under his breath, but he wasn't the one who commanded them. "Slaves, slaves," the lips mumbled. He stopped again, this time in the doorway as if it were his first time there, like it had been on his first day when he was nervous and shy, as if they were going to throw him out. He didn't feel like himself. He was unrecognizable. Yes, *he* was the unknown force whom he had wasted so much time on. He was the thief. He might as well have clasped his hands together like Harpagon and screamed, "Thief! Thief!"[12] But since there's no thief who wouldn't defend himself and lie, Minas protested and made accusations, and at that moment a miraculous light dawned in his mind. All of a sudden, a summary of evidence in his defense was handed to him, as, once again, his lips started to mumble, "slaves, slaves," in spite of himself. Yes, Vahakn was the thief and Minas was the plunder. So Minas wasn't the one who offended Apkar, the one who had led him to do evil. Before leaving, Vahakn had stolen his soul and taken its place, taken the place of his soul where he settled in as lord and master and now ran everything as he pleased.

Cleansed of his sense of guilt, Minas pushed through the door in good spirits, greeting the night guard with a "good morning." "You're early today," the guard said in surprise.

"Those bastards!" screamed Apkar as Minas came into the kitchen.

With his sleeves rolled up, he had already started washing the dishes from the day before. He leaned over the sink without lifting his head and stayed in that position as he spoke.

"Who?" Minas asked. "Who are the bastards?"

"What? Don't you know?" There was ridicule in his tone.

"*What* do I know?" Minas said.

"Weren't you the one who avoided me on the street today?"

A shudder passed through Minas's body. He couldn't finish the work he had started. He was in the middle of preparing the milk, coffee, hot chocolate, and teacups, when his limbs stopped obeying his will. Apkar saw it. He knew. He also knew about all those other times that Minas had walked behind him early in the morning on their way to work.

Gripped by shame, Minas was destroyed, engulfed in the flames of a firestorm. He almost threw himself at Apkar's feet, driven by an uncontrollable urge to confess, tossed like a tree toppled by the wind.

"No, oh no. Ziya again. With his never-ending apologies."

He fell silent.

He fell silent like he had late that one night when they were all sitting around the table, tired of the jokes and the waiting. The spring chill had pierced their skin and started to numb them. A weary Minas was sinking into his chair, miserable, hoping that his friend would finally take out his wallet, pay for their coffee, and say it was time to go. But Vahakn lingered as time passed in vain, aimlessly. Still, a strange feeling brought his heart to life. It flared and died down in bursts. Slipping his hand into his pocket, proudly paying, standing tall in front of Minas, and saying it was time to go had created a true struggle in him. Giving—giving for the one who had always known how to take. And yet he expelled that strange musing from his heart. He couldn't. He wanted to but he couldn't. Something intangible and slippery resisted his habit. The more he lingered, the harder it became to leave. But only by leaving could he put an end to that new feeling, which grew progressively more complex. The contradiction snuck into that intricate jumble that was his mind at that moment and settled there slowly and obstinately, but with certainty and control like an injection of poison. The café was almost empty and the crowd on the street had already thinned. The stillness of the night slowly took position like the riot police during an uprising.

On the other side of the street, the night was sleeping with one eye closed.

Suddenly an unusual commotion broke out, escalated, and rolled down the boulevard. Heads rose all at once and turned toward the street. It felt as though the enemy had penetrated the city from a newly conquered trench. The supply train, making a racket and spewing smoke into the air, shot toward the central part of Les Halles.

"It's one o'clock," said Vahakn anxiously.

Then he jumped up as fast as lightning and ran without looking back. Minas hadn't had a chance to figure out what was going on until Vahakn stopped in the middle of the boulevard, with his arms hanging and a strange look on his face, and screamed, “Wait for me. I’m coming!”

The train had passed Pont Saint-Michel, but people still followed it with wide eyes. The street took on an unusual, unfamiliar look in its wake. The stillness of the night, barely settled, had scurried away in fear and then little by little reclaimed its position, hesitant and trembling.

Vahakn turned and started running again. He feared he wouldn’t make it in time. As soon as it reached Les Halles, packs of vagrants would attack to empty the carts.[13]

Vahakn had become an expert. He knew how to shove people aside to take their place. He was more amused than insulted by their curses. He was clever and didn’t shy away from work—the faster the better. The faster he finished, the sooner he would be free to go stretch his legs in the sleeping streets or parks, where no one dared lay a finger on or awaken a meek, sleeping flower. In his mind, he was rebelling against Minas, who had made him late, and now he ran without turning back, his elbows tucked under his shoulders. And yet he couldn’t help thinking as he ran, “Poor boy, how is he going to get out of this?” There seemed to be two people in him. One ran toward Les Halles, toward the line of train carts about to be unloaded, while the other thought. He thought about the person sitting worried in the café in front of two empty cups. He tried to go back, slowing down only for a second, but then picked up speed again and ran faster with a larger stride, panting.

A sun rose unexpectedly around him. Of course this was impossible in the middle of the night. He was on the Pont Saint-Michel when it happened and it seemed that he had walked into a night illuminated by an invisible sun. The light in his heart radiated from his eyes and lit the darkness. The streetlights, whose light had grown pale, were fading. He wasn’t sure whether he had stopped or was still running behind the train, which, having almost reached Les Halles, shortened its breath like a dying man whose gasps had slowed, and the street fell back asleep, watched over by the cold, uniform light of the streetlights. “Give, give,” a voice in him said—he who was only used to taking—and waves of happiness crashed in his chest, which surged with a blissful sense of pride. “What would happen if I go back?” Already it wasn’t the same Vahakn, despite his attempt to justify himself. Perhaps because of it. There was a split in his mind and confusion that appeared as a result. "Give, give, but give what?" someone protested for him. He looked around and the only thing he saw was Minas's face at the café, desperate because of his own unexpected exit. He couldn't prevent that old, gurgling laughter in his chest, usually reserved for when someone played a bad hand. Why did he try to console himself with words he hadn't summoned, but which rose to his lips nonetheless and made them move? "What would have happened if he had gone back?" Yes, what would have changed? Perhaps he could have found the calm, indifference, or joy that he had lost. Suddenly he grew sad. It was impossible. How could Vahakn be sad out of an inability to help someone? True, there was something heart-wrenching about Minas the day before, something he saw in his imagination—a Minas who roamed the streets and riverbank, forlorn and abandoned and quite possibly trembling, his sleepy eyes flooded by the confused image of a hotel, which he had chased hopelessly. "Oh," he sighed as he stopped. "What an odyssey." With his surging emotion, the image grew and a simple, banal phenomenon turned into an odyssey, in which perhaps he recognized his own life. But why did he stop? Had he stopped? No, he hadn't. It seemed that way to him because as he looked up, he saw the train, which had stopped ahead of him. He had walked fast and without stopping, because he was already there. Hundreds of derelicts threw themselves onto the train. Mountains of goods were piled high on both sides. He made an effort, as though there were someone tugging at his arms, jumped, and threw himself into the fray for bread, but this time what gave him strength were the two unsettled cups of coffee holding Minas hostage. This is why he was sad? A sadness like alcohol, slow but assured, had penetrated his brain, his blood, and he did his work in a stupor. "No one would even bother to get him out of the water on this cursed night." His mind was not on the work. Minas's image swam and flipped in the water. Unable to work or even move, he suddenly broke away from where he stopped, jumped down from the cart, and ran, panting, toward the café on Saint Michel.

At the same time, the images in Minas's mind were replaced by Apkar—not his image, but the real Apkar who worked silently at the sink, focused inward. The boss had left. Why wasn't Apkar saying anything?

Surely he was holding a grudge. He had the right to feel wronged, but Minas was just waiting for a few words to muster up the courage to throw himself at his feet and beg for forgiveness. Not a word, not a single sound from Apkar. Minas didn't even hear the unusual clanking of dishes and glasses that Apkar would make in the morning. Was he upset? He hadn't even turned around once, but Minas, drained by impatience, fell to his knees and freed a whole flurry of words to express his regret and beg for forgiveness. Apkar didn't move, didn't look at him, and what was even more surprising was that he, too, stayed exactly where he was, even though his devastated face kept staring back at him.

"You'll see. A letter is going to come for you today from his wife."

As much as the prospect of the letter bothered him, Minas was glad to have established that Apkar was not angry at him after all. Like him, Apkar was preoccupied with Vahakn, too.

In fact, there were two letters waiting for him at the hotel office at noon. One was from his mother. He glanced at the other one. The postal seal was smeared. He could only make out one word, the name of the *département*: Isère. The letter was from Arshalouys.

He immediately went to lie down on his bed. He opened his mother's letter first, but, holding it in his hand, he waited a moment before reading it. There was a strange silence in the room, inhabited by a whisper, the presence of the absent Vahakn. An absent presence. Yes, that was it. He didn't find anything else and there was no need to look. The explanation had imposed itself with the undeniable force of reality and it was up to him just to accept it. Of course, it was a presence that was invisible to the naked eye, but it was present nonetheless, despite its absence, when Minas listened very closely.

My dear Minas,

We received the letter and the money you sent. Why do you do things like that, son? Why do you trouble yourself? We're doing better now. Thank God. I'd written that Shoushan finished her apprenticeship. Now she's making a good living. You should see what a stylish seamstress she's become. She works in a nice factory and has a few French customers on the side. They pay her well. The poor girl has to work nights at home. Since my illness, your uncle has kept sending us some money every month. I wrote to you about this in my last letter. Take care of yourself, son. Make sure you're not lacking anything. Don't worry about us. I'm not as strong as I used to be, but I still manage to do some sewing. I don't understand anything about that Sorbonne of yours. Will you at least come out having learned a trade? This century belongs to the tradesmen. There's no other hope for us around here. Armen has his mind set on leaving school and going into a trade, too. As it is, the boy isn't good at school. He didn't turn out like you. It breaks my heart, but what can we do? Maybe he's making the right choice in this cruel world. He just turned twelve. I wish your father could open his eyes just once more and see this. He dreamed of university for his sons.

Let me add that I don't see any other way for Armen. He's not going to give up that old habit until he goes into a trade. Don't think he's stopped, even now that we're doing better. I'm scared that something bad is going to happen to him one day. God spare us this misfortune.

Take good care of yourself. How did you end up like this, my son? My heart breaks when I think that you've become a dishwasher in a restaurant. Everyone is making something of himself, but you've fallen into this situation. That must be our luck, I guess.

Love,
Your mother

Sitting on a rickety chair in front of his desk, he read his mother's letter once more under the electric lamp, while outside, the spring sun had given luminous clarity to the air, which, although cool, could have fanned his warming forehead, had there been a window that opened out onto the street. His window, permanently closed to the "courtyard," made the room look like a blind face. It was as though a blind man were staring at him.

Leaning his head against the letter, he thought about what he would write, which was always the same. Why didn't his mother, who was pained by the thought of his work, want to understand that he wasn't a dishwasher? He did have a "trade." He was a breakfast cook in a small, but elegant hotel. He was lucky that he could leave at two in the afternoon to go to his classes at the Sorbonne. He offered this last lie as the salt and pepper on a flavorless dish, so he had an excuse to live away from them. And, why not, if it put his mother's mind at ease?

When he lifted his head out of the letter, the other one, waiting by his left arm, came into focus. Now he understood why he had read his mother's letter a second time, and instead of responding right away or waiting until later, he fell into his thoughts, which stripped time away and let him put off reading the other letter. Suddenly he stood up, put the letter in his pocket, and went out.

He sat on a stone bench by the Grand Bassin in the Jardin du Luxembourg and took the letter out of his pocket. He wasn't too fond of the area around the Grand Bassin. He liked to sit with a book in his lap near the Fontaine Médicis, under the thick foliage of the trees, until the park closed. Afterward, he would slowly walk down the street and join Vahakn at the Billard. But since the day he had seen Nicole arm in arm with her friend, carefully walking down the stairs, passing the Grand Bassin, walking back up with the same caution, watching their steps, and disappearing into the woods at the top the opposite staircase, Minas abandoned the Fontaine Médicis and kept an impatient eye on his surroundings, with a hand on his heart to soften the blow. Often he would sit in the woods across from the stone statue of Verlaine. That was where he had finally talked to Nicole for the first time, and after, it was only there that he could meet her and dare to speak as he had when, trembling with the fear of losing her, he had approached her, not without his chin quivering, and asked, so that something of her could remain after she was gone, for a scrap thrown to him as charity: "What is your name, Miss?"

"My name?" she answered. "What's my name to you?"

At this, she and her friend, who was resting her head on Nicole's shoulder, broke into riotous laughter, suddenly adding a new dimension to the depth of the woods.

"I need your name, so that I can walk around with it, lie with it, take it with me everywhere, when you're out of sight."

"You're crazy," she had said, standing up.

"Your name, Miss. Your name."

Conquered by Minas's tenacity, she unhooked her arm from around her friend's shoulder and gestured as if she were tossing him an apple.

"Nicole," she said. "For you."

Since then, whenever an emotion crept into his heart and blood rushed through his veins like a fawn chased by a hunter, Minas sounded that name in his chest like someone in danger screaming, "Help!" He did it just as he took hold of the letter in his pocket.

Dear Sir,

I just received your letter and I wanted to reply right away by express mail. Your letter was entirely unexpected. I'm frantic, Sir. Forgive me for bothering you, but I don't know whom to open my heart to about this. Since you're a friend of Vahakn's, you can understand what I'm feeling. Look at what Vahakn has done to me. I don't know where to go, where to run.

Once again, please forgive my candor. My soul was stifled and needed to scream. Now it has, but not without causing you this annoyance, for which I apologize.

Your friend's inconsolable wife,
Arshalouys Vahakn

Two boats collided. Sails drenched, the boats toppled into the water and took on the sad look of fragments.

"It's windy," he thought, shrugging his shoulders. Was he cold? Whenever a sense of loneliness came over him, he would feel cold. A little later that evening, that inescapable conqueror would suddenly come down from the sky and lay claim to his land. Minas would be left all alone before the "open heart" in Arshalouys's letter with a chill that would drive him to enter it and find solace in its warmth.

That began in him an endless monologue before the image of this inconsolable stranger, gently turning it into an outline of a letter, which he stood up to write, already picturing himself in front of the desk and throwing himself head first into the "open heart." He left the park and walked down the sidewalk along Saint Michel at the busiest time of day. The words in his mind quickly followed one after the other, making it impossible to form sentences. He wanted to give them poignant twists based on the needs of his own heart, but the shoving of the passersby chased away a terrified word here, another there, as Minas worked to collect them and squeeze them into a sentence. The letter became necessary to stubbornly rein in disobedient words, despite his hidden fear that they would take his freedom prisoner. An indistinct, faint premonition hovered in the expanse between his mind and heart, leaving the shadow of a ferocious bird with its claws spread, and creating an unformulated second reality that fed greedily on the reality that had already begun to shatter around him. He stopped in front of one of the cafés where the great poet—almost always by himself at the same corner table, his exiled forehead leaning over a pocket-size notebook, pen between his fingers—chased a word, a comma, a verb for years, so that the poem that burst out from within could reach completion—neat, polished, and refined, suddenly illuminated from within like a diamond in the hands of a jeweler. Every time Minas passed by his heart pounded—a pounding that prevented him from approaching the poet, to whom he owed his first feelings of pride. He didn't know how, but that day, he found himself standing in front of the writer's table—something had brought about his boldness, which was not boldness at all, but an escape to the only refuge that could make him forget the persecution at the hands of the ghost lingering inside him. Now his entire field of vision was filled with the pensive face of the poet, who stared at him, his heavy head tilted upward, controlling his annoyance at being disturbed, but affording an imperceptible, forgiving smile, after he took off his glasses and held them in his hands.

"Excuse me, Mr. Tekeyan," he said finally, at once firm and wavering. "I know I'm disturbing you, but I've waited a long time for the chance to express my gratitude to you. Do you remember? You published my first poem in your newspaper in Constantinople."

"I do remember. I do," the man said. "I think the next day you left for Europe. For Marseille, right? I was there, too, when I was your age. I was in the same situation. The day before, we were passing by your house in Scutari and Shahan showed me your front garden. I remember it well. You were sitting under an acacia tree. But you're a poet."

The blood buzzed in his ears. It rushed to his brain and he lost his sense of time and space. He was walking through the streets of the gigantic city that had borne witness to his anguish, where he had felt its cruel, ruthless tension. Now he felt bigger. Now he was the giant in whose eyes the city seemed tiny. Then he saw himself sitting at a desk between the four walls of his room, where the silence rocked him in its arms late at night and drifted toward sunrise. The piece of paper was in his hand and he read the lines he had tossed onto it over again. They didn't form a letter, but had now turned into a poem.

At that, he took his hand to his chest and breathed deeply, like an inmate just released from prison who opens his arms into the air, breathes, looks up at the sky and at the life ahead of him.

Then he rested his head on his folded arms and fell asleep.

He wouldn't pay, even if he could. It was a matter of principle. It was an immoral sense of morality that drove him not to pay for anything. Therein lay its pleasure. What am I saying? That was his way of protesting against the ugliness of life. This is why he had invented the feet game. Sitting outside the café, he would play the feet game—a marvel, really—with intense concentration. He kept an eye on the comings and goings of the waiter, so that he could "fold his tail" at a moment's notice.

Even when he was asleep, Minas couldn't find peace. As soon as free space opened up in his mind—sleep was the best way—Vahakn's past would storm in and lodge itself in Minas's present, which is life itself, since the past is no longer life and the future has yet to be. The future is calm and patient, that which will become tomorrow's present, and it waits inspired by the confidence of not yet having failed, whereas the past—always turbulent—comes to a boil and rises, torturously steaming swirls of incense up to the gallery of the present.

Look, with his head on his arms and surrendering to his inner vision, Minas won't move until morning, until his alarm clock wakes him. It's the alarm of reality, unforgiving and cruel, that puts people in front of the interrogator of existence.

The act of "folding his tail" was not as simple or as easy as it sounds. Sometimes it took hours, like a game of cat and mouse. The longer the game lasted, the closer pleasure inched toward perfection. It wasn't always the people in the café who fell victim to his mischievous games. Acquaintances, friends, especially friends, would fall into the trap he set. "Excuse me," he would say. "I'll be right back. I'm just going to get myself a pack of Gauloises." And he would get up to wander the streets with the utmost sense of calm, cheerful, his head held high, his face contorting, chewing, and swallowing the act with ecstatic delight. "I pulled a fast one," he would muse, even as he rehearsed the reasons and excuses he would give the next time they met, which meant that a flicker of human frailty remained in him despite himself.

"Pulling a fast one" was a complicated thing that required constant vigilance. It was not a straightforward act, rough and primitive, but rather a convoluted one, serpentine and insidious, pampered and relished—a civilized act. "Pulling a fast one" was more than a struggle for existence; it was also a game, a diversion, but above all, an addiction whose tail was tied to the navel of life.

"After all," he would say. "What am I really stealing? A cup of coffee, a couple of pieces of bread, a ride, a room?"

And so he wandered from city to city, preferably large, crowded urban centers, with his mouth half-open—probably the result of his habit of mocking—stretching his legs and exploiting the gullible, who, as he said, were born for his tricks. He lived in a mysterious state of waiting, in the future to come. It would certainly come and save his soul from the pettiness, taking aim at the target hidden in his line of sight.

Never had his dark conscience been visited by a flash of compassion. He had an explanation for each misdeed. Minas, awestruck, listened and laughed "like a crazy person." Vahakn sometimes took on superhuman proportions. If he didn't pay for his cup of coffee, the waiter probably would. If he didn't eat the food he didn't pay for, it would end up in the trashcan. The trains would leave with or without him. Nothing changed. The balance remained the same. As for the hotel manager, he didn't lose anything, because the room would have been vacant otherwise, since Vahakn always came at the last minute, around midnight, when the rooms would all be rented. There were many, many issues with the linen, but that was a different story, since hotel managers are not keen on changing the linen. Only idiots are affected by the word "theft." For the serious-minded, this is not theft, because in no way has the economic balance been disrupted. Only its base has shifted. Since long ago, people have declared theft a sin, a despised threat to the public order, as if the public felt anything when, for instance, Vahakn ate a meal he didn't pay for. Whose stomach went hungry that night? The rich have come up with a law and imposed it on others to protect their property. The powerful have reserved legalized theft for themselves. And, my God, what kind of theft that is! The theft of your strength, your blood, your life, your dignity. "But Minas, careful." Stealing from a big thief requires genius. Sometimes I wonder why the greatest geniuses don't concentrate their power on theft but instead waste their time on works of art. I mean, why don't they focus on the great art of theft? Because I think rather than taking the plunder for themselves, they would distribute it to everybody by the handfuls. Whatever is yours is mine, because whatever is yours is everyone's. What an ingenious idea! What do you say? Heroic theft and plunder—think of François Villon.[14]

"Do you know of François Villon?" he asked suddenly and, without leaving time for an answer, added, "Him? No? But what is your profession?"

Minas was taken aback. His mind quickly reviewed the situation before the "events," but a fog had settled on the past and he couldn't see anything as he searched for the traces that would one day become him. A beam of light fell on the darkness surrounding him—clear, pure light. His heart ached. His sense of guilt came to life and grew in the darkness that the light had cracked open. Yes, why didn't he have a profession? How could Vahakn have managed to have one? When had he had time to learn accounting? Curiously, these questions gave way to the surprising revelation that he was prone to a constant numbness, or to be absent from the world. Where was he? Where did he live? It was as though he didn't belong to this world. And now Vahakn's question, which he hadn't shown any particular interest in, had taken him by surprise and brought him face to face with the present. But the present was not just facing him; it stood against him, fierce and accusatory. He lowered his head toward his chest. Was he embarrassed for not having an answer? As he lowered his head, he felt that there was conflict between them. Like him, Vahakn was divorced from the present, too. The difference was in the fact that while Minas lived with harsh inner tension about the future, Vahakn was immersed in the chaos of the past, which explains his ravings and jumbled mental images.

"I . . . I," he stuttered, almost apologetically. "I don't have one. I'm a poet."

No, his answer was neither a justification nor an assertion of superiority. He didn't even know why he said it like that. His lips didn't express his intention. The proof was in his cheeks, which immediately flushed and burned. It was as though he had confessed to something shameful and was at a loss as to where to turn and hide his gaze, which distanced itself from Vahakn.

Suddenly, in an effort to scatter the discomfort, he slipped into a laugh and said, "In a word, I don't have a profession."

He was going to go. He had made the decision just like that, all of a sudden. At ten o'clock, he would walk through the revolving door, the one protected by caryatids on either side. By then, Hortense would be ready to make her official entrance into the day's affairs. Dressed and ready, she would come down the marble staircase covered by a narrow strip of carpet, walking tall and elegantly with slow steps, as though she were counting them one by one. Hinging slightly on her hips, she would look down at the tips of her toes and into the foyer, where the employees would be lined up in respect. She would prepare her face with a smile and walk toward the hotel guests, extending both hands to say, "Bonjour! Bonjour."

Yes, he would certainly see Hortense descend the staircase like a countess. He was going precisely for this. Submitting his letter of resignation was just a pretense. A lie. He wanted to fill his eyes with this beautiful sight and offer an image of his own pride to her eyes. The rich don't realize how fortunate they are. Had sorrow entered her heart? She would get away, travel, and come back with her heart cleansed and pristine. Sorrow is born of environment and circumstance. It sticks to the layers of the heart like glue and spreads slowly and stubbornly, drop by drop. Sorrow doesn't like to migrate.

He would go. He would walk in silently through the revolving door and watch Hortense's arrogant descent down the staircase. Today he would make the trip, his eyes wandering between the folds of her dress, trembling wave by wave as her delicate knees and slender legs grazed the fabric. As she moved from one stair to the next, her body seemed to stretch toward the ceiling and her gray eyes filled with insolent reverence. That was enough. He wouldn't be able to resist. He has no strength left to resist the coffee, milk, hot chocolate, porridge, omelets, and Apkar. Apkar? And this tiny woman crouched behind the door, her lovely, mouse-like chin lowered toward her chest, which watched and followed your each and every move. He wouldn't reply to Arshalouys and her paper factory. His eyes yearn for beauty. Yes, yes, he would quit his job. To hell with the factories. But where would he go? He would go to the Fouquet. He would forget about the Billard and Boul'Mich. He would walk along the Champs Elysées, calm and unmoved. He would go to the Fouquet, yes. Finely dressed waiters would be at his beck and call. "What does Monsieur desire? Duck à l'orange?" Ah, duck à l'orange! Very well, duck à l'orange it is. The wine list, please. And then? Then he would retire to his foul-smelling room, and to make it even more nauseating, would open the window that had been closed for months, the one facing the "courtyard." And when the stench from The Ani would rush in, he would sleep on the floor, exactly where Vahakn had been.

The screech of the alarm clock made him jump out of bed, although it wasn't the usual sharp, resounding, overwhelming screech that made him jump in fear. Instead it was a hoarse, timid sound, like an apology, that buzzed around his head, seeking a crack to slip into. The sound of the clock was so sad that morning. He was struggling to reach someplace, to settle someplace, and without it, he would be self-serving, aimless, and above all, dishonorable. This is why he passed through the crater between sleep and consciousness, like a worm undoing its rings in the damp earth. He was a worm that tried with great difficulty to clear a path in his mind through the thick night, while Apkar, unusually chatty, told a story in a sweet, saccharine tone—entirely unlike Apkar.

He said that one day, nearing evening, they were sitting outside the Billard, you know, at the corner table, on your left when you go in, at their favorite table. At the table next to them, there was a girl, a student I think. Vahakn was very witty, very personable. He struck up a conversation with her right away—a discussion about literature. I can't understand those kinds of things, but I was amazed when the girl said, "That's very interesting. Very interesting!" That was the power of the way Vahakn spoke.

Bravo! The girl was amazed. "Those authors of yours," Vahakn said. "I couldn't care less about any of them. Art is for cleansing the soul. If it's not for that, what else is it for? Life is constantly dirtying the soul, art must constantly wash it. Of course, it's not like washing your hands. It's hard. It's hard to cleanse the soul. But what a wonderful thing it is to live with a clean soul." What did I see next, Minas? The girl's hand on Vahakn's. They talked without moving their hands. When Vahakn gently pulled his hand away, the conversation hung for a moment. When it started again, it wasn't the same. The flavor had changed. It was like food without salt. After she left, I laughed as I said to Vahakn, "I think it was about to happen if you hadn't pulled your hand away." "Oh, no," he said. "Everything is good until that point. Beyond that it's dirty, Apkar. Dirty. Women are dirty things. It's the emotion they give that's wonderful. Can I tell you something?" he continued after a period of silence. "We're all wasting our time. My mind was only preoccupied by the prospect of having someone pay for our coffee. I was deceived like an idiot."

"How did it happen?" I asked.

"Emotion, Apkar," he explained. "It was emotion."

Right then, Hortense came in. The work had been done. Everything was in order—washed and cleaned. As usual, Hortense said in a tone of voice equal parts request and demand, "Minas, don't forget my coffee before you leave."

Minas handed the tray to Apkar and left. He didn't go to the Jardin du Luxembourg or to the Billard. He wandered outside the city until evening—in the forest where spring had awakened nature and tree blossoms had started filling the air with their sharp fragrance.

His feet stepped lightly on the sidewalk, where evening had begun to make way for night. There hadn't been any wind or rain that day. The sun had slid freely across the sky, from east to west, while above the Colline de Chaillot, its palette had decorated a few clouds with bright patches of color. They reminded him of lost lambs that had strayed from the herd. Clusters of sunlight hit the glass windows and here and there the houses smiled at one another.

His feet were slower than usual and more hesitant. There was a whole list of enigmas to which Vahakn remained indifferent, since his mind was thoroughly preoccupied. In a forest of feet, his eyes searched for the particular pair that would finally make him call out, "That's it!" He directed all his energy to his eyes and ears. The other parts of his body had ceased to exist. He bundled them up and tossed them aside, telling them to wait for him over there. He was all eyes and ears. Even though his coffee cup wasn't empty, he didn't know where he was. His mouth, his stomach, his intestines were not a part of him. He had left them in that bundle. When the waiter asked him if he wanted to order something, his mouth answered from inside the bundle: coffee with milk. His being had divided in two: past and present. His eyes and ears ran with time. The rest came to a halt with the bundle, which was separated from him not only by time but also by space. The night before, his feet had taken him all over—from bench to bench, street to street. He hadn't felt his feet or his body. He knew he wasn't a ghost. He definitely must have become a ghost. The money he earned at Les Halles was still in his pocket, but he was saving it for the next day's two cups of coffee. No, he must have definitely gone crazy if he was actually thinking of paying for something. He couldn't sit still as he tried to get rid of that idea, but he couldn't shake it off completely. All of a sudden, he stopped in front of a hotel, went in, rented a room, and got into bed in an attempt to use sleep to flee his obsessive thoughts. But he couldn't fall asleep. He collected his strength. "I will fall asleep," he said, but his eyes defied him and stayed open. The night stretched out in his mind as morning was about to break. Suspicion stayed perched on the edge of his thoughts. Where could Minas be at that moment, the moment that was constantly renewing? But for Vahakn it remained unchanged, clinging to an awareness of guilt that lasted through the entire day. In the evening, Minas finally arrived with the shadows, leaning against the post of the streetlight. Vahakn couldn't bring himself to yell, "Hey, compatriot!" like the first time. He choked on his own voice. All he could manage was a little jump—a jump forward that remained suspended, incomplete, with his ears attentive and a stare that was more of a scream, an unvoiced scream like a fish's stare. Minas's eyes looked at him through a haze and, of course, didn't see anything. Vahakn's image didn't reach his pupils. Between his eyes and his image, there was an unnecessary haze and yet he was staring directly at the spot where they had sat together the night before. His gaze—as heavy as lead—gradually sunk below his eye sockets, despite his effort to pull it back up. This is why he couldn't see. He looked, but couldn't see. Looking is not the same as seeing, especially since he was convinced that he wouldn't be able to see for the simple reason that Vahakn wouldn't be there. He couldn't have been. "Why did I come here? Why am I lingering around the café? I know he won't show up. He'll stop coming because of me. His sole purpose was to deceive me. He's already done it once. He deceives everyone. He doesn't know what to do. He's irresponsible. He made it clear that he could even *kill* someone without a strike to his conscience. The minute after committing a crime, he can forget his despicable act and, with this sheer ability to forget, he can be ready to commit new criminal acts.

Minas wandered near the café and refused to admit to himself that he had come to meet Vahakn. He knew that he wouldn't see him there, even if he suspended his disbelief, as he was now, leaning against the lamppost and looking into Vahakn's eyes like a fish moving closer to its bait. "Who knows where he is now? Busy hunting for new prey." Faith is blind, as they say, like addiction. And there, sitting outside the café, Vahakn searched for his mouth. He didn't have one to scream with and had a wild urge to scream to keep from raving. He had left his mouth in the bundle with the rest of his body parts. His eyes looked more like noise than a gaze—a scream that couldn't rise. It fell with sharp, tragic laughter. In his veins, he felt a movement akin to the coiling of a snake, which pulled him down toward the earth, toward the ground, toward the mud. He realized then that the bundle in the distance had come undone. His mouth had fallen out. Like a caterpillar taking on a new form, he felt complete. After a short, almost imperceptible jolt, the parts came together and he could at last scream aloud: "Hey, Minas!"

~

Dearest Sir,

I wonder if you have received my letter. I'm getting impatient waiting. I'm constantly waiting for the mailman, as if you were somehow obliged to write to me. I know we all have our own pain, but what can I do? I've lost my mind. I was fine until now. I told myself that once he got tired of wandering, he would just come home one evening and it would be like he had never left. He would come home after work. Every day I imagine making his meals, setting the table, sitting and waiting. I tell myself that he will sit down at the table as soon as he gets home. Now that he never will, I don't know what to do. My heart is restless. Before at least I used to fill the time by thinking about him and the meals I would cook for him. I constantly want someone to talk to about these things to avoid thinking about them. But I don't have anyone to make my heart feel lighter. Can you understand the void that I've fallen into?

How is it that he reached that point? No, he shouldn't have done this to me.

Yours sorrowfully,
Arshalouys Vahakn

The sheet of paper on his desk was still blank, but he had already started to fill it with his gaze. For more than an hour his eyes furrowed the page, which surrendered to the caress of his pen. Like an expectant father, he anxiously anticipated the result. He vacillated between writing and not writing. In that moment, he took hold of the pen and rested its tip on the paper. The black pen waited with extraordinary patience to run across the pristine whiteness of the page, while he, taut with resistance, refused to obey the order. And yet, based on a natural inclination, he was filled with a sense of compassion and gave in. Pen in hand, he drew some quivering lines that represented the words "Dearest Madame." Why "dearest" and not "dear," as he had written before, reserving for himself the simple role of relayer of information? The current carried him away and it was too late to swim against it. He realized he had come into a game that had already begun. He gently laid the pen on the desk, outside the margins of the paper. There was something so provocative about seeing the pen on the sheet of paper that it made him empty his heart in a flood. He seemed somewhat serene, but it was a false serenity, like a dog that buries a bone it's been thrown in a sign of protest, but having kept an image of it in its mind, drools and dozes sweetly with its head resting on its paws.

He rested his head on his right arm and closed his eyes, too. He tried to sleep. He stopped thinking. He felt sick—at least he wanted to believe he was. Thinking of work in the morning, he wanted to go to bed. He couldn't move. Now he could finally write. Did he have to? No, he didn't. So he slept like a baby. The evening had been crushed at the edge of the night. The deepening silence in the room had become overstimulated to the point of becoming audible. The silence was a faint buzz in his ear canal, while beyond him, its wide waves spread endlessly across the city and beyond. Suddenly he felt a jolt. He sat up and took hold of the pen. The silence in his ears was no longer a buzz.

Dearest Madame Arshalouys,

Please accept my apologies a thousand times over. Believe me, it has not been unwillingness or indifference that has kept me from writing. If I say forgetfulness, I would be wrong again. It's not that I've forgotten to write, but more that I haven't written like this before. How can one remain indifferent to your inconsolable pain, particularly after Vahakn entrusted me with the responsibility of consoling you? Neglect on my part would be unforgivable. In your letter, you write about an emptiness that doesn't take much effort for me to understand. We share a similar condition. I say "we" because whenever Apkar opens his mouth—Vahakn must have written to you about him—he talks about nothing but our unfortunate friend. All of a sudden, you will see him fall into a profound inner void before he finishes his thought.

Of course, it would be impossible to go on like this forever. It would be impossible to carry around a dead person with us like this. Life is for the living. We must wait and be patient until the storm passes. Time takes care of everything. They say that there is calm after the storm—the bigger the storm, the greater the calm.

Let's wait and be brave until that day, which I hope comes soon.

Your grieving friend,
Minas

Apkar was furious that day. He was exactly the opposite. He was calm after a dreamless night. As he dropped the letter into the mailbox, he already felt a change in his mental state. He felt that he must have done good work. He thought he had freed himself of the letter's disturbing consequences.

The consequences were now seen in a different light. Even an image of Arshalouys had been sketched in his mind's eye as he arranged the words of his letter and saw a kind of harmony—not calm and still a bit distressed—bring about a knowing smile in the relaxed lines of her face. Arshalouys seemed beautiful—perhaps he wished she were. Why did he want her to be like that? Beautiful Arshalouys. In his imagination, he beamed at her blooming smile, but it was intercepted by Hortense whom he had forgotten was there, hunched and leaning against the door, just at the moment he glanced at her. Her preoccupied expression opened to draw in the light of a smile that Minas had intended for somebody else. Hortense couldn't have known the journey that smile had taken to faraway places where fog always descends on the roads. Hortense smiled back with a look that exuded gratitude. In that moment, her unpainted lips were about to move when Minas stopped her.

"Yes, I got it," he snapped. "I'll bring you your coffee. I'll bring it."

He didn't recognize himself. He was a completely different man, confident and self-possessed. Ever since last night, the Hortense who leaned against the kitchen door had retreated and the Hortense who descended the marble stairs like a countess, Madame Hortense Bédier, had emerged. Now he was in control of the game. The apprenticeship was over. "Now I'm the professor," he said to himself. He wasn't the same person who jumped when Hortense gave orders. He was inexperienced then—shy and weak—when Hortense, with the gentle touch of her delicate fingers on his head, silently guided those love games with such care—yes, I must admit it—with such refined care that he didn't feel as if he was being coaxed. She spared his sense of male pride, while his head, innocently subjected to Hortense, traveled over the sensitive parts of her naked body, greeting them with kisses as he passed from one to the next.

The heavy velvet curtains were drawn. Their deep red and fragrance had made the air heavy, almost palpable. Minas kept going like a swimmer in the water, a tray in hand. Hortense was lying on the bed. She was reading a book, or pretending to read to give her waiting some kind of purpose. When she lifted her head, she suddenly blushed and grew nervous, like a bird folding its wounded wings and waiting on the edge of a bush for the helping hand of a kind stranger. And that's what happened. Her petite body, naked under her lingerie, fell into his arms with all her warmth. He wanted to make her melt with his kisses, with the little love games he had learned from her. Now he wanted to return them to her, multiplied, perfected. Minas was up against Minas. After the wrestling match, what remained in his arms was a small woman—a girl, practically—whom he looked at intently, like an executioner looking at his victim. She was so tired that she couldn't move—it was as though she had already ceased to exist. But he kept staring, not at the creature immobilized by his gaze, but at that thing that, born of his sudden lust, was the embodiment of his lust and came to life slowly, imperceptibly, her breasts heaving with the waves of air she was breathing in. He threw his arms around her neck, forming a firm, passionate ring. His lips perched on her mouth, like the bee on a flower, not to offer a kiss, but to extract one, to pack into the kiss the jumbled, scattered, and shattered fragments of his inner being.

The silence, hanging from the curtains on the windows, was a group of sleeping bats that weighed heavily on the room. In that oppressive atmosphere, he struggled to find what was tormenting his imagination. The mingling odors of bodies, dirty water, and wasted semen prevented his mind from chasing after a lost image that, at times, was a body falling from his limp arms, the countess descending the marble stairs. In particular, it was an image that fled to the edge of his thoughts and lingered there, irrefutable and shapeless. That was the misery of his search, because it was at once the product of his imagination and its immediate disappearance. He shook his head, as though it would help untangle his thoughts, and the heaps of image shards spilled out like bats that, terrorized by the light pouring through the window, fled in every direction toward the dark folds of the curtains. And yet the image remained unbreakable, disturbing his search with perfect effort. He tried in vain to stand up and walk through the ruins that filled the room. He was tired of those endless ruins, because they kept resurrecting an image of the Armenian, of the essence of his nation.

Then he gave up, called off the search, and tried to sleep.

~

Early in the morning, he tiptoed down to the kitchen, carefully avoiding the night guard. Throughout the night, there was something unsteady and tender in his soul, something that suddenly thickened, hardened, and took shape when he stood in front of the stove. The shape was the letter he had written to Arshalouys the day before. Profoundly amazed, he cried out, "*Ah ! ça alors*." A match in his hand, he was about to light the burner to make coffee, but immobilized, petrified, he couldn't do it, because out of the confusion of the night clearly emerged the object of his torturous search, right there facing him, just as they say that one day the Earth burst out of the ocean fully formed. Emerging from his thoughts, that object stood across from him. If he had wanted to, he could have held it in his hands. It seemed so clear and so tangible, even though it was just an image, like an image born of a painter's mind, that is to say, a concept turned into a painting, hung on the wall, materialized. Minas stared at it in bewilderment. "*Ah ! ça alors*." It must be said parenthetically that this French expression of amazement, which is often used in daily life, is a way of remaining disconnected from the story of an interlocutor. "*Ah ! ça alors*" is just another inconsequential interjection thrown into the air that allows listeners to continue developing their own mental image, preventing interaction between two beings and therefore running counter to the idea of language as a tool for communication. Of course, this wasn't the case for Minas. In fact, quite the opposite was true. By repeating it three times, one after the other, Minas not only communed with his interlocutor, which in this instance was the letter, but also became it completely. The night—a master of the business of spoiling a game—can so easily blur the line between a Hortense, lovestruck in his arms; a Madame Bédier, elegantly descending the staircase; and an Arshalouys, born of his mind who withdraws into her lair like a shadow, retreating with the dawning of the day. The first task of the day is to put everything in order and arrange it to be able to make use of life, except in the case of someone who dwells eternally in the night, like Minas. So in plain daylight, he returned to his night mode, taking with him the residue of the day's thoughts: regret. He couldn't understand why he had written the letter. Well, he had written it. Let's suppose that writing it had been a responsibility, that he had to write it to calm the heart of a distraught young woman, Vahakn's wife, except that he had had no right to slide across slippery emotional ground. The more he reread the last letter in his mind, the closer he examined the words he had used—first one by one, separated from one another, then as part of the composition as a whole—and the more he realized that he had corrupted a sentimentalism that his words could not have conveyed if he hadn't wanted them to, consciously or otherwise, and which could easily capture a heart weakened by misery. Why so informal a tone? His very first words were like two heads leaning in close, "Dearest Madame Arshalouys." What right was there for this intimacy between two strangers? It could also be interpreted as impudence. Then he could shamelessly retreat and slide into the dim light of easy sinning. Apologies—offered by the thousands as he assumed his self-appointed role of consoler—soften the ground under her feet with the stomping of emotion, circle her heart, besiege it, then suddenly leave and do from afar what the fisherman does when, in a calculated final move, he casts a net, supremely confident in his catch.

And this hadn't been enough. He still needed to settle her into Hortense, to enjoy an entire night of sex, surrendering to frenzied rapture.

It was already clear to him, beyond any doubt, that he had shamelessly tried to take possession of her as though she were abandoned property. This was the reality, even if his responsibility was legitimate and their correspondence had already become part of a routine. Sitting at the rickety table in his room, the power of their correspondence invited him to plunge deep into the transgression that had already begun, because Minas, pen in hand, was searching for words to entrust to the white sheet of paper on the table to correct the misunderstanding in the previous letter. Fortunately, he did not go through with it. Rather, he couldn't go through with it, because he became distinctly aware of its impossibility as long as there existed in him two opposite worlds that deliberately flowed into each other, distancing him from his original goal. He couldn't decide on the phrasing he would use once and for all—at least that was for sure. It wouldn't do to swing one way and then another. For instance, to write "Dearest Madame" now and another time write "Dearest Madame Arshalouys" or "Dear Madame." At that moment, he considered this last one the best, but also saw in it a deliberate attempt to break off ties, which he likened to cutting tightly wound rope with a sharp knife.

Meanwhile, night had reached his door. He set the pen down on the paper and put both hands on the table. In that same moment, the silence, which had taken refuge in the closed box of his room, fell on him like a lid. Minas felt the terror of loneliness. It had been the first time since Vahakn's death that he felt it. He closed his eyes, thinking that it would help him to avoid feeling it, and listened closely. The silence flowed into him, seizing his entire being. Now there were two silences: one was him and his own loneliness and the other was the room, throbbing like the heart of a huge animal. It was probably the impression of an animal that reminded him of the caryatids. Seeing the Hotel of Silence curving the caryatids' shoulders under its massive weight as well as their silent suffering, people held their breath even before going inside. It was there that the widowed Hortense Bédier guarded the silence like a high priestess and, watching her steps, raised her finger to her lips as she came down the staircase, chiding those who disturbed the stillness: "*Allons, allons, silence là-dedans*." Minas knew very well that nobody was disturbing the silence. The concierge walked on his tiptoes to avoid clacking his heels on the marble, while the porter gently turned the revolving door. If he made the slightest noise, he scrunched his head into his shoulders like a student bracing himself for a beating. But every day, Madame Bédier repeated: "*Allons, allons, silence là-dedans*." Suddenly he saw Hortense's face in his imagination. He saw how her right nostril twitched, raising the corner of her mouth and distorting her entire face as she took her index finger to her lips to deliver her daily refrain.

Minas also understood the secret of the other face, which gave her the look of a schoolgirl as she stood in the doorway of the kitchen, leaning against it with her shoulders slightly hunched, staring at him as he worked. Her sharp stare and pursed lips made her face look like a mouse's snout.

~

"He has his hat on." Of course he didn't own more than one hat. How could he? He was homeless. "He doesn't even have a bag."

His monologue ended when he heard Vahakn's voice: "Hey, Minas!" His eyes were drawn to the hat. He saw only the hat. Such a strange thing. Vahakn was entirely a hat. The confidence that came to him was drawn from the hat, not from his voice. His voice was the hat and perhaps simply a wish, born of a wish, so that he would be able to say to himself, "He's got his hat back. His pockets must be full," and be happy about it. Minas didn't even have time to be surprised, but he *was* surprised that he hadn't needed words for all of this. He hadn't seen the need to move words into a sentence. His conviction had been immediate and spontaneous. It was at that moment that his ears caught his name and he saw another mouth opening and taking the shape of his name. The important thing was not his voice or the shape of his mouth. It was the hat that dictated the rest, because a belief in the hat already existed. His ears were able to immediately assume their role, while his thoughts slowly made their way through the dense forest of inference and speculation. With his sense of hearing near the door to his soul and his ears sliding the bolt to it closed, Minas managed to redirect his attention to the outside world.

"Bravo, Minas," Vahakn said with satisfaction as Minas came to sit on the chair next to him. "How did you know that I left my hat behind because of that? Didn't they give you any trouble? Oh, this hat. It's a treasure—a treasure. You drop it wherever you have a drink and leave. This isn't a hat. It's an insurance policy."

He was sitting in the chair next to him, mute, and it might be said, motionless. They had found each other. This was enough for the time being and he needed, first and foremost, to take a deep breath and settle into himself. Vahakn was satisfied, too. He enjoyed where he was sitting and didn't even see Minas sitting on the chair next to him. Perhaps he was sleeping. His eyes were closed, but they might just have been closed to help him collect himself. He was gathering the fragments of a self that had been scattered during the day. The fear of being alone had broken him. He had gone to Rue Saint-Jacques again, but they told him that his friend had moved without leaving an address. It was then that, as he walked down the street and reached the banks of the Seine, he stopped in front of Notre Dame. The fear of being alone, the fear of having been abandoned, had surfaced and suddenly broke him. It was in that tattered state that he had arrived at the Billard in the evening, drawn by a hopeless glimmer of hope, like a moth dancing around a fire before throwing itself into the flame. Fortunately, it wasn't a flame he had thrown himself into, but a bistro chair. Despite being so close to Vahakn and so far from him at the same time, he couldn't stop talking. He spoke endlessly and his words, beating down Vahakn's wall of indifference, took on the appearance of a monologue. "*Ah, par exemple*," the monologue began. "It was the only way to meet you. That's for sure. Do you understand? The hat, the hat."

During the day, when everything is in motion, it's impossible for thought to pause for a moment and concentrate on the details in which it's often possible to find a quintessential moment of life. It cannot be found in the jumble of ever-moving images on the surface of life, especially when they are—willingly or unconsciously—engaged in the business of disguising themselves like actors.

Minas was confused. Despite every effort he made to emerge from it at any cost, the confusion had yet to relent. His mind flowed freely like a river and the more he tried to cling to something, the more he was plunged into the water and pulled away by the tide. The river was a torrent of mental images that didn't stop. The powerlessness of his will to stop them was what tormented him. More than the weakness of his will, there was in him a kind of complacence toward the images. With their descent, he sunk further into their inner depths, where he hoped to finally find peace of mind. But, as always, the deeper someone goes. . . . Like a drowning man whose anxiety swells as he's pulled toward the ocean floor, Minas fluttered and rose to the surface of his own mind, where everything suddenly stood still. A frozen image appeared to him on the surface, as if a film projector had stopped. It was an image of Hortense. The stillness had made the twitch in her right nostril disappear. Her will had been incapable of eliminating it; it had, rather, at most succeeded in hiding it, though the effort had distorted her face even more. Hortense had finally been able to make something pleasant out of the ridiculous, which was the very charm of her personality. Minas registered the surprising transformation that took place on that still, trapped image and his heart filled with inexplicable compassion for Hortense. The spontaneous, heartwarming charm of her mouse's snout engulfed him.

~

And yet he didn't see Minas in the chair next to him. Minas himself didn't hear what he was saying once he sensed him in the other chair. That was enough. The words had no meaning. His presence was what gave meaning to the words and also what gave him the right to relax into his chair. Now his bones, spine, and muscles no longer saw the need to remain alert, to keep watch, or to hold themselves upright. Sitting in the bistro chair, Minas was a defeated army whose soldiers—exhausted and wounded—took refuge in the shadows of the bushes at the side of a long road to forget in a deep sleep the horror of the day's events. Even though the back of the chair kept his torso upright, Minas was immersed in horizontal sensations. Like the soldiers at the side of the road who had evaded danger, his line of sight was overcome with images of a house, a room, and a bed, when he suddenly stopped in front of a run-down hotel near Rue Danton. Like a fish tossed onto dry land, he sprung out of his thoughts and his throat released a hoarse sound: "I found it!"

Vahakn immediately understood. He had a strange capacity for discerning the unspoken. He even understood that Minas was not paying any attention to him. It was as if he wasn't there. He looked at his half-open eyes—impenetrable, dull, and hazy—in which lethargy lingered idly out of hunger or sleeplessness or both. "What did you say?" he asked, but the question didn't quite come through. It didn't come out of his mouth because a slight shift happened in his brain and imprinted barely noticeable movements onto his lips. Minas didn't interfere in the battle that his will was waging against sleep. It appeared that sleep was in fact the master of his will, which failed to restore his features to their original position. They roamed around his face, abandoned like him, while his forehead—smooth and polished—invited Vahakn's attention. His forehead assumed surprising proportions under Vahakn's gaze. Sitting in that chair in that café on Boulevard Saint-Michel, his mind was lulled to sleep beneath distant purple horizons. His eyes were entranced by his friend's forehead, which had gradually grown brighter and more luminous, because with sleep, a childlike innocence had come to visit him and stir a sense of fatherly affection in Vahakn's heart.

Sooner or later, the regret of failure will manifest itself in everyone. The wrenching, scorching regret of a father who sees his child as a kind of rose, an ornament worthy of his pride, until the moment he finds himself before a new reality. In the child is an autonomous, distinct, and independent being. With this realization, the father decides to make a person out of the child, a person who will be the embodiment of his dreams, the one who he had not been able to become, since every life is a failure when it stands before death. Every father sees himself in his child. And through the child, he gives life to his consuming fantasies. This is how the sacrifice of a father begins. But fathers will never understand why one day their children will suddenly flee their dedication and turn into wanderers in search of their own fantasies. Every rejection is an act of construction.

And he still kept looking, his gaze having merged with the forehead of the other, while his heart was filled with feelings of supplication. He had forgotten about the procession of feet on the sidewalk. He turned his head toward the street out of habit, but no sooner than he turned did his gaze return to hang on Minas's forehead once again. The man sitting next to him was a trembling creature. He was a shipwreck flowing with the water of the river within him, carrying along with it treasures that remained unknown to him.

Vahakn extended his hand, almost warmly, and gently shook Minas's shoulder.

"Hey, get up. We haven't come here to sleep."

Minas was startled.

"What? Am I sleeping? Of course I am. It's been two days since my eyelashes have touched. Last night I was so hounded by sleep that I dragged my feet from street to street looking for the hotel. You know what? I found it, I found it. I finally found it, but . . ."

"You found it?" Vahakn screamed joyfully as a brilliant idea came to him.

"On Rue Danton," Minas continued. "I mean, on that narrow little street opening onto Rue Danton. But if you only knew how I found it . . ."

"So you can go now."

And with clown-like gestures and words coated in honey, he tried to convince Minas.

"Look at me and listen very closely. You'll go now, but not in the state you're in. Collect yourself a bit, get a room there and have a nice nap. Then you'll tell them you have to leave to take care of something urgent. They know you, so they won't make you pay right away, especially since you have the right to two months. Don't tell them anything about that, though. And don't be scared, I've done this kind of thing many times before. Early in the morning, you'll pack up and go."

Minas contorted his face, as if he had figured out the extent of the deed.

"No!" he screamed. "No, I can't do this kind of thing."

There was terror in his cry. Vahakn knew that Minas needed some serious rest. If he spent one more night on the street under the open sky, his strength would abandon him entirely.

Vahakn stood up. "Wait here, I'll be right back," he said calmly.

He had barely taken a step before turning around. "Don't run away," he added. "I'll be back in a half an hour, at the most."

Minas couldn't have run away if he'd wanted to. He slouched in his chair. Now he was sinking, powerless, and surrendering himself to the dense haze around him. Only a voice reached his ear. It was his own voice coming from within. All of his body's doors to the outside were shut. It cannot be said for sure, just assumed, that his disconnection to the outside world can be attributed either to somber resignation or despair, but when once again he heard the voice say "He's gone," he made an imperceptible motion like someone pulling a bed sheet over his head to fall asleep.

But since it was impossible to sleep outside the café, on the sidewalk, he closed one eye to trick himself and kept the other open to trick the waiter, who was working just as much as he was watching him. Sometimes both eyes would suddenly close, encouraged by some inviting mental images formed by memories of home and bed. His chin—as heavy as lead—fell to his chest, despite his struggle to ward off sleep.

Vahakn was not gone for long. But to Minas it felt as though he had awakened from hours of sleep, when he noticed Vahakn's footsteps out of the corner of his hazy eye. Yes, Vahakn's footsteps drew closer on the sidewalk and he was carrying a bag.

"Come on," Vahakn said.

There was a joyfulness in his voice. This was why Minas could jump out of his thick inner turmoil, as if he were pushing away an obstacle with his shoulders.

Vahakn paid for the coffee in that particular way of the rich that reeks of arrogance, but he did it explicitly to inspire confidence in Minas. They crossed the street and passed a bakery on the corner of Rue Racine, where they bought small loaves of bread made with milk. Then Vahakn stopped in front of a hotel across from the Sorbonne. He squinted, pretending to read the name of the hotel and, like someone who had found exactly what he was looking for, said, "Right, this is it," in a way that immediately dispelled the suspicion that had already begun to grow in Minas.

The hotel reception desk took care of the formalities—Identity papers? Where are you from? Where are you going?—and Vahakn, refusing to hand the bag over to the concierge, accompanied Minas to his room, walking behind him and giving the bag and its owner more authenticity. The room had every amenity—*confort moderne*: hot and cold water; a clean, large, imposing bed; an armoire with a mirror; and a table and armchair. The floor was covered with coarse, bluish carpet, and above the headboard was a lamp that could be turned on or off without even getting out of bed. After he finished reading, he could just press the pear-shaped button. Minas felt like a phoenix rising from the ashes. He couldn't stay in one place. He walked back and forth across the room; put his hand under the cold water, under the hot water; turned the faucets on and off; and then stopped in front of the mirror on the armoire, still silent, stirred and restless. In a moment, he transformed into a new man and filled with happiness. At times, he was almost choking on his emotion. He didn't know how to express his feelings, which had gathered in his throat to form a hard lump. He moved to the left and right to hide the tears welling up in his eyes.

"Well," Vahakn said, moved. "Go to bed now and get some rest. Tomorrow morning, you'll come to the Billard. I'll pay the bill downstairs."

Vahakn was almost out the door when Minas ran after him, finally able to open his mouth.

"Where are you going?" he asked.

"I don't know," Vahakn said. "Paris is big."

"Haven't you had enough of this life, Vahakn? Let's find work tomorrow and we'll have a room like this every day."

"I can't."

"Why not?"

"I don't know. I'm waiting. It'll happen someday."

He walked down the carpeted corridor with his head bowed, while Minas, deep in his sad thoughts, followed Vahakn's steps with his eyes. When Vahakn reached the stairs, he lifted his head and started walking down them proudly like an actor coming out onto the stage.

Minas was alone now. His back against the door, he looked at the room without moving; he feared that any movement would suddenly displace everything and make everything vanish. What did all of this have to do with reality? Reality was a combination of happiness and fear. But what if it's all an illusion? He was careful not to let his hand graze the bed. He didn't touch anything. And yet there he was in the mirror. His hand accidentally touched the cold surface and suddenly all the objects in the room surrendered to him. Then he could touch the rest of the objects, too. He could put his head under the hot water that flowed from the glittering faucet, pull open the covers on the bed—that miracle—and stretch out underneath the fresh, white sheets—which he did. Everything was real. Quick, quick, enjoy it while it lasts! It could soon turn into a dream again. And it was already a dream. "Don't concern yourself with us. I wrote that your uncle is keeping his promise until the boys get older. Take care, son. What are you up to? You never say anything about yourself. Don't let my health worry you. The doctor said it's only heart trouble. Soon you'll feel fine, he said." How rich a life of security can be! Rich with both sadness and happiness. And all of this, all of it crashing into each other, turns his mind upside down. Instead of closing his eyes and falling into the sweetness of sleep, look how a rose meditating in a vase awakens emotion in him. Whistling ships head toward wide horizons, while in the circle of their masts, his sister's grieved face smiles at something invisible beyond the rose. Across from the "horned" church, the girl selling perfume in front of the barbershop suddenly turns her head away, seeing lust in his sharp gaze.[15] Why so sharp and lustful? Why did he scare the girl, the one with a fake black beauty mark on her left cheek? Only now did he see that she had a beauty mark. How had it been that he hadn't seen it before? How naïve he had been. But he got his punishment. My God, how did he get here? Leave the barber's daughter in peace. The ship leaving the harbor whistled. Ghevont must be done with his work over there. What is

Ghevont doing? The ship whistled once more and he felt like he was about to fall. He was at the edge of the bed. Quick! He stretched his hand out to reach the button above his head to turn off the light, pressed it with his thumb, and all of a sudden darkness invaded the room.

He won't look for the towering Hortense walking down the narrow strip of carpet on the staircase anymore. He had made this decision the day before. He would love this slim, petite woman who two nights before had known how to make herself small in his arms. So much so that she dissolved in them as he held her tight, kissing her ears, eyes, and lips. Now he smiled at her in a way he had never smiled before, especially at a woman who was the object of his affection—Hortense—she who was always compelled to become small, to become childlike out of love, whose chest beat surprisingly fast and swelled under the moons of his kisses, and in whose gaze lived a gloomy light. The scent of her breasts was still on his palms. Sometimes he couldn't help staring as he cupped them in his hands and felt them tremble as he released them onto her slim body, which would have taken flight like a bird if his tense fingers had allowed it. The grip of his fingers, under which her body stiffened in obedience, brought a new, unfamiliar shudder.

No, he wouldn't love the coquettish, conceited Hortense on the staircase, who was already prepared to shout orders with each step. He would love this tiny woman who looks at him so tenderly, with the glassy eyes of a fish, admiring and beseeching, while he prepares the breakfast orders and arranges them on trays, as though he were a war commander on the front, bringing thousands of captives to throw at her feet.

Sometimes he laughs out loud; a smile wouldn't be enough to express his joy and his triumph over this woman who knows how to behave like a child. For months, she worked quietly to teach him all the secrets of her body without a single word, carrying out her strategy in silence. It's in the temple where love matures and is refined, where words kill mystery. When he looks at her, laughter rising, his heart—brimming with pride—fills with gratitude. Recalling the love games during the night, led by

Hortense's silent orders that threw them both into a supreme moment of union, he sees the road that brought him to victory, to the place where love is achieved by taking possession of something beyond even the body. Of course, Minas could not explain what "beyond the body" possibly meant. There are things that defy explanation, and if they are like that, it's probably because they are of pure inner emotion that transcends the boundaries of language and remains out of reach for the mind. It may be said that what Minas felt was a profound sense of satisfaction and happiness, which came to him not through Hortense's body, not from possessing it, but from the presence of that which is called Hortense. This was the novelty of what Minas called "beyond the body" and perhaps his curious mind had already begun to create a theory around it. He actually felt her presence just as powerfully, if not more powerfully, when she was gone, which was something he realized after Hortense had left the kitchen. It meant that the question came down to being there. Even if Hortense left, she was always there, invisible, because she was within him—"beyond the body."

"Long live the Revolution!" Apkar said all of a sudden.

Minas looked toward the door at the speed of lightning. Hortense was gone. Apkar, on the other hand, did not need to look toward the door. He felt Hortense's comings and goings on his back, as if setting down a heavy weight or picking one up. Besides, he wouldn't have seen anything if he had looked. The door created depth between the wall and the room service elevator. Yes, a heavy weight fell off his back. He felt lighter whenever Hortense quietly opened the door, trembling, and then disappeared. Her presence silenced him. Holding his tongue, he turned back to work diligently, not because he was afraid of her, but because he wanted to make his disdain known.

Apkar's exclamation was followed by a burst of laughter mixed with bold derision, which he pulled along behind him at all times, like dragging a dead animal to the dump by the end of a rope.

Minas pretended not to notice, not so much because of the laughter directed at Hortense, but rather because of the sorrow that roamed the caverns of Apkar's hoarse voice, like rats roaming through the sewers of the city, not alone but in packs.

Apkar hurriedly paced to the elevator and back and then arranged a few things on the stove. "The bitch left," he growled.

Without stopping his work, Minas turned his head mechanically toward the sink. Apkar was standing there, his back against the sink as he dried a plate with slow, well-oiled movements. A disdainful smirk softened the lines on his face.

"She's gone, but don't worry. She'll be back," he said, drawing out his voice to convey hidden meaning.

"Why?" Minas asked.

"Come on, you're really asking *me*? You know better than I do."

"I don't get it, Apkar."

"Really? Do you take me for a fool? Did you learn that from Vahakn? Listen!" he said suddenly, raising his voice. "Before you started, that woman never set foot in here. She'd stay for five or ten minutes and then go. Now she'll go on talking for an hour. She doesn't even come up for air."

Minas preferred to keep quiet, especially since defending himself with lies didn't sit well with him. But his heart ached. True, the pain wasn't physical—it was some kind of sadness that gathered to form a lump that weighed painfully on his heart—but having turned to Apkar, almost face to face, he realized that his silence would be insulting. It already was insulting, because Apkar quickly turned his head away and Minas broke the silence:

"So it's my fault," he said in a low, humble voice.

"No, it's mine!" Apkar shot back even more harshly. "But I know a way to keep her away. You'll see."

The next day, when Hortense came in, Apkar started to make a terrible commotion, singing "Les bourgeois, on les pendra." With that popular song of insatiable vengeance, he added his own lascivious laughter that made blood pour out of the walls. Hortense covered her ears with both hands, turned around, and left. When, with her hands over her ears, she looked at Minas to express her astonishment, he noticed something new on her face. Despite the snarl that appeared to show her displeasure, Minas saw a strange serenity that made the twitch in her right nostril disappear. This usually forced the corner of her mouth to twitch, which in turn made her constantly bite her upper lip.

~

He strolled down the boulevard. He was already nearing the bridge. The boulevard was filled with people and cars. Elbows pushed through the crowd. Sharp, hateful glances were exchanged. Near the bridge at the top of the stairs leading to the riverbank, the clock on the iron railing read eleven o'clock. Entirely numb to feeling, he didn't notice anything going on around him. As he walked, he cursed the day he met Minas and that game they played. Suddenly he felt something. It was fatigue. He looked like he was coming back from a funeral. He had buried his old carefree attitude along with the dead. No, this wasn't why Minas was sleeping peacefully in a soft bed at that hour, while he was going to unload carts. The job was a guard against his old carefree attitude. Perhaps it was its absence that now made his thoughts, as sharp as the blade of a knife, stand in front of him and threaten to cut through space? The more he walked, the deeper the image became in his mind and the more he was pushed to the edge of the crowd, alone and isolated. There he was, standing at the base of a well, throwing a stone and watching its effect on the water's mirrored surface. It should have shattered, but instead he only saw himself, sinking into his own wound. He was tired. He was exhausted and he hadn't even reached Pont Saint-Michel yet. Leaning against the stone edge, he watched the flowing river below. Across from him was the black mass of Notre Dame, standing tall in the darkness. The noise of the cars and passersby didn't reach him. He was alone in the night, in endless desolation, which rejected him and pushed him back so far that even the desolation wouldn't have him as a friend. There was nothing, nothing that told him, "Come here." The city had closed its eyes to him. The city was getting ready for bed. Everybody rushed home, while he was forced to keep walking. He was forced to keep walking to forget the passage of time. His waiting strained to suspend time to prepare him to accept the unknown object of his anticipation, which could have been a person or an event. This is why he was always alone and unable to look anyone in the eye in a sincere, friendly way. He thought about this when he began cursing Minas, who at the moment, was sleeping sweetly and innocently in his soft bed. If Minas had only been with him, he would have looked without blinking into his eyes beneath the streetlamp. Minas had a startling gaze. It exuded an elegant serenity that infected his smooth cheeks with an enchanting sheen—the sheen of innocence—that suddenly revealed trembling ghosts rising from his wounded heart, gripped by the fear of life. Now he tried to look, through his imagination, into the eyes of the absent Minas, but he only saw himself, as though he were standing in front of a mirror, but he couldn't hold his gaze and, before he felt his eyelashes touch, he had erased his own image from that gaze.

It was still early. He reached Les Halles and stopped in front of the Église Saint-Eustache. Its clock sounded the twelve strokes of midnight, careful and measured. The big trains arrived one after the other and dumped the food they had been carrying, invading the surrounding streets with piles on Boulevard de Sébastopol, Rue Réaumur, and the Poste Centrale. The nightly stir of well-known restaurants released cheerful notes into a night filled with the commotion of work. The cafés looked like lanterns dangling over the edge of the night. The clock on Saint Eustache had just struck twelve, covering Vahakn with silence, as he suddenly saw himself transported to an unfamiliar place. A splendid place, which was his everyday environment, so ordinary, and yet that night it seemed so foreign to him, so otherworldly, as though an imaginary reality was being constructed behind a curtain and he was standing at the edge, ready to walk on stage as soon as it opened. There was still time before the panting, tumultuous arrival of the day's hero. And when it did arrive, the curtain of the night would open and the gang of vagrants would storm the stage. Vahakn, quicker and nimbler than most, would shove them with his arms, elbows, and shoulders and push his way through to the front of the line to get his share. And in a frenzied atmosphere filled with curses, the carts would be unloaded as quickly as the vanishing of the proverbial piece of cheese thrown to the rats.

But he was already under the lights on the large boulevards. And he was not at all surprised, because a secret thought would often pursue him from within and occupy the entire space of his mind, disrupting his schedule and daily reality. This is where the imaginary curtain game came from.

Driven by that impatient idea, he couldn't wait for the curtain to open and, gently pulling up one corner, he slipped out. He was on the verge of confessing to himself the reason for escaping to the other side of the curtain, but the spineless idea fused with his footsteps and kept pushing him onward. He escaped from himself, but he still had to break through the crowd and get to the opposite sidewalk, and at the exact spot where the two boulevards converged, people ran underground to catch the last metro. These rushed people were not the usual crowd. It was just as the theaters and cinemas were closing. Vahakn stopped to avoid colliding with them and once again found himself alone, entirely numb, and stranded in the corner of an alleyway, trembling. He had once again fallen into his whirlpool of inner images. There was his main idea, the main impetus for his walk that night, which like a solitary, dazed fish making its way among thousands of fish, appeared clearly before his eyes. Vahakn was running away from Minas. Leaving the neighborhoods on the left bank, he plunged deep into the ones on the right bank. He was on the corner of Boulevard Haussmann when the thought came to him. Before him stretched the wide, nearly deserted boulevard in magnificent serenity. The streetlights winked at him from behind thick foliage. But it was in front of Printemps, in the overpowering glow of the windows, that he stopped and confessed. Yes, he was running away from Minas. He said it to himself right then and there, the secret behind his nightly escape attempts, as though he were talking to someone else. The lie was no longer bearable. He needed to walk, to keep walking, to pull himself out of his own head, like pulling a cork out of a wine bottle with a pop. He was thinking about this as he came to stand in Place Saint-Augustin and beheld before him the mass of the church jutting into the dark canvas of the night, its large, round dome thrusting into the heart of the sky. Unusual activity was going on around him. He was in front of the enormous Cercle National des Armées. Military officers in full regalia and white gloves, along with men and women in civilian clothes, headed toward the building's big, wide door. Naval officers shuffled across the sidewalk. Suddenly, as the crowd grew denser, a black car pulled up to the curb. One of the naval officers rushed to open the car door and let out a soft noise into the night that lodged itself in the gaps in Vahakn's concentration. A woman extended one leg and then the other out of the car door. She stood and started to walk, stopping two steps later to cast a heavy look over her shoulder. For an instant, her eyes closed, as though she had grown tired of the weight of her gaze. Vahakn could see long, black eyelashes hovering above her rosy cheeks like tiny little fans. The woman was followed by an admiral in a ceremonial uniform adorned with medals. The woman was tall and slim—perhaps owing it to the dress that fell to her gold shoes and, with each step, made a silky rustle pass through the glimmer of her diamonds. The purplish strands of her hair and starry eyes reminded Vahakn of a sweet spring evening. Stately and erect, she held her skirt in one hand, more for the effect than out of necessity. The rustle of the silk was music to Vahakn's ears. When she passed by, he followed her with his eyes, mesmerized, until she reached the entrance to the building, where she vanished at the admiral's side like a dream disappearing as sunlight falls onto our beds just as the room is breaking free from the night's clutches. Vahakn stood still, rubbing his eyes nervously, as if to anoint the lingering vision with gold dust. Then, suddenly, he started to run, run like a wounded animal looking for safety.

He finally reached Les Halles, but the train was long gone. He was glad it had left, because it required such considerable effort to make his way through the pack of vagrants.

What Minas has done since the moment he gained something "beyond the body" must finally be said. The following evening, as usual, he went upstairs through the service door and discovered something completely new. It was subconscious at first, but slowly became conscious little by little. For a moment, he stood halfway up the stairs, which he would never normally dare to do. He realized he wasn't rushing. He was calm. Usually he climbed those same stairs secretly, his ears trained to detect the softest footsteps and ready to hide at a moment's notice. He feared chatter, especially from the maids, who—always jealous, always gossipy—would waste no time spreading rumors, folding them into their whispers. He wasn't holding a tray for the simple reason that it wasn't time for coffee yet. It would come at around two o'clock, before he left for the day. But the tray was just the pretext. Reaching the second floor hallway, he sauntered the two meters to the end of the hallway, where he found Hortense's room, half-covered by the thick, saber-shaped leaves of a giant cactus. The door seemed to be protected by a brigade of knights with their swords drawn. He opened the door without knocking. "It's me," he said, seeing a big, wide smile that seemed to embrace him on the face of the woman lying supine on the couch. He almost ran to the couch and jumped into the woman's arms, which were open to welcome him. That woman—Hortense—pressed him to her and whispered, "My child, my child." Minas fell to his knees, put his head in her lap, and started to cry. His crying lasted a while and was now and then interrupted by sobs that threatened to tear out his heart. But what happened was exactly the opposite. Once he stopped crying, his heart was stronger, bound more tightly to his body. He sensed the presence of his strength, which resembled a ripe piece of fruit. He was not at all upset that Hortense stayed silent as he cried, unable to relate to the source of the pain that remained obscure to her. But Hortense rested her hand on his head tenderly, and although there seemed to be indifference in her voice, she now and then repeated, "My child, my poor child." If Hortense had known Armenian poetry, she would have adjusted her normal refrain to say, "Cry, my son. Cry so you may grow up," which would have better suited Minas's state of mind.[16] But Hortense didn't know Armenian poetry, and even if her own words meant the same thing, her indifference was anointed with mild scorn. Not only had Minas not been unsettled by Hortense's detachment from his pain, on the contrary, it made him press his head into her with an unfettered soar of the heart and expel a flood of emotion through his sobs, like a child clutching his mother tighter and tighter to stifle his tears.

Then he stood up. His heart was finally calm. At last, a callus had fallen off his heart and disappeared. He wiped his eyes and noticed Hortense half-naked beneath her long, gauzy nightgown. Hortense gave him a curiously languid stare. Minas moved closer, warmly and respectfully covered her naked breasts with her nightgown, and stretched out beside her on the couch. He dozed for quite a while.

It was already dark when he found himself on the street. Someone bumped into him. He turned to the man and apologized. The man, who knew he was at fault, looked at him with surprise and both of their smiles brightened. The man apologized in turn. Minas was happy. He felt like singing. How long had it been since he had last sung? Yes, he would sing. He would sing right now on the boulevard, where the streetlights made it look like a stage. He began mumbling "Pamp Vorodan."[17] He continued singing under his breath. It had been so long that he had forgotten the words, but they suddenly exploded like a bomb: "Down the fields of Ararat." "Oh!" he called out. His heart was calm and the passersby didn't make him feel the least bit shy. It was his right to sing. Now he would always sing. He made his decision and kept walking down the boulevard. Porte Saint-Denis was still far. He passed by Apkar's street, where the girls waited for propositions or did the propositioning themselves with a "my darling" or an "are you coming?" So why not? Just like that, maybe to test his new strength or for no reason at all—none—he picked a girl and found a hotel. He tortured the girl with his tender games, against which she resisted on principle. But when she stood up to fix her hair and try to calm her racing heart, she said with playful anger, "You're a pig—a pig!"

There was something strange in him now, outside of him, which he still couldn't grasp. The people, the streets, and the city offered him intimacy and approached him, whereas before he had only seen hostility. Everyone seemed to recognize him and might as well have greeted him, but he didn't recognize himself, what he had become, the new Minas whom he would meet outside the Billard. Indeed, that was where he felt the transformation. Ever since he found himself "beyond the body," sobbing in Hortense's lap, encountering the girl on the street and longing to go "beyond the body" with her too, he had completely changed, matured, and dropped the pursuit of his inner images. He looked around with new eyes. Only yesterday, sitting in the same spot, did the passersby represent a forest where Vahakn went to hunt every night. That was what had changed. The forest had disappeared and was freed of people roaming along its paths. Yesterday he still saw them through Vahakn's eyes. Now Vahakn had disappeared from the horizon in his mind and had suddenly become a distant memory. Memories are what became of those days of hallucination, which Vahakn had used to weave a spider's web that trapped him with the startling threads of his life. He was like a spider that weaves a fateful web around its prey with the threads of its own body. He looked over at the chair next to him, where Vahakn had sat only yesterday. Today it was empty, but he didn't feel emptiness inside, because he lived in the presence that he found during his excursion into the world "beyond the body." He chuckled. In a single moment, his laughter purged the entire past. He had been so stupid. And he had a violent desire to get on a train or go to the barbershop, but this time the barber's daughter wouldn't be afraid of him. She would smile at him. He wouldn't stupidly say to the girl selling fish, "Your cheeks are the color of trout." He yearned to set off, to revisit the places where he had known so much heartache. Once again, his gaze wandered around the street and the café. Everything was familiar. There was nothing foreign to him. The foreigner had left him. Resisting, obliging, no longer faltering or retreating. On the way to his room, he remembered Vanadour, who had left him on the sidewalk. He was embarrassed by the fragility of his emotions. He walked with certainty. He began whistling—never mind that Hortense had called him "my child." Her voice was in his ears, her gaze in his soul, and the length of her body, now taller after his sobbing, had emerged mature with the presence of her "beyond the body."

Vahakn's letter was still on the desk. He picked it up and read it over again all the way through. It felt as though Vahakn were there. Minas also saw a change in Vahakn, which reminded him of his own transformation. In the letter, Vahakn attributes his emotional insensitivity to being dead, which would have only inspired a laugh had it not been for his tragic end. But now, a closer, more composed look revealed a certain truth to those words. Here death should not be understood in its physical sense. The man who died a month before his death, from the moment he decided to kill himself until the day of his suicide—the time during which he wrote that letter—was not dead himself, of course, but rather he was a man defined by his psychological state—the source of his words and actions. The change—the old psychological state, in his words, dead, vanished, making out of him a seeker of a lost thing, like we all have been at one time, endlessly in search of something lost—had not happened during that month alone. Similarly, if we were to rely on the individual words in the letter, we must also be convinced, as he says, that with his symbolic death, the general givens of the psychological state that made Vahakn seem like

Vahakn to us no longer applied, and from that moment on, Vahakn was no longer Vahakn and a new Vahakn emerged. That moment, however, had not begun the first time Vahakn had stared at the ash on Ziya's tie, finally putting his finger on it and saying, "It's nothing. Just some cigarette ash." Death, following Vahakn's logic, had occurred the moment he had put his finger on the tie: the moment he *touched*, not the moment he *looked*. The observation is so indisputable that now, when Minas visualizes Vahakn, the first instance of surprise lies in the latter's change of facial expression. First and foremost, his face. One day, while they were walking along the banks of the Seine—on one of the days after the scene with the tie—Vahakn was in a cheerful mood, chattering away, when he stopped and looked at him straight in the face. Vahakn kept talking. First, his usual distractedness was nowhere to be found in his voice. And then there was a seriousness, a seriousness about his own words, a sense of respect. He seemed entirely focused. But what surprised Minas was Vahakn's chin. His weak, ever-drooping chin had gone to join the healthy parts of his face, forming with them a previously nonexistent harmony that made him look like the buffoon he already was and turned him into a slimy, deceptive creature. It must be said that Minas had not particularly grasped this idea at the time. Now it dawned on him as he replayed the scene with the letter in his hand, sitting in front of the table in the room where they had lived together. In the floodlights of his consciousness, Minas saw so clearly that Vahakn had appeared to him with two faces: one distant, extending further into the distance and giving way to the new one, which, on the contrary, drew closer and came into Minas's field of vision, compressing his features and fashioning a new face, which—born of the other, out of the other's death—came through as that of a handsome, loving, amiable new man—a brand new man. With a quick leap of his mind, Minas made a connection, confirming a similar change in Hortense—on Hortense's face. A short while ago, just a short while ago, Hortense—supine on the couch—stared at him without that twitch that gave her a contorted, tormented expression, which often suggested her effort to conceal an evil thought. That face had calmed, illuminated by an inner sun, which in reality came from the space "beyond the body" that they had both reached the day before.

Indeed, just as the sweetness in Hortense's voice and gestures had cleaned the stains of past desire, Minas saw in Vahakn a nobility, a confidence of feeling when he spoke and acted. For instance, he partly gave up or ignored the feet game beckoning him from the sidewalk, until one day when he cheerfully referred to the girl whom Minas now knew to be Arshalouys. It seemed as though Vahakn had, piece by piece, begun to think about organizing his life. He came to consider his work at Les Halles to be real work. Vahakn's reckoning with life—starting with that simple touch on the street, through which the long wait for the unthinkable would seem to reach its end—made the loss of a friend all the more poignant. When he thought he was safe, Vahakn climbed another floor away from the mysterious sense of anticipation within the haze of his soul by bringing his fingers to Ziya's tie, which revealed to Minas the prototype of the man Vahakn would become after Ziya's murder. And who knows? Maybe Vahakn was right when he said he was dead, because he had instinctually murdered Ziya not on the night in the Square du Vert-Galant, but on the other night when, sitting outside at the Billard, a finger resting on his tie, his touch was like the blade of a knife on the vulnerable hollow behind the silk.

The main problem was not having a plan. For eight days, I've been trying to make my pen dance across the page. I shouldn't rush, but how can I not? From the day I conceived of the idea, I've had no rest. Putting it like this isn't quite sincere, either. It is inexcusable to accept the first word that comes out. The issue of word choice is the most important and the most difficult, at least that's how it seems to me. I haven't even started yet and I'm already using words improperly. The words "idea" and "conceive" don't sound quite right to me. Often people are driven to create new words, or just new sounds. It's possible to agree that here the word written as a note might be of no importance. We must be vigilant, so that imprecise words don't enter real work in the future. But this point of view is wrong, too. If I allow myself to be easily pleased now, everything will become difficult later. Absorb the difficulties now, so that the work will be easier later. Otherwise, a bad habit will take root. We must be demanding from the very start. Herein lies the seriousness of the work, because above all else, seriousness is what is needed. How can we convey the identity or authenticity of a thought or a feeling if the words cannot find their place? Inspiration is not enough, especially for someone like me, who is just taking his first steps in prose.

Now, conception supposes consistent mental effort. By excavating the object of its pursuit, the mind at last brings it into the world. From within the plowed field, the seed grows to see light. Who knows? Maybe I'm wrong. I don't imagine that my words and I were born together, but when suddenly the thought captures its object and traps it, an expanse comes into being, a stockpile of words at my disposal, outside itself, and here the words help hold the vision. For a long time, I didn't know what a mouse was. No, this isn't true. I knew. They said it was a rodent that gnaws on everything. This much I knew. But I had never seen it gnaw on anything. Gnawing is an abstract image, like the mouse itself—the mysterious animal that fled like a shadow as soon as it saw me. The mouse was also something of an abstraction to me until the day I saw a cat pounce on one before my very eyes. Only then did I know it to be a mouse—a poor, pitiful, tragic thing that lay motionless in front of the cat. It was the unfamiliar that stirred my fear—the gnawing was all I had heard. When it knows the words, the thought extends its hand in an invitation to dance and takes hold of whatever it likes, whenever it likes, like a cat with a mouse devoid of mystery, yet still terrified by its loss.

It never crossed my mind that I could one day express myself in prose, although now I realize that I've used it in life every day, without feeling as amazed as Monsieur Jourdain.[18] But I'm not altogether convinced of what I'm saying as I recall the sentences I've used with people that have surprised them. For example, the girl selling fish opened her eyes wide in amazement after I told her, "Your cheeks are the color of trout." Rather, what I realize more now is that what I took to be fiction was something else, since it prompted amazement in others and set me apart from them, keeping my life disconnected from theirs. Hence my desperation.

Was it nine or eight? Yes, exactly eight days ago, I was sitting outside at the Billard, where I can be found far less frequently since Vahakn left us. I sat there and thought of the time we spent together. I felt so good, as if Vahakn had been sitting in the chair next to me. Sometimes I even tried to turn and talk to him, but my movement consumed and digested itself, while I remained confused and disappointed, my heart racing.

It was at a moment like that when he was forced on me. Just like that, with no warning. From outside, he was thrown inside and stayed there, expanding, imposing himself, and my will became his will. He said, "Write!" Now tell me, please, which is more agonizing? To be a slave to an inner obsession? Or to be handcuffed and taken to jail through the streets, flanked by two policemen?

Whatever it may be, I'm like a prisoner who has been plotting his escape for eight days.

Here, however, the problem becomes more complicated. I ask myself how a personal issue could possibly interest others—readers, I mean—since ultimately writing supposes a readership. The written word is a medium for exchange and communication, so why not also for borrowing things that must be returned? Thinking is more individual. It's possible to think without borrowing. We think to steer our own lives. In this there's no connection with another person. There is no give or take. It's thinking about what to do, then either doing it or not doing it—walking, for instance. Who cares? But when you write or walk, thought also takes on a peculiar quality, multiplying in the exploration of the self. It doesn't know how to end. Nor how to exhaust itself. The meteoric rise of thought in solitude is exactly how people give themselves over to madness. But I don't have any intention of going mad. This is why I want to write. Not because it was Vahakn's wish, but because when I turn to him sitting outside at the Billard and look at his demanding eyes, they tell me, "Write!"

In this case, one must reflect on the law of exchange, which brings us face to face with those like us. In other words, as the aesthetes say, change the subjective into the objective. Leave yourself behind. Slip into someone else's skin and hide there. Become universal, so that they will listen to you. Appeal to your listeners. Make them listen. Enchant with a story that will capture the reader's attention. This way you will accord a function—not to mention a message—to writing. But not Vahakn's message—no.

Here is Vahakn's letter. It will be the axis of the piece, around which the characters in the story must be gathered, because what is being told is, after all, a story. There's only one issue. Usually authors have already jotted down the events that took place, when the fate of each instance is decided, accounted for, and concluded with all of its effects. Writing is bringing the past into the present. In this case, only Vahakn and his victim, Ziya, belong in the past. Apkar, Arshalouys, Hortense, Nicole, and I still continue to remain in the present. We cannot be part of history, and in the end, it wouldn't be possible or fair to relegate us, with the stroke of a knife, to the past, just to pull us back into the present. We have no right to leave readers desperate to know everything and make them wonder, "What then?" Yes, what then? We need to wait, although if we were to look closely, it would be easy to predict the future through the chain of events, so that it becomes easy to roll the future up in the past with your thumb and hunt it down from there. There is still the matter of deciding how accurately the reactions to each event can be predicted. This is still an object of contention. Events will take unexpected courses sometimes. For instance, a moment ago, I saw no point in recording how my heart skipped a beat when I mentioned Nicole's name. Who knows how simply recalling that unremarkable, insignificant feeling could have an effect on the future? It might one day change the course of a whole life, destroy it, or give it wings, the way Hortense, as we already know, brought stability and guided it toward a satisfying conclusion. It's possible to write in the future tense, and not because it falls into the realm of prediction or fiction, since even novelists write about the future in the past perfect, transporting themselves to a distant future where everything has already happened. It would be smarter to wait and be satisfied with writing down the events of the day. At the same time, it's possible to be truthful and write, "a novel based on a true story," on the cover. Zareh's mistake shouldn't be made. Those arbitrary, contrived notations must be avoided. I had an argument with him about it back then. He knows just as well as I do that he did it deliberately. The incident under the bridge was made up. Nothing like that ever happened, since he was the one who paid my travel expenses and the only one who knew about my escape. How could it be that after having naïvely squandered the money I got from selling my books on prostitutes I didn't even sleep with, I shamelessly used that beggar to satisfy my lust and then steal her modest savings? His explanation didn't convince me.

By attributing the act to me, he was seemingly raising a cry of protest against humanity. See how far your injustices can take a man? Shameless! Whatever his intention, I was the one humiliated. People looked at me with disgust and I was ashamed to be around them. According to him, the novel is not about what happened, but what *could* have happened.

In a way, maybe Zareh is right. I think I need to wait for the events to take on a certain sense of completion or an outline, at the very least. How long will it take? Is it possible to wait a whole lifetime with this heavy weight on my shoulders? If honesty is required when addressing the reader, just as much as honesty is required of the writer, whose soul is perpetually gripped by the imperative to be rid of inner obsessions, how do we reconcile these two conflicting stances, dear reader—my friend and enemy?

If we were to take a closer look, it would also become clear that the fate of the dead is still uncertain. I understand the utility of taking notes. It drives thoughts to think. Thought dives deep into itself, then rises like bubbles. It amasses wealth like travelers who keep collecting treasures on their trips.

I shouldn't have said before that Vahakn and Ziya were dead—because they aren't. They have just gone somewhere else or entered a new realm. Perhaps to die is to change realms. Some people will laugh at what I am writing. Why doesn't anyone laugh when someone talks about changing an old, stained shirt? Everything changes. The body is the soul's shirt. People are not merely bodies; they are paired with souls in one room, like Vahakn and I used to live in this room. I haven't forgotten the first time we opened the window; Vahakn shut it, saying, "It smells like shit," and afterward we never opened it again, to spare our souls from suffering in the room in which we lived together. But the soul doesn't suffer after it's buried in the ground. The soul is very cunning; it flees and always finds a body in which to dwell. Only the body rots and decomposes in the earth, abandoned by a deceitful soul. So if this is how it is, Vahakn's life couldn't have ended on the day he died. Now what do we see? We see from the notes here that he is present in our acts and thoughts. To be more honest, I will even say that he expresses his thoughts through us, while we naïvely believe them to be our own. Often our acts amaze us because we never think that they are, in fact, the realization of thoughts that Vahakn is controlling within us. They feed on us like the parasite he was when he could still be found in our universe. The same goes for Arshalouys and Apkar. And for Hortense, too, as a corpse. Yes, Hortense, too. Her gaze has been transformed by the vision that Vahakn's death has ignited in us. If acting out our thoughts is not living, then what is life?

~

We're leaving. Wouldn't it have been better if we had sat and had some milky coffee? I could barely control myself when he paid for just his coffee. Maybe my happiness rubbed him the wrong way. Am I to blame? He was the one who brought me. Of course I slept wonderfully. Why wouldn't I have? "You just got a week's worth of sleep," he said. "Twelve hours, to be exact." What was I supposed to do? Not sleep in that soft bed? My bones even rested. I always need them to stay on my feet—to walk. What does he have against me? Sure, I understand. It lasted a bit too long. I still have my hopes pinned on Apkar. I'll have a word with him in private when I see him. He got up as soon as I sat down. The waiter stood there, expecting an order. "No," he said. "We're leaving." Where are we going? I was so surprised that my gaze probed his eyes inquisitively. "For thine is the power," he said, opening his arms and trying to laugh. It was the laugh of a buffoon, his face hideous and his teeth almost rusted. I'm certainly not saying that he should feed me. But what I find criminal—yes, criminal—is that first he gives you hope, fills your heart with joy, and then suddenly it's like he's screaming "Die!" in your face.* Ok? I don't need anything from him. He has bound his luck to my bad luck on his own free will. He taught me incompetence, as though I hadn't been incompetent enough. If he regrets it, well, then, let him be sincere and say it openly. It's obvious that I won't be spending tonight at the hotel. I'll let him know that he's finally free. He can leave. I could go to Les Halles and unload the carts, too. He thinks I don't know. Why does he hide it from me? Arakel told me the story, but I haven't said anything. It's none of my business. I want a job—a decent job—like everybody else. My mother was right when she said, "I

* As he was writing these lines, Minas didn't know what he would learn and write down later. See the section on the Cercle National des Armées. That day, Vahakn was completely broke.

hate poverty. I hate it. I don't like the poor." She didn't say it, but she hated the rich even more since becoming poor. His miserable mother. If she knew . . . what, am I crying? Yes, I must be crying, since here I am wiping my eyes with the back of my hand. We're in front of the park. It looks like he wants to go in. I don't know. I'm walking behind him, following his steps like a loyal dog. I don't need to think. He is thinking for me. I'll go crazy if I start thinking. Yes, we're already in the park. Let's see what he's going to do. Oh, the sun has filled the park. I like April a lot. I mean the month of April, because I'm not sure that I like the other one too much.[19] They didn't give me enough time to like it. Life is beautiful. I have to admit it. The sun, my God, look at the sun. Look how the trees, which have already begun to cover their bare branches with blooming flowers, are smiling. I could never understand this. Why do the trees strip bare in the cold of winter and put their clothes back on only beginning in spring?

It's true. I was carefree when I was alone. People can deny themselves this or that. It's not the same when you're dealing with somebody else. The slightest movement can often uproot everything and leave a big, gaping hole in its wake. This is why I hate Minas. Yes, I hate him. How should I put this? Hate is not quite the right word. What I feel is something similar, but not hatred. In any case, it was from the expression on his face that I learned to recognize shame. I don't understand why I hide my work at Les Halles from him, why I play hide and seek with him. Yes, it's nothing if not shame. He must be stupid not to get it. But why? We could have gone and worked together, but I kept it from him. It wasn't just that. Now my shame is even heavier and it has caused me to feel disgusted by Les Halles. I was so ashamed last night! It was because of him that I walked right past Les Halles. I wasn't thinking straight. I walked and walked and passed right by my usual turn. It was because of him that I felt shame seeing the wife of that man dressed up like an admiral. I was embarrassed beyond words. Heat rose to my cheeks. That bitch! Today, too, I feel disgusted by everything. Everything? No, just by myself. The glory of her breasts expanded before my eyes and from the height of her indifference, she made it clear that you were nothing—a worm. Finally someone understands! Nothing else existed but the glory of her half-naked breasts, as though they were calling out, "To deserve these, you have to be at least an admiral." But behind them, beyond them, beyond them, there was Fatma. I hate Minas. He was so happy when he came to the café with renewed energy, soothed, brave, rejuvenated after a good night's sleep. He was only missing a cup of coffee for his bliss to be complete. When I told him, "No, we're leaving," he seemed to lift his hand and give me a resounding slap across the face. I can still feel the sting of that slap on my cheek. We left the café unaware of each other. It was as if we weren't together. Hey, we've reached Luxembourg! What for? Who told us to go? But we went. We're in the park at the most crowded time of day. The place is jam-packed. I wish there were a corner to sleep in at least. I'm tired. The roots of my eyelashes are burning. I figure we're here because no one can think in a crowd. You must be alone to think. And I'm alone. Minas is so far from me. My brain is twisting like a screw, uncontrollably. It's twisting. I'm like a crippled man who, forgetting his handicap, or not even realizing he has one, considers himself an equal, until the day when, forced to flee from danger, everybody runs and he's left behind in the middle of the square, his bad leg failing to save him. The world suddenly goes black. I am that cripple. Minas conspires against me with his silence. It's nothing else. Silence is the distance that separates us and I can't run after him. I'm crippled. Strange—that's how it feels to see his brain ruminating. His head is a shop window and through it I can see his brain ruminating. Here his mouth took on a different shape. He's going to say something. Speak, Minas, speak. I'm going crazy. There's a slight twitch in my lips. Perhaps it's a thought looking for words. Lips preparing for a kiss assume a similar position to carry out their function, like a soldier attaching a bayonet to his rifle before a charge. He opened his mouth slightly, very slightly, almost in repentance, only to close it again. The poor thing was being tortured terribly. Look at his tense lips. It seems like he's about to bite them. I have to help.

"What are you thinking about with your head hung like that?"

"Nothing," he said.

They were sitting on a stone bench in front of the Grand Bassin. They were lucky to have found a place to sit amid the crowd. There were chairs, but you had to pay for them. It's wonderful to sit under the sun, basking in its warmth and not thinking, or letting your thoughts wander into the distance like worker bees moving from flower to flower. But Minas was on edge. He was thinking. Let him try to hide his thoughts all he wants, but they began to show in the quivering at the edges of his mouth, opening like a split pomegranate.

"Let's go get the bag from the hotel later."

Vahakn answered with a monologue. The words buzzed around Minas's ears like a gnat. He worked to grasp their meaning from within his daydream. Stubbornly and slowly, the words crossed into the realm of understanding. He was looking at Vahakn with wide eyes when he screamed, "No!"

"Oh yes! What did you think? That I would have let you in on it and have you betray us like an amateur?"

"So you mean . . ."

"You wouldn't have had the chance to take it with you. They would have kept the bag, but who cares? It was only filled with paper and sand."

"Would they have arrested me?"

"No, they're not as stupid as you think. The police are of no use to them. They would have just taken your identity papers and kept them until we paid up."

Minas was stunned as Vahakn broke into riotous laughter. His exuberance instantly scattered the heavy silence between the two friends. Satisfied with himself, Vahakn opened his arms, extended them, shrugged his shoulders, gave a long yawn, and said, "To the one who doesn't love this life . . ."

And he immediately added, "Let's go to the Billard and write a letter to Arakel. Do you know Arakel? The tailor on Rue Descartes? 'Dear Arakel, we're leaving on unexpected business. Your bag was left at the hotel. Forgive us for not having time to bring it back to you. Please show them the enclosed note to get your bag. It's right near you: Hôtel Claude Bernard,' etc. On to the next one. Your French is good. Write, 'Monsieur le concierge, please be so kind as to return the bag in room number thirty to the gentleman with this note and request payment from him . . .'"

The sun had left the park, but there was still a sweetness in the air. The sky had grown white. As the evening drew closer, the white turned to a pale blue. Minas's hand stopped moving across the paper.

"Look," he said, pointing at the two cups of coffee. "What are we going to do about these?"

"God is with us. We'll figure something out."

Minas kept writing. He finished the first letter and began writing the next one. "Monsieur le concierge . . ."

"Did you used to catch sparrows when you were little?"

"I don't remember," Minas said.

"I used to love to. I started when I was five. I had an uncle who liked to play like a kid. We used to catch birds together. We would clear the snow in the garden, enough room for a small circle, where we would put a mesh. Held up by a stick, the mesh had an opening on one side. We would tie a string to the stick, and when a sparrow hopped inside, we would pull the string from the window above, where we used to spend our days. The mesh would fall and the poor sparrow would be trapped. Then I would slowly put my hand inside to catch the bird. I could tell which sparrows, nibbling on breadcrumbs, would be trapped. There were nimble ones that used to jerk their heads and come and go with crumbs in their beaks. Then there were the slow, hesitant, fearful, suspicious ones. They deliberated far too long and faltered. You would think, look, they're about to go inside the mesh, but no, one hop and they're back out. By the time they made a decision, they were trapped. They would definitely make a decision. They are hungry in the winter with snow everywhere. Don't you get it? Not a single worm in the trees. They have no choice but to go in, but by the time they figure it out, the mesh has already fallen over them."

At that moment, Vahakn noticed a pair of feet on the sidewalk, a pair of feet among an untold number of others that were walking straight ahead. This particular pair knew where they were going, or their master did, at least. Vahakn didn't move; he was in position, his gaze fixed, afraid even to blink.

"It's happening," he said.

"What?"

"Here's the one who will pay for our coffee."

Back on the sidewalk, the pair of feet paced up and down the boulevard, but not toward Vahakn. His gaze was glued to them as he beckoned, "Come here, come down here, dreams. Come down here, sweet dreams." He mesmerized them, enchanted them. He knew the expression of their master: one corner of his lips raised, one eye open and the other closed.

He no longer felt the need to look at the feet. It couldn't be any other way. He hopped like a hesitant sparrow, jumping more confidently into the mesh, the toes of his shoes turned toward Vahakn. They started walking.

"Excuse me, is someone sitting here?" he asked with extreme politeness, sitting down.

Minas was overwhelmed. He barely heard Vahakn's comment. "Didn't I tell you this was going to happen?" Vahakn said, utterly confident and pleased. Minas didn't know if he should introduce the newcomer.

From the next table, he pricked up his ears and straightened his tie. He looked at the man out of the corner of his eye. He looked handsome in his black coat and white shirt.

Minas overcame his confusion to introduce him.

"Are you Armenian, too?" he asked Vahakn. "I had the honor of meeting Minas effendi." Turning to Minas, he said, "You see, I haven't forgotten your name." Turning back to Vahakn, "It's nice to meet you. I love Armenians. Back in Istanbul, I had friends who were Armenian."

He spoke with his delicate torso leaning over the table. He drew his head toward Vahakn and noticed the reluctant beginning of a sweet smile appear on his face.

Minas left the second letter for later. He put away the paper, envelope, and pen. The mutual affection that seemed to be created spontaneously promised a long conversation, especially since Vahakn never forgot his intentions.

"Forgive me," he began. "Monsieur . . ."

"Ziya," he said.

"Forgive me, Ziya effendi. We aren't students. We have to get up early for work tomorrow morning. We'll see each other again."

Vahakn stood up and gestured for the waiter, but Ziya grabbed his hand.

"Let me get it. I would be offended otherwise."

At last the manuscript is finished. True, there are still dozens of pages of notes strewn across the table, but they don't have any direct bearing on the story. After shuffling through the pile of papers, I can see that an impulsive choice has already been made. I don't mean to say that the notes that have been left out are unimportant, just that including them would have burdened the reading and Vahakn's portrayal wouldn't have become any more interesting. The notes are mostly about Vahakn's antics, which are described in enough detail here. But I need to add the following, which, at the moment, is imposing a fierce sense of compassion in me. But it's better to quote from notes written in the heat of the moment.

We were walking down Boul'Mich. We had reached the corner of Rue des Écoles in front of the bank. I stop short. On the sidewalk, someone, breaking through the crowd, comes toward us happy and smiling, as if he'd recognized an old friend. But there is something broken in his smile, which is moving like a mechanical spring. He is clutching a pamphlet in the hand he extends to us. His forehead is strained by the effort it took to extend his hand. His big eyes seem to be about to burst out of their sockets. He has a beard that hasn't be touched by a razor in at least eight days. His whole body exuded supplication, contorting his face like a mute unable to speak.

But finally he spoke: "In order to save the nation!"

Only then did I recognize his voice and called out, "Hey, it's Mr. Bentham!"

The crowd streamed along the boulevard and jostled us where we were standing. The man's hairy cheeks attempted a smile, but failed. The smile couldn't spread from his muscles to his eyes to form a real one. It stayed on his cheeks like a dying light.

"He didn't recognize you," I said painfully, turning to Vahakn.

"Do you know our Sarkis? He writes poems and sells them."

"He's from our school. One day, our philosophy teacher was lecturing on Bentham. At the end of class, Sarkis raised his hand."

"'In your opinion,' he began. 'Mr. Bentham . . . ' but couldn't keep going. Hearing the 'Mr. Bentham,' the whole class broke into laughter. Since then, the name Mr. Bentham stuck."

As I was explaining, we'd walked away without realizing it. By the time I turned around, Sarkis's face had vanished into the crowd.

Until now, my work has been eased by the pile of old notes and Vahakn's letter. Now I'm facing serious problems. They have absorbed me so much that I've been completely cut off from reality. In its place has emerged another reality. My effort to overcome the difficulties plunges me incessantly into that other reality, the one in which everyone else's life becomes secondary, like a reality spinning behind a shop window, alien to me, irrelevant. When I pass through the streets, and especially when I'm in my room, they seem entirely different to me. They are the streets of my new reality, the new reality of my room where others have no place, no access, and where I work alone, constantly surrendering to a strange search, where I am the lord and master—its absolute ruler and its absolute slave.

Once again, I start running to the Jardin du Luxembourg right after work. Apkar himself and Arshalouys with her letters are at my disposal. They follow my orders. But Nicole? Nicole, who has been on the margins of my heart and mind since the day I cried in Hortense's lap, had suddenly—I don't know how—slipped inside the boundaries of the new reality. She wasn't with the others behind the shop window. On my visits to the park, where I tried to give Nicole a sense of her responsibility to the new reality that she had become a part of, I found that my old, smoldering feelings had reignited. I am truly scared of her. She's so unapproachable and elusive, and still so ethereal, that I don't understand what her function can be in this vast world that I call mine. I went to the movies in the afternoon, more to arrange my thoughts than to pass the time. I was hoping to think in the dark theater, but the news segment showed a report on summer collections at the major fashion houses. Nicole suddenly appeared on the screen. In a hall full of spectators, she paraded down the catwalk with dainty, tantalizing steps as light as a bird. Her arms hung from her shoulders in a way that made it seem like she had relinquished her body to draw the audience's attention to her clothes. Another twirl as she struck a new pose, then another, always with a slight, airy thrust of the hips, which, from one moment to the next, transformed her into a dancing dream. The dream didn't last long. Turning her back to the crowd, she was about to disappear backstage when the graceful expression on her face, which the audience no longer needed, suddenly hardened. Her eyelashes quickly fell over her eyes. I was so mesmerized by her that it surprised me to see the moment her fake smile waned and her eyebrows descended like clouds chased by the wind. It sent shivers down my spine. It was as though something ominous had happened to me and only me. "Where are you?" she asked, her gaze sinking into my eyes. "Where have you been all this time?"

Despite the sting of her reproach, it was the same reproach that once weakened my attempts to get close to her during our chance encounters in the park. I left the theater abruptly with an indescribable sense of joy, because through her unexpected appearance on the screen, Nicole had not only entered these pages once again, having been away for a while after losing to Hortense, but there was no doubt that she had just made a date with me beyond the shop window. Holding my breath, I ran straight to the Jardin du Luxembourg with the trembling heart of a lover rushing to his first tryst.

~

In the morning, he met Apkar at the entrance of the Métro Saint-Denis. Rain was falling on the city. The sky was so gloomy and low that it seemed to touch the rooftops. Fog rose heavily from the sidewalk, waiting for the sun before evaporating into the air.

Apkar did not immediately cross to the opposite side of the street as he normally did. He walked straight ahead, hunched over, his chin to his chest and his left foot dragging behind him with extraordinary torment like a loose limb. Sometimes he moved his arms, lifting his head at the same time to stare straight at an invisible yet stubborn opponent.

Minas caught up to him at the corner of Rue Cler and gently put his hand on Apkar's shoulder. Apkar jumped as if he had been stung by a bee, but smiled kindly when he saw Minas.

"Oh, it's you."

"What's going on?" Minas asked. "You look upset again."

Apkar didn't answer right away. They passed to the other side of the street without a word and walked side by side in silence. Suddenly Apkar seemed as though he were about to burst into flames. He stopped on the sidewalk, which seemed to shrink him. He was forced to lean on his bad leg to stay upright. Now taller than Apkar by a head, Minas looked down at him expectantly, but Apkar didn't say a word out of respect for his friend's silence. Minas kept quiet, but not without a kind of anguish that melded compassion with affection. Even though he felt a powerful need to empty his heart, the jumbled words swarming around his head didn't obey him.

They were at work when he finally exploded.

"Slaves, ha!" he said. "I wish he were alive to see what slaves can do."

Their eyes met and Minas saw a smile begin to shine on Apkar's grieved, rebellious, and rough face, reminding him of summer at dawn. Minas had never seen anything as beautiful as that smile. Sometimes, when Apkar's face was at its ugliest, a smile would suddenly spread across it like an extraordinary narcissus living in the filthiest of waters. Not even Nicole's smile was as beautiful on the day that it exploded in resounding laughter underneath a grove of trees in the park, bringing fiery clouds to the sky.

Encouraged by Minas's disarmed, enchanted gaze, Apkar raised his fists. He was about to open his mouth when Minas whispered in his ear:

"Be quiet! They might hear you."

It was simple. Minas understood where his friend's frenetic excitement came from. He had been in the same overexcited state last year. The day before the first of May, he was already sensing what was to come the next day, which would put an end to the farce of this world.

Dear Monsieur Minas,

Forgive me for my delay in responding to your letter. Thank you for your brotherly advice. But this storm will not pass. I cannot reconcile myself with what happened. Why did Vahakn do this to me? Why did he leave me alone like this? Lancet is a very small town. There were a lot of Armenians here at one time, but almost all of them left for the big cities once their work visas expired. Many went to Lyon or Grenoble. They said there was no way to make money for them here. We thought about leaving, too. Vahakn left, promising me that we would move to Marseille, Lyon, or Paris as soon as he found work. Every day I came up with big, big plans in my little brain. Big dreams. It's an unbearable life, Minas, the life of a laborer. We hadn't been prepared for a life like this. Why am I telling you these things? Forgive me. Please forgive me, Minas. I have no one here to whom I can empty my heart. What should I do? Where should I go? I feel that I can't even stay here. I must escape this place. Memories of Vahakn are at every turn. But how? How will I escape?

How many times have I written this letter only to tear it up! I know I'm bothering you, but this will be the last time. I thank you for your sensitive, brotherly letters.

I beg you not to forget your sister,
Arshalouys

Sweat beaded on Minas's forehead. Somebody had gripped him by the neck and started strangling him.

"What do I care? Who am I to give advice about someone else's business when I can't even handle my own issues?" he screamed all of a sudden.

He felt fingers slowly tighten around his neck and tried through a flurry of words to save himself from who knew what kind of danger. "What do I care?" he repeated. "Let's say I give some advice and she's grateful for it. Look at this situation!" But he couldn't resist. The hopeless whisper of the letter wound around his heart, became his master, and picked him like a flower. He took a piece of paper out of a drawer and hastily, illegibly, and without any hesitation wrote "Get married" and signed it. Then, without putting it in an envelope, he tore up the letter. The tearing of the paper became the whisper of an aching heart, warming his body, and Minas weakened with the tenderness of compassion. He couldn't bring himself to behave like that desperate woman. He decided never to write to her again. After all, he didn't owe her anything. What did they want from him? But what would Vahakn think, the same Vahakn who supported him by working at Les Halles? If he knew how badly his only friend was treating his devastated widow . . . Of course there wasn't an assumption that he would support her. All she wanted from him was a few words of comfort, words that would span the expanse between them. Suddenly that distance became a lament and the lament transcended space, where he felt he could now talk face to face and whisper words of empathy. He could even see her eyes already, wide open and gazing at him from behind a curtain of grateful tears. Yes, he could see them now. His head was leaning not on Arshalouys's shoulder, but on the table in front of which he was seated in his tiny room on this side of the expanse. But he saw in the pained eyes staring at him more sadness, recalling what Apkar had said about Vahakn's white wedding. He took another sheet of paper out of the drawer, laid it on the desk, and started to write. But he felt, however, as though he were following orders like a man sentenced to death and forced to sign a confession.

Dear Madame Arshalouys,

Your letter has truly moved me. But what can I do? What can I say? If I were able to do something about it, believe me, I would spare no effort. But I beg you, get married. I see it as the only way to ease your pain.

Minas Yerazian

This time, he emerged victorious and reveled in the feeling of victory. With one word and one stroke, he had, almost unexpectedly, wiped the cellar of his inner illusions clean. He finally felt the satisfaction of a man who had done his duty. He looked at the letter, which was already in the envelope with a stamp. It was already out of reach, waiting for the first hours of the morning to take its fateful course.

He stood up. He paced the length of his room, whistling and glancing at the envelope now and then, contented and satisfied by his triumph over himself and his vulnerabilities. It was the first time that Minas felt something akin to self-respect, but like after all triumphs, a penchant for arrogance slowly settled in his numb heart. The more he thought of Arshalouys and the blow his letter would deal her, the more he saw the parallel between her and a singing bird in a tree, whose chirping would be buried in sad silence in a split second, cut short by a bullet.

With one word, Minas had cut Arshalouys's song short. He had left her without a song. As he paced the room, he stopped suddenly in front of the envelope waiting for morning on his desk, jumped into bed, and buried himself in it, recreating the silence that forms after a bird has stopped chirping. He covered his ears with the blanket and fell asleep without shutting off the light.

The rain stopped at around two o'clock. Following the relatively beautiful days of March, April had disappointed Parisians in need of sun. The moment the sun appeared, people filled the parks, turning their faces toward it with their eyes shut as if in prayer. And yet here was May, beginning with a downpour. By the time he reached the corner of Boulevard Saint-Denis and Boulevard de Sébastopol, the rain had stopped. Only once in a while would a shower run through the streets like a mob. In the sky, the warm, luminous sun would suddenly appear between the gaps in the black clouds, descending on the city and laughing along the length of the sidewalks like a mischievous prankster. It was in that kind of moment that voices seemed to say, "They're coming! They're coming!"

From the depths of Boulevard Saint-Martin approached a dark throng. The mass of people at the four corners of the intersection moved into place and took position, forming a square with an open center like a circus ring. Anxious to see the conflict about to happen, everyone's eyes were directed more toward the empty space than the approaching crowd of workers. It wasn't only the onlookers who took position. On the nearby streets, a mass of police units had lined up at the entrance of the boulevard, barricading strategic points that the march would have to pass in order to reach the Place de la Concorde, the Chambre des Deputés, and the Champs Elysées. This was the traditional May Day route: from the Bastille toward the rich neighborhoods. Boulevard de Sébastopol was the only street open, with no access to any of the ones on the right side—Rue Réaumur, Rue Étienne Marcel, etc.—up to Châtelet and Hôtel de Ville. Its sole purpose was to push the throng back and shatter the collective strength of the workers, who would continue to carry on the fight in smaller groups, here and there, like the rear guard of a retreating army.

Suddenly "L'Internationale" erupted. The procession was already in sight and spread wave after wave—decisive, immeasurable, and impatient. The entire length of Boulevard Saint-Martin was filled with people, like the cork in the neck of a champagne bottle, slowly edging upward to explode with a pop. And that's what happened by the thousands and tens of thousands. The tail of the march had barely left Place de la Bastille when the front reached the intersection and the hopeful refrain of the battle cry rose along with the growing din of stomping feet, followed by "La Jeune Garde" and "La Carmagnole," at once jumbled and united, in harmony, as if it were the song itself that would open the street for the procession to pass, unhindered and victorious. But then came the first clash. The chants and the crowd now become a mob in front of Boulevard Saint-Denis and collided with the police. They started elbowing, then escalated to punching. They shifted positions. In the tussle between the police and the workers, a torrent of merciless blows poured down from all directions. Cobblestones were thrown into the air, shattering store windows and cracking skulls. They ran, chased them, and launched a counterattack. Minas watched in horror as a white baton rose in the air and landed on a head. Blood poured out and stained the cobblestone street. The fighting lasted for an hour. The procession from the Bastille had kept going, splintering and breaking off in the square, extending down Boulevard de Sébastopol, creating a number of separate pockets of resistance, while other groups still managed to penetrate the big boulevards, still pursued by police, fleeing and fighting back, until the firemen finally arrived. From the fire trucks parked at the end of the four boulevards, a rush of water shot into the crowd and made the battle unequal and impossible to win, even though the torrent often blindly fell on their very own men. Then they started to retreat. As the crowd in the intersection thinned, Minas saw Apkar. Wild and foaming at the mouth, he dragged his bad leg behind him as he threw punches left and right until he found himself face to face with a policeman. The policeman lifted his baton, but in that moment, a boy—his eyes breathing fire—stepped in front of Apkar and, tilting his head to the side, bore the blow aimed at Apkar's head on his own shoulder. At that moment, another policeman struck Apkar over the head and threw him onto the sidewalk. Minas saw all this from across the street, but it was impossible to cut through the twenty-some meters separating him from Apkar, who was lying right on the corner of Rue Boulanger. The water hoses and swinging batons on one side and the flying cobblestones on the other made crossing that stretch not only dangerous, but impossible. He needed to wait until the crowd dispersed, but suddenly it occurred to him that since the police would come to collect the wounded, he might be able to take Apkar away. The police interrogation would confirm his identity as a foreigner and he would be treated even more harshly. They could even deport him. What would happen to Apkar then? That idea left Minas unsettled. He ran left and right to no avail. He went to the Porte Saint-Denis, passing under the arch, skirting the police, and made it to the opposite sidewalk. The fighting was fierce there too. He veered through the thick crowd. Slipping by with difficulty and trying to avoid the clashes, he made his way through Faubourg Saint-Denis and then on to Rue de l'Échiquier, where he cut across Boulevard de Strasbourg behind the firemen and finally reached his friend, who was still on the sidewalk in front of the Théâtre de la Renaissance. He quickly pulled him up, put Apkar's arms around his neck and, propping him up, carefully retraced his steps out of the conflict zone, even though the police were still chasing small groups of demonstrators who had infiltrated the forbidden zone down the side streets.

On Rue de l'Échiquier, Apkar hung from Minas's neck. Minas thought his friend had lost all his strength, but Apkar lifted his head off of Minas's shoulder, turned back, and yelled, "Vazken! Where's Vazken?"

There were police cars on the side streets as well as on Rue de l'Échiquier. The cars were already filled with the arrested and the wounded. Minas walked faster. They could be stopped and interrogated. Unfortunately no store, café, or pharmacy was open. Blood continued to flow from Apkar's nose and the wound on his head, though not nearly as heavily as before. The entire neighborhood looked like it was at war. It was impossible to find a taxi, at least near Opéra. There was no other way. The hotel was the closest place. They hadn't said anything to each other yet. Apkar didn't struggle and let Minas do what he thought was best, but as they approached the Hotel of Silence, he put up some resistance. He leaned against the wall and refused to go any farther. Minas paused for a moment too. He took a breath and then put his arm around Apkar's waist and started walking in silence. In the same moment, a voice called out from behind them. Minas turned around and saw the boy who had thrown himself in front of the policeman to protect Apkar from the baton.

"Are you both all right?" Apkar asked, once the boy and another one his age caught up to them.

"He's just a little kid," the boy said, looking at Minas. "He's not one of us, but we're friends from the orphanage. We go everywhere together." And turning to Apkar, he added, "I'm fine. I've got a trick. As soon as I see the beating coming, I turn myself into stone and stiffen my body, so I don't feel it when I'm hit."

"Is that right?" said Apkar. "How can someone stiffen their head?"

The boy, whom Apkar had called Vazken before, took off his hat to show him the shirt he had stuffed inside.

"It can soften a blow to the head too," he said and added cheerfully, "We fought well today. Didn't we, Kegham?"

Noticing a group of demonstrators running away from the police, the two boys went to join them.

In the kitchen, Hortense took care of Apkar herself. She washed the wound with hydrogen peroxide, rubbed it with iodine, and wrapped a clean bandage tightly around his head, making him look like a mullah. Apkar and Minas broke into laughter. Hortense stared at them in bewilderment, not understanding why they were laughing, and rushed to lift Apkar's arms up against the wall to stop the bleeding from his nose.

"We went to watch the procession," Minas started to say.

"Right, right," Hortense said skeptically, not letting him finish. "What difference does it make?"

May was about to end. It had barely begun before the days passed in rapid succession. Things of beauty tend to be short-lived. Sunrise, sunset, and look, the day has entered the heart of the night from which a new sunrise and sunset will be born. Winter is endless, gloomy and wet—long, snowy hours that strive to become a day, but only manage to be endless stretches of time. The nights were dark and the days were filled with work, continuous work without an end in sight, where night and day remained indistinguishable in the presence of the city's almost perpetually burning lights. In this vast gloom, only working hours create a kind of movement that renders the passage of time perceptible.

There was, however, another reason. If time can be understood through the changes generated by its evolution, the trees grow bare and once again grow green leaves that turn into pale scraps that fall to the ground. Night follows day like a dog follows its owner. Nails grow. Hair whitens, falls out, or needs to be cut. It wasn't the same for Minas. For Minas, the quick course of May was purely psychological. Since the day he signed the letter to Arshalouys, he had put an end to his anguish. Time had made a giant leap. History had been emptied of its contents and there was nothing left to happen. During the period when he noticed and recorded the sequence of events, it was in that state of anticipation that time passed with heavy steps. The waiting was what gave time a gauge. After waiting a few days—in reality, he was waiting without really waiting—for Arshalouys's reply, he at last came to the conclusion that she had discerned the hidden meaning in his letter, namely his rejection. Let's remember that he wrote "Get married." Yes, it was because of those words that she had fallen silent, perhaps into a half-dead state. It could be said that the Arshalouys issue had been taken care of, at least he thought so, considering that he now finally enjoyed a serenity that at times troubled his heart, which had grown accustomed to unease.

Ever since May Day, Apkar buried himself in a self-imposed silence. There was so much silence around Minas!

In the early days, Minas was scared. He thought Apkar's injury might have impaired his speech. Minas often insisted on a medical exam, but Apkar didn't understand what Minas was saying. A quick, faint ripple appeared underneath the skin on his face before fading away. Neither his mysterious smile nor his concentration at work could dispel Minas's concern. He kept an eye on Apkar, who didn't show the slightest glimmer of verbal life. If it was a grudge he was holding, Minas couldn't explain it. He never did him any harm. He had never even thought about it. On the contrary, he had treated him with brotherly concern and compassion. That day, he had saved him from imminent danger and tended to his wounds. We could even say that he hadn't hesitated to put himself in harm's way. It was in these thoughts that an idea came to him. No, that kind of thing was impossible, however strange the human mind could be. So he drove those thoughts away and looked for another solution, but again his concern came to stand in front of him. Was it possible that he had turned into the target of Apkar's hatred after having seen him being beaten? He knew, he understood Apkar's childhood, which had been a constant string of beatings and insults. From this perspective, Minas empathized with Apkar's rebelliousness. He fought heroically to turn the world into an ideal, so that children would never see the face of beatings or deprivation. Could it be that Minas didn't show the extent of his admiration, or that Apkar didn't notice it and thought less of him? After that, Minas resolved to express his admiration more often and to raise Apkar onto the pedestal of his admiration to help him overcome dejection and feel encouraged and valued. He thought this idea could help cut through Apkar's vengeance, but he quickly decided against it because—who knows?—maybe Apkar needs that feeling, maybe it feeds and nurtures a rebelliousness fueled by hatred. So that was it. Now he remembered that when he rushed to Apkar in front of the Théâtre de la Renaissance, Apkar immediately turned his head away and didn't look at him once during their escape. Maybe he was embarrassed. It must have been shame—shame of having been seen degraded—that instantly transformed into hatred and added to his inner capacity for rebellion. People don't like their morals to be laid bare. Of course, it's one thing to talk about them and quite another to have them be seen. In the first case, degradation told as part of a story sounds like an exploit. However, the more we feel pity, the more admiration there is in our compassion. To tell a story is not to expose, but to dress it in another way. The second case is not the same. This is true exposure: seeing with the eyes—and not with the imagination, as he did the first time—the ugliness of someone around you, because degradation is ugliness. Minas saw it before his very eyes when Apkar was beaten on May Day. Slowly but surely, Minas was convinced that it could be the only reason for Apkar's silence. The fact that a friend had seen him during the beating must have been intolerable, even though the beating was followed by an honorable act. Apkar had left home to batter, break, and lay things to waste, but there he was cruelly defeated and trampled, as he had once been by his father, an authority figure indistinguishable from the one he saw that day. So on the day of the beating, as he lay sprawled on the sidewalk with a head wound, he was the same boy he had told Minas about. How could Apkar reconcile himself with the feeling that had now left him unable to talk? Minas couldn't reconcile himself with that fact. He chased it from his mind and returned, perhaps for his own sanity, to his original suspicion that it was the result of beatings to the head that Apkar had lost the power of speech. And so he confirmed his conviction for himself and settled into it to stop thinking about other possibilities, which not only didn't correspond to the truth, but also drove him to despair, whereas the illness theory filled his heart with such feelings of exaltation that he saw something beautiful in Apkar's fight. He should do the impossible to help his friend regain his words. It lasted like this for a while with Minas using every opportunity to convince Apkar to take his suggestion and see a doctor. Apkar would always refuse outright, until the day when, lifting his arms out of the soapy water in the sink, he finally said with utter calm: "Did you hear? They've taken him away."

"Who?" Minas asked.

"Sarkis."

"Where did they take him?"

"Where else do they take crazy people? Charenton."

Minas didn't know whether to be happy that Apkar had started talking again or upset by what had happened to Sarkis. Poor Mr. Bentham—a sweet, harmless, humble man who wanted to "save the nation" with poetry. But no one, no one at all, took an interest in his poems, and yet the poet had a wonderfully innocent smile for all those who turned their backs whenever he extended a hand with his book.

"But Apkar," Minas said, jumping out of his daydream. "They only take dangerous people to Charenton."

"Didn't you know? What kind of poet are you who isn't interested in the Armenian people? He needed to be restrained. He would attack anyone who didn't want to save the nation. Every day there would be a fight in the street. Do you know Arakel, the tailor? He took Sarkis's book and threw it right back in his face, sneering. Our Sarkis lunged at him like a lion and started throwing punches. Then the police came to take him away."

On a nice May evening, Minas walked up the boulevard thinking about Sarkis, whose pained expression would no longer be seen around and who, perhaps at that moment, had gone crazy out of a feeling of infinite time and punched a heavy door that only opened to those coming in. He stopped in front of the Billard, but didn't go inside. With Vahakn gone, the café had lost its charm for him. It seemed foreign to him, as if it had never even been part of a fraction of his life. On the sidewalk, there was no longer an invisible hook cast by Vahakn's gaze and the passersby, who, with their footsteps freed, no longer saw the need for self-defense. They walked, bold and carefree, with a kind of disdain for the absent. He quickly walked past the café. He couldn't stop in to the upstairs part of the café, where he was heading now, despite Vahakn's opposition to meeting old classmates from Constantinople who shared his memories. He glanced inside through the door and saw, as always, a meditative Vahan Tekeyan, head bowed over his pocket-size notebook. That evening, with June not too far away, he wanted to go straight to the hotel. For a while now, since the day he finished his manuscript, his mind had been calm. Crumpling up the story and tossing it aside, there was nothing left to do. The curtain had fallen. But instead of staying in his room, he found himself in the Jardin du Luxembourg. He had specifically not said anything to Hortense. He wanted to spend the night in his room. He could have mail waiting for him. He also wanted to read through his manuscript to see if he could give it the structure of a novel. The revisions would take an entire night. It didn't matter. The next day in the afternoon he could take a nap in Hortense's room. It would be a deep sleep made even deeper by Hortense's attentive caresses.

He had already spent the entire month of May with Hortense, ever since the day that her slight body had rocked him in her arms for hours. That day had put an end to his training period and replaced the burning of his senses with tender warmth. Sometimes, under the guise of checking his mail, he would go to his room, take a stroll through a world of memories, or have dinner with friends at The Ani. Life had found its equilibrium. In the ruins of a passing storm, one way or another, the swallow rebuilds its nest. Minas would build his nest by writing poetry, or by loving Hortense. Loving Hortense? Why did his heart skip a beat whenever that idea came to mind? His vision had darkened, but he could still see fine. The eyes on his face could see. He was by the Fontaine Médicis. He stood in front of the stone statue near the fountain. Around him, here and there, couples were kissing. Across from him were the Palais du Luxembourg and the Palais du Sénat. If he wanted to, he could even see what was hidden from view. Yes, with his eyes closed he could see the museum on the other side of the *palais*, where there hung a *nature morte* by—who would have thought?—an obscure Armenian. If he closed his eyes even tighter, he could see the details of the painting, especially the almost trembling light that so sparingly marked the canvas. He saw all of this even as his vision darkened, but he was seeing with his heart and feeling pride in the trembling rays in the work of an Armenian like him, unseen by the world. Under that dim light in his mind, he saw Hortense, as if born of that light. On the narrow, grainy screen, he saw a wavering image of the woman who would always silently caress him and look at him with a deep, pensive furrow between her eyebrows, as if looking from afar, as she had once before, from very far, like a slave or a beggar with an impossible wish. In that humble gaze, he saw her femininity, that passivity that suddenly turns a shy man into a lion. He remained a lion until she rocked him in her arms like a child. And yet it was not *that* Hortense who made his heart pound, the Hortense who quietly left him alone with his thoughts; who calmed him whenever he dreamed, resting his head in her lap; who inspired the poetry that was given a silhouette by his work each day; who was the clock watching him at night, always waking him up for work with a cheerful song that would renew the day, but also bring about the return of another one briefly hidden, because he found himself feeling that time was endless. Here was the crowd of the city's workers, whom he met every morning on his way to the hotel, half-awake yet rushing, as though still chased by lingering ghosts from the night before. There is Hortense with her caresses and her warm, smooth body, and then there's Apkar with his miserable girls. No, it wasn't *that* Hortense who had turned him into a sleepwalker in his waking hours, but rather the one who just told him, "The room next door is empty. If you move there . . ." Look, it's always in the same way with a kind of female finesse, the key to which she had given him herself. She leaves the initiating up to you while she does the ordering, just like the one time she instinctively used her fingertips to guide his head toward the most sensitive parts of her body, where his kisses sowed and reaped love in a way that made him believe he wasn't an inexperienced boy just discovering those soul-stirring sensations. And this still wasn't all of it. Now he was seeing clearly. How hadn't he understood the hidden meaning in her words as she was saying them? He hadn't felt it in the song, because she knew how to anoint its words. We don't often fall victim to the chill a snake's stare can cause, but rather to its mystical song. Before he left, Hortense put her whole heart into a kiss, as if putting his hand to her chest, locking eyes with him, and saying, "Look how it beats for you." This is how the images fell one after another, with her gaze pensive and searching. The deliberate, cautious movements that accompanied her words tore through their bitterness. "Don't you think your miserable girlfriend might need to go for a walk or to the theater once in a while? I know, you don't like to do it. You've thought about it already, I'm sure. But you don't dare, do you? Dare, my friend, dare! Come on, take me. You know I'm yours. I don't even belong to myself." Yielding and obedient, he listened with his lower lip hanging open, though not without a certain sense of pride. He was about to say that he would be happy to take her out, but he resisted. His heart hardened in anticipation of an attack and his inner self felt a distant, unattainable absence, when Hortense added, "Tomorrow let's go to Kilisse and order you a suit jacket." She hadn't finished her thought when she took his hand to her face and held it there for a moment, trembling, holding her breath, and then continued in a softer voice, "It'll be my gift to you. My very first gift." From the shaking in Minas's hand, she sensed the hurtful words to come. She had put in a year and a half to reach the moment when she could finally say the words she had prepared with such care, to prevent causing any offense, only slightly scratching the surface of his dignity. She knew the reaction of a kind young man. She offered her love and her body without reservation as a training ground where an inexperienced, fragile boy could mature into a man, so that one day she could say, "It'll be my gift to you." Underneath each and every leaf on the stem of a rose is a thorn. It was for this very reason that she put her index finger over his mouth. Her lips immediately followed to seal the silence and perhaps his approval, too.

But now, as he sat by the Fontaine Médicis and recalled that moment, his wounded pride gained momentum in his heart, like ripples growing into a tidal wave. He felt the full weight of the goal that Hortense had pursued for months, which, now unexpectedly unmasked, appeared to him clearly, while the entire reel of images played in front of him and made everything so clear. A chuckle escaped and turned into uncontrollable laughter. As it went on, the chains binding him loosened link by link. Once he had broken free, without vengeance or even obligation, he saw himself next to Hortense on a night out at the theater, where a friend approached them and asked, "Is this your mother? It's nice to meet you." His laughter was now tinged with scorn and left a bitter taste in his mouth. He understood that one way or another he was going to be faced with the need to make a decision. But whatever that decision may have been, his agitation fed continuously on the imaginary, yet innocent, exclamation of his friend, as though it had actually been said. "Is this your mother?" My God, how had he not thought of this? How could he have kept himself from seeing that Hortense was old enough to have a son his age? Where did this obsession with age come from? And why? What purpose would it serve? Of course it was his own mind that invented the idea and invited it inside, as though subconsciously looking to destroy something. He stood up. An almost audible cry needed to escape from his chest. He walked to the part of the woods where he and Vahakn used to sit for hours. He could still feel the echo of the scream he had let out near the Fontaine Médicis a little while before. He didn't know why he had said Nicole's name. But Nicole wasn't in the park and now, as he passed through the streets, the one thing that stayed with him was the sharp glance she had shot at him from the big screen right before he left the movie theater. He wanted to go back to his room and yet he wandered from street to street. Who knows? Perhaps he needed, first and foremost, to purge his mind of the images that haunted him. It took him a long time to get to his room. He went up the half-lit staircase, slowly and hesitantly, pausing for a moment before making a decision. "Yes, I'll get my bag and go straight to my mother."

He still can't come to terms with what happened a little while later after he had pushed himself out of his room like a crazy person and started roaming the streets, ultimately trying to make sense of everything, taking himself by the wrist and asking, "Is this really me?" He started to think an illusion had taken hold. Where was he? Where was reality? He couldn't have made up such a dramatic ending. Having reached this point in the story, he had already considered the ending, and a happy one at that. He didn't know where to turn. If this kind of scene had been written into a novel, I'm sure that any reader would have snickered skeptically, and rightfully so. What a strange turn of events that, in the span of one evening all the characters, or at least those still standing, would seal their fates—unconvincing fates at that—while also leaving him responsible for everything in the whirl of unresolved disorder. When, after the moment of hesitation in which he had decided to leave, he finally continued up the stairs and reached his door, he didn't realize why the key was in the lock and the door was ajar. He stood in the doorway and looked inside, first straight ahead, then in surprise and amazement. He squinted. Yes, that was her. Who else could it have been? There was no need to ask. It seemed as though he had been waiting for this. It was not in vain that he had agonized over those letters, fearing they might be construed as an invitation. He had tried to avoid that tone, clearly with little success. And here he was. He was always the guilty one wherever he went. Impulsively, without thinking twice, he called out her name as if she were an old friend.

"Arshalouys, what are you doing here?"

Arshalouys was sitting on the edge of the bed, her bag at her feet. She stood up confidently as soon as he shut the door, as though she had carefully studied and planned this moment.

"I'm here," she said.

"Yes, you are. But who told you to come?"

"Oh," she said, visibly taken aback but not crushed, the back of her right hand over her mouth. "You've forgotten. My God, how quickly you've forgotten!"

"What have I forgotten, Madame?"

"What you wrote."

"Which was?"

"You wrote 'Get married,' so I came."

Minas, his head in his hands, struggled to keep his composure. He still couldn't believe it. Was this reality or was *this* a dream too? What was a dream and what was reality? But this wasn't a dream. Pulling his hands away from his face, he looked straight at the woman standing in front of him. She was still trying to smile, to turn something into a smile and make it a source of infinite happiness.

"But I didn't suggest that *we* get married. I told you not to be alone. It was just brotherly advice."

"Well, you left me with a choice to make. And so I made my choice."

"Just like that, all of a sudden?"

And all of a sudden, he leapt toward the door, which was still ajar, closed it behind him, and left.

He roamed for quite a while. It was like back in the old days when Vahakn would mysteriously disappear at one in the morning, panting down the boulevard right before the train arrived. Now Minas, mentally adrift, walked through the streets by himself and came to stop in front of the closed shutters of the Billard to find shelter in Vahakn's shadow. He didn't go far—to deserted spots along the river, then from street to street, always convinced that he had left the incident far behind, that he had forgotten it, erased it from his mind. When his knees gave way, he stopped walking, deep in thought, and decided to take a trip. He decided to go much farther to his mother, whom he should never have left in the first place. At this, he finally lifted his head. The street sloped straight down, it's true. It veered slightly in the middle, but what was closer—within view even—was the closed door of his hotel room.

~

Paris, June 6, 1927

Dear Zareh,

You know about the ongoing French literary debate surrounding "La Marquise sortit à cinq heures."[20] *Each new generation in search of itself collides in the very beginning with this issue and treats it with contempt, because it's the hallmark of the old, conventional novel. By fighting against it, the French novel has achieved the stability, or introspection, that has expelled the marquise. I feel the same kind of contempt. Disgust would be more like it. You can imagine that I feel disgusted when I read, for instance, in one of the last paragraphs of this text: "And all of a sudden, he leapt toward the door." And this right after the "all of a sudden" in the line immediately above. Here I am debilitated now that the draft of Vahakn's story is done and I'm supposed to start working on turning it into a novel. The marquise comes out of nowhere and tries to leave. And I can't keep her from leaving, because when I see her standing arrogantly in the doorway with a look that is both present and absent, cunningly sizing up everything near and far, and when she is about to take a step, exactly at the moment she opens her parasol, it seems as though an entire dream comes undone, disintegrates, scatters, and simmers. Where will the marquise go? This is the question on everyone's mind and we follow its development with trembling rapture. Where will the marquise go? To the Marquise de Sévigné?*[21] *To a mysterious date in Bois de Boulogne? Or to leafy corner on Île de la Cité? What interests me is the story of Vahakn's inner world, but what do I see? I see that what I've written is something else entirely, if it isn't just* "La Marquise sortit à cinq heures." *Everyone thinks they know why the marquise leaves. This failure saddens me, but also gives me the chance to reconcile with you. It was precisely because of that failure that I didn't like the first book in your* The Persecuted *series. It was a bit too marquise-like and yet I fell victim to the same inescapable temptation. I was naïvely convinced that on my own, away from you, I could write a purely psychological story better—on a side note, when will it be published?—as if it were possible to see the soul anywhere else but in the sways of the body. It entails a return to the marquise, who will now leave, and before taking a step, will cast an inexplicable glance all around, as though to put out the light in the curious gazes staring at her, so that she can continue her journey through the story.*

I won't be able to get out of this myself. I'm sending you my manuscript. You can finish the work however you'd like. Stick to what you know. As for me, I will return to playing in verse. I would have liked to deliver it to you in person as I'd originally planned, especially since I could have told you more about it. There are still so many things that I couldn't squeeze in anywhere or introduce any kind of inner logic to without upsetting the rules and standards. But it's precisely these rules and standards that refuse to accept all those other things that happen to form them. So many precious fragments of life are lost when you try to turn reality into art.

Yes, I'm sure you would have been happier—I know I would have been—if I had brought the manuscript myself. Three years have passed since that evening when you took me to the train station. I miss the old days when we used to sit in the cafés on La Canebière until late at night. Needless to say, I miss my family, too. Whenever I think of my mother, my heart aches, but there is also a sense of fear when I think that in that city is a hidden force that can render me powerless. I packed my bag and was about to leave, but I felt I couldn't. I couldn't leave without at least seeing Nicole once more. I'm going to stay here. As soon as I leave work, it would be enough to spend entire days in the Jardin du Luxembourg waiting to meet her. I've been going for eight days, but so far there has been no sign of Nicole. I wonder if this is the reason why I unknowingly packed the events into the last pages of my manuscript, bringing everything to a neat ending. Is it possible to imagine the fateful convergence of all the characters in my manuscript happening in one day, having them reach a conclusion one after the other—like a group unexpectedly rising up to topple a tyrant—had it not been for my own exhaustion? Don't you think that literary work is like a tyrant? That it constrains us and takes us prisoner? Now I understand. So that's how it is. Who could have imagined? Do you see what can happen downstairs when you're busy upstairs? Look how it happened. At the last minute, intent on freeing himself from the tyrant, the prisoner hastily organized everything, brought it to a close, giving each one its share, and came here to the Jardin du Luxembourg to wait and dream of Nicole, who seems to be my freedom. I'm breathing. I'm breathing now and yet I feel a new weight on me, some kind of yoke that might disturb my peace. Don't disturb me while I wait for Nicole! I'm afraid that I've inherited the inclination to wait from Vahakn, too. When you read my manuscript, you might wonder how that kind of inheritance could have such an ending. Maybe it's not the same, but it's close. Do you see the mess your friend has fallen into? Of course, reason tries to save the day and shine light through the haze, to think about the part imagination was able to play in the most recent events. What? Is all of this imagined? What about Arshalouys? At least Arshalouys! How can we believe that she is anything but the product of my overactive imagination? If you had been here, you could have gone to my room and seen for yourself that Arshalouys actually existed. There is no doubt in my mind, even though I escaped like someone fleeing a bad dream. But she is in front of me at this very moment: alive, real, about medium height with a dark complexion, as thin as the flame of a candle with fiery black eyes that consumed my own as she said, "Ah, you've forgotten. My God, how quickly you've forgotten!" There's still more. If words can trick us, then how can we deny my seeing the unusually strained tendons on her long neck? As I was about to leave, Arshalouys, visibly upset, yelled after me, "Don't leave me alone! Please, I beg you." I left nevertheless. I left like a coward. I know, what use is regret when the fact is that I fled like someone running from a house in flames? Before leaving, I told the concierge that my sister would be staying in my room until I came back from my trip. No, what I said wasn't a lie. Isn't my quest to find love a kind of trip? The roads I'll take are the most unfamiliar and the most mysterious. All the countries of the world seem familiar when compared to the country of love, where we walk through memories left over from books and school desks, whereas with love, "Who knows how to read the heart?"[22]

I was at the entrance of the Jardin du Luxembourg about to go in with Arshalouys's plea still ringing in my ears, when I turned around. Do you think I went back to Arshalouys? No, I didn't want to be rude to Hortense and leave without a proper goodbye. And besides, I had another reason to see her.

Fortunately she agreed, perhaps figuring that she would be leaving a door open. I told her that I was going to visit my mother. Arshalouys would replace me until I came back. I didn't keep my plan from her. By having Arshalouys work with Apkar, who knows, maybe the two of them would one day . . . ?

From Hortense's apartment, I went to Arshalouys to tell her the news. It was quite late. I knocked on the door gently with the knuckle of my middle finger. My heart was trembling. If I tell you my hand was trembling too as I knocked on the door, don't doubt it. A few hours before, I had rushed out of that door like a coward. It's hard to come back to a place where you know you have done wrong, especially knowing that I would find Arshalouys, overcome with grief and miserable because of me. I couldn't arrange the words in my mind, not knowing if they should be used to repent or console. I ultimately didn't know what I should say. The door opened right away. The key was in the lock where I had left it. It seemed that Arshalouys was waiting for me.

"I was sure you'd come back," she called out, clapping and throwing her arms in the air.

Of course I was happy. I was happy that Arshalouys wasn't overcome with grief or miserable. But I hoped from the bottom of my heart to see her eyes flood with tears. I wanted to be moved by her sobs, so that I could break through the regret accumulating in my heart by lavishing kind words on her, exhausting my reserves in search of words that would bring a smile to her face, while all that was left to hear was a parched reality: an overjoyed Arshalouys.

"Arshalouys," I said. "Tomorrow morning I'll come to take you to where you'll be working. I'll be here at five-thirty."

The following day, I brought her to the hotel. True to his misogyny, Apkar welcomed her with his usual crudeness, but still eagerly took charge of helping her adjust to the job.

If you want, you can find a place for this somewhere. At any rate, the truth is that both Apkar and Arshalouys were happy: one to be of use and the other for having gotten a job the very day she arrived in Paris.

Yours,
Minas Yerazian
Summer 1965

[END]

Afterword

Zareh Vorpouni's *The Candidate*

Testimony, Sacrifice, and Forgiveness

MARC NICHANIAN

Translated from the French by
Jennifer Manoukian and Marc Nichanian

Forgiveness and Testimony

Published in 1967, *The Candidate* (*T'eknatsun*) is one of the most representative novels of the Armenian diaspora and allows for the greatest understanding of the singular figure of the survivor, who never ceases to haunt imaginations in the endless aftermath of the genocidal event. The novel is forthright and impressive, the product of the blood, sweat, and tears of its author, Zareh Vorpouni, who spent nearly forty years writing it—forty years of silence, and therefore powerlessness, after the publication of the first volume in his projected series of novels, The Persecuted (*Halatsuatsnerë*). The first volume, The Attempt (*Pordzë*), was published in Marseille in 1929.[1]

In the interim, Vorpouni published And There Was Man (*Yev Yeghev Mard*) in Paris in 1964 to break the silence between novels as well as the silence of mourning that he carried despite himself. And There Was Man was praised by its few readers, who saw it as signifying a shift in how the genre of the novel had been practiced by the Armenian-speaking diaspora, which was essentially limited to the Armenian communities of the Middle East. With And There Was Man, Vorpouni had finally mustered the strength to put the Armenian mother and the French woman side by side in a cemetery—a crude juxtaposition whose charm has never dissipated in the minds and culture of the survivors of the Catastrophe. He laid bare the mathematical law for their shared, reciprocal dominance over the Armenian psyche and heralded the arrival of a new diasporic man, cleansed of his contradictions and indulgences, released from the indelible mark of the recent past, and prepared to accept the foreign in him.

The series of novels, however, was put on hold. Vorpouni needed to return to his first project to finally confront the obstacle he had continued to face during all those years of silence. In the end, why had he decided to embark on a *series* of novels as a young man? He certainly had Marcel Proust in mind, a legendary example for a burgeoning novelist, but there is very little in common between Vorpouni and the author of *In Search of Lost Time*. Vorpouni's novels have a strong psychoanalytic dimension and their relationship with time is entirely determined by the nature of the catastrophic event. They complete the difficult, if not readily apparent, task of demonstrating that the temporality of the catastrophic event is situated beyond the historical understanding of time and, therefore, naturally beyond the grasp of historians. The catastrophic event is independent of or seeks to free itself from their grasp. But these two observations about the psychoanalytic dimension of Vorpouni's work and the temporality of the event do not argue in favor of Proust's influence. So why did Vorpouni begin this project as a young man? The question can easily be reversed. How could we have known that the time of mourning and the time of forgiveness had been pulled out from under us forever? How could we have known if that collapse had not been recorded in a piece of writing or in a body of work? In order for it to be recorded, the long gestation period of a series of novels was required.

The "time of mourning" is a familiar concept. Through reading the work of Zabel Essayan and a few others, we might even understand that the genocidal violence of the perpetrator begins with a persistent yet implicit will to forbid mourning in the victim, and that, in more peaceful times, once the moment for reconciliation has come, it also continues, in a way that is not any less persistent, through a general manipulation of mourning.[2] The process undertaken by the Truth and Reconciliation Commission in South Africa and the state of exception that has reigned for several decades in Turkish Kurdistan have given us good examples of this kind of manipulation.[3] The same cannot be said about the time of forgiveness. We know nothing about it and do not concern ourselves with it very much. In an excerpt from 1921, Walter Benjamin describes this time of forgiveness as a "tempestuous storm . . . that precedes the onrush of the Last Judgment against which [it] cannot advance. This storm is not only the voice in which the evildoer's cry of terror is drowned; it is also the hand that obliterates the traces of his misdeeds, even if it must lay waste to the world in the process."[4] Forgiveness, then, is superhuman. But without the time of forgiveness, no matter how inhuman or superhuman, and no matter how destructive, there would be no humanity. The victims and the survivors of genocidal will may have been deprived of this human superhumanity. It is true that we have been deprived of the time of mourning. But maybe we have also been deprived of the time of forgiveness, or at least of the capacity to forgive. In this way, the genocidal will of the perpetrator has been transformed into a catastrophe for the victims and for the survivors, which explains why "Catastrophe" (in Armenian, Աղէտ [*Aghet*]) is the only proper name that suits the event. But it is a name suited for the future. It will return at the end of the time of forgiveness, even if the entire universe must be laid to waste in the process. The Catastrophe has not yet reached us. Consequently, Vorpouni's plan for a series of novels assumed a private agreement with time in hopes that one day everything would make sense and with the expectation that the turn and return of the Catastrophe would coincide with the time of forgiveness.

The following analysis of Vorpouni's work will resemble what I have called elsewhere a "phenomenology of the survivor." Vorpouni could not have known from the beginning that the phenomenology of the survivor was at the heart of his undertaking, that it was what he was expecting from himself as a novelist, that it was where the novel would lead him, or that it was what the novel was expecting from him. The survivor was demanding a series of novels. I examine how this idea operates by focusing on this particular novel in the series, *The Candidate,* which restarted the machine in 1967. Who, then, is the survivor? The survivor must first be understood as the dead witness. But he can also be understood as the one who has been deprived of the time of forgiveness. In any case, forgiveness would require the acknowledgment of what there is to forgive. As a dead witness, the survivor is perfectly incapable of this acknowledgment. By killing the witness in the victim and rendering him incapable of mourning, the genocidal perpetrator has also rendered him incapable of forgiveness. Here the perpetrator has stripped the victim of his humanity once and for all. How can I forgive the very act that has rendered me incapable of forgiveness?

In this strange phenomenology of the survivor, the one who speaks, writes, describes, and dictates what is to be written is the dead witness. Because all of these elements will occur in a novel, it is the dead witness who will justify the novel as a framework, as an echo chamber, and as an instrument of reception. He will be the candidate of the novel and for the novel. The injunction to write—which is not quite an injunction to tell—will come from the dead witness and will form his legacy, the only legacy that he can leave. Because there is a survivor testimony in the middle of *The Candidate,* it is the very act of bearing witness that will become an object of examination, forcing us to repeat a question that we have asked on many other occasions: What do all "real" narratives—those that are not literary testimonies—bear witness to? What do all the narratives that we call testimonies, in which survivors recount their journeys, their odysseys, their suffering, the death of their relatives, and their painful returns, bear witness to? Since they claim to bear witness, they do not originate from the dead witness. Should we infer from them that it is *possible* to bear witness? What are they bearing witness to, exactly? What are they really doing? What purpose are they serving? What hidden injunction are they responding to? By putting a survivor testimony in the middle of a novel, Vorpouni examines, for the first time, the intimate, conflicting relationship between novelistic and testimonial narratives. He examines this relationship from within literature and therefore without unnecessary questions. As the heirs to his work, we are now the ones asking the questions.

A Three-Tier Structure

The Candidate is written largely in the third person and its narrator is the same Minas who appears in the other volumes of The Persecuted series. At the end of The Attempt, Minas had fled Marseille, leaving his mother's corpse on the floor of their kitchen. In a fragmentary way, with constant temporal cracks within the narrative, the new novel recounts Minas's encounter with Vahakn, another young Armenian, in 1927 on the streets of Paris; the friendship that unites them; the life they share for five months in a musty hotel room; their conversations with Ziya, a young Turkish student who came to study in Paris; Ziya's murder at Vahakn's hands; and Vahakn's suicide one month later. The novel begins immediately after the suicide with a letter from Minas to Vahakn's supposed fiancée Arshalouys to inform her of Vahakn's death. As a secondary theme, the novel also describes Minas's sexual awakening through his boss, Hortense. In the middle of the novel is a letter from Vahakn to Minas explaining the reasons for the murder he committed and for his suicide. The letter forms the core of the novel because it sets the narrative in motion. It can be read as a survivor narrative—one among thousands of others—but it is the only survivor narrative situated at the center of a novel.

First, we must discuss the status of the narrative within the novel, that is, within the other narrative that Minas offers about the production of Vahakn's "original" narrative. But the explicit structure of the novel forces us, at the same time, to examine the status of testimony in general, not only within the novel. This call for examination is unique in Armenian literature and perhaps beyond it.

As previously mentioned, the external narrative of *The Candidate* was written almost entirely in the third person, seemingly by Minas, the narrator. In contrast, Vorpouni wrote The Attempt entirely in first person. In *The Candidate*, the few shifts from the third person to the first person are explained in a passage toward the end of the novel: "The main problem was not having a plan. For eight days, I've been trying to make my pen dance across the page. I shouldn't rush, but how can I not? From the day I conceived of the idea, I've had no rest. . . . It had never crossed my mind that I could one day express myself in prose," says Minas. He decided to write Vahakn's story. Minas is a poet and readers are led to believe that he has never written prose before. This revelation indicates that Minas did not write his story in the first person in The Attempt. Someone wrote it for him and turned his story into a novel. This seemingly anodyne remark is essential, and we will discuss its importance later on.

Minas is writing because he is obeying Vahakn's injunction, which drives him. The first time we encounter this injunction, Minas is sitting at an outdoor café, the same café where he used to sit with Vahakn: "It was at a moment like that when he was forced on me. Just like that, with no warning. From outside, he was thrown inside and stayed there, expanding, imposing himself, and my will became his will. He said, 'Write!'" From this moment on, Minas begins doing two things at once: he resists Vahakn's will and obeys it. That said, he is astonished by his actions and questions himself. Why write, he says, "a personal issue [that could not] possibly interest others." He is looking for reasons and excuses. It is not as if he is refusing to write. On the contrary, he wants to write, but he wants to write independently of Vahakn's will. He wants to write by evading the injunction to write. He says, for example, that people cannot keep their thoughts to themselves without going crazy. In this idea, he has found what allows him to justify writing: "The meteoric rise of thought in solitude is exactly how people give themselves over to madness. But I don't have any intention of going mad. This is why I want to write. Not because it was Vahakn's wish, but because when I turn to him sitting outside at the Billard and look at his demanding eyes, they tell me, 'Write!'" He even finds a number of other reasons to write: to get the reader on his side, to go beyond the subjective point of view, to universalize, to create interest, to give purpose to the written word, or even to give it meaning, "But not Vahakn's message—no." He resists and justifies the act of writing to himself. He does not want to obey the injunction, but he eventually yields. It is then that he records in his notes the project he has in mind and the apparent structure of the entire book: "Here is Vahakn's letter. It will be the axis of the piece, around which the characters in the story must be gathered, because what is being told is, after all, a story."

Let's suppose that we are reading Minas's notes in the first person—his reflections, his doubts, his decisions—and that they naturally find their place in the remarks and narratives that revolve around the central element. But this simple structure is complicated and faces an added twist when Minas suddenly mentions "Zareh," seemingly Zareh Vorpouni, who has become a character in his own novel. He could be the author of The Attempt, in which he told Minas's story but added absurd and outlandish incidents, which leads us to a reflection on the art of the novel. "Zareh's mistake shouldn't be made. Those arbitrary, contrived notations must be avoided. I had an argument with him about it back then. He knows just as well as I do that he did it deliberately. The incident under the bridge was made up. Nothing like that ever happened, since he was the one who paid my travel expenses and the only one who knew about my escape."

Minas broke free from the writer who created him, mustered the courage to confront him, criticized his literary choices, and corrected them, if necessary. The final episodes in The Attempt—all of which relate to Minas's escape and form a strange ballet of mourning, writing, and sex—are declared fictional by the fictional character of Minas. "How could it be that after having naïvely squandered the money I got from selling my books on prostitutes I didn't even sleep with, I shamelessly used that beggar to satisfy my lust and then steal her modest savings?"

But when Minas discusses and corrects Zareh's writings, which deal with his own character's biography in the novel, it is certainly Vorpouni who is correcting what he had written forty years earlier. And if this structure were not complex enough, it is complicated even more in the final pages of the novel in which Minas writes a letter to Zareh asking him to put his notes in order and, accordingly, to become the editor and the publisher of the book. Once again, the letter deals with the art of the novel and with the need to go beyond banal, conventional methods of novel-writing. These are Minas's concerns and there is every reason to believe that they were Vorpouni's concerns as well: "What interests me is the story of Vahakn's inner world, but what do I see? I see that what I've written is something else entirely, if it isn't just '*La Marquise sortit* à *cinq heures.*' Everyone thinks they know why the marquise leaves. This failure saddens me, but also gives me the chance to reconcile with you. It was precisely because of that failure that I didn't like the first book in your The Persecuted series. . . . I won't be able to get out of this myself. I'm sending you my manuscript. You can finish the work however you'd like."

We now clearly have a three-tier structure. Vahakn kills himself but leaves a testimony that explains his act. Minas inherits the manuscript letter from Vahakn as well as a pressing need to save the testimony from oblivion and give it a semiliterary existence, which means that, by itself, the testimony would not have had an audience. It could not play its role as testimony. It would cancel itself out. Together with the manuscript, Vahakn's experiences have to be saved and emphasized. The survivor is not enough in and of himself. Minas not only receives the letter that will function as testimony; he also clearly receives the injunction to complete it by adding a truthful narrative and providing context. Minas completes his task conscientiously, but it is Zareh's responsibility to have these notes organized and published. With the help of this three-part structure and the transformation of author into character, Vorpouni writes into the novel not only his idea of writing as a constant process of retouching, but also the very injunction that originates from the survivor.

Vahakn, Minas, and Zareh: aren't all three survivors? Why arrange this complex interplay of transmissions, injunctions, and orders to render the testimony of a survivor readable? Let's suppose for a moment that Minas's notes had to be stamped as art to create an audience for them. Without this stamp, they would have been abandoned. But such an explanation seems rather simple to clarify the passages between Vahakn, the murderer/survivor whose suicide coincides with the murder he commits; Minas, the amanuensis of the survivor who receives the injunction to write; and Zareh, the actual novelist who organizes the notes and signs his name to the book. It is implicit that the role and function of testimony are at play here. Secondarily, but logically, literature itself is at play as a form that shelters testimony within itself, whether it is hidden or obvious. Readers are caught in the back and forth between them, in the double and reciprocal questioning of testimony and literature.

The Issue of the Signatures

What would have happened if Vorpouni had been satisfied with a two-tier structure, if he had only kept the pair of friends, Vahakn and Minas, and eliminated any reference to Zareh? The heir to the survivor would have kept the testimony in his notes and talked about himself in the first or third person. In using the first person, he would have taken on the role of narrator in the conventional novel. Readers would not have necessarily understood that even the pages written in the third person were his own. The story would have coincided with the story they were reading. The novel itself would have been the heir to the dead witness. The reader, not Zareh, would have been the third tier in the three-tier structure. And since Vorpouni did not entirely master his own novelistic invention, at times he gives the impression that Minas is addressing the reader without Zareh as the intermediary—the final signatory, the one called "the author." In these passages, the book takes on the structure of a conventional novel; for example, when Minas reflects on the difference between life and the novel by criticizing novelists who do not respect the incomplete nature of life as Zareh does and by recognizing that the narrative has to stop at some point. Here he addresses the reader, saying: "How do we reconcile these two conflicting stances, dear reader—my friend and enemy?" In this instance, Minas is the writer and the author of his work. But we know that this is not the case. When Vahakn tasks Minas with writing, he certainly does not want to make Minas into a novelist. He wants to make him into the heir to his testimony. In fact, he does not want anything at all. It is the testimony that transforms Minas into its heir and keeps him under its yoke. Before the suicide, he and Vahakn were joined by friendship. After the suicide, they are joined by testimony, by the strange necessity of bearing witness. After Minas collects his notes, he does not work on them as a writer or an artist. He works on them as an heir and as a subject: an heir to a testimony and a subject to its injunctions.

It is true that Minas is a poet in the novel, but he is a poet independent of the function assigned to him by the survivor. This is why, in the letter he writes to Zareh at the end of the novel, he adds: "As for me, I will return to playing in verse." Minas is not going to sign his work with his own name. He sends it to a third person to sign it: Zareh. Indeed if it is true that Minas is writing to Zareh, "[You can] organize [this work] as you please," in the novel, Zareh does not come to the fore in his own name. We do not know if he has done anything more than sign it. We do not know and have no way of knowing how he has changed Minas's writing and rearranged it to his liking. The assumption is that he did not change it at all, that he published it just as he received it. All he had to do was sign it. Of course, this issue of the signature is quite central. And to make the ambiguity or uncertainty surrounding the signature more apparent, Vorpouni ended the novel with a letter from Minas to Zareh. Minas's signature—"Yours, Minas Yerazian"—is followed by "Summer 1965" and then "End" in brackets. We can assume that Vorpouni himself put the finishing touches on the novel in the summer of 1965. But the final signature of the novel is Minas's signature. We can always read the pages we are given as if Minas himself were their author. In fact, he *is* the author. This approach might be seen as formalistic, but it touches on what is at stake at the heart of the novel. Behind the interplay of signatures is the status of this testimony and of testimony in general. Behind the status of testimony are the nature of the catastrophic event and the terrifying question of forgiveness, implicitly lingering, forever awaiting our attention. The three-tier structure and the interplay of signatures force us to ask ourselves: Who is the author of a testimony? As suspected, it is what we assign the strange name *testimony* that is at play here. The purpose of this mise-en-scène is for us to ask ourselves: What is a testimony? How does it function? How is it structured? How does it come into being? What does it require to exist in general as testimony? What does it require of us? The novel is the beginning of a perfectly unexpected response to these questions. In one way, it says that what we call testimony demands and supposes a link—both as an injunction and as a legacy—with the suicide of a survivor, then with a dead witness. In another way, it says that testimony comes into being through an odd exchange of signatures and that it presumes this exchange in all cases, even in the most ordinary testimonies or in those written by the highly literate, who sign their work with their own name without any ambivalence, murder, or suicide. There are many conclusions to be drawn from this state of affairs regarding the reflection on forgiveness. But neither the link to the dead witness nor the issue of the signatures would have appeared, been recorded, or invited reflection without the three-tier structure.

Two transmissions, two dispatches, and two injunctions are henceforth needed to create a testimony. The second dispatch, from Minas to Zareh, highlights the issue of the signatures, but we must begin by examining the first dispatch, the one sent by Vahakn and received by Minas. We have already said that Minas is an heir to Vahakn, that he is his legatee. He inherits the testimony and the will (or the necessity) to write. The word "legacy" appears for the first time when Minas sees his boss, Hortense, staring at him at the hotel where he works. "'Vahakn's legacy,' he muttered under his breath." The reflections that follow highlight how Minas and Vahakn are interchangeable. It is the necessity of the dispatch that differentiates them in the same way that Minas and Zareh are only differentiated within the three-tier structure by the necessity of another dispatch. The day Apkar came into the Billard and announced that the hotel needed someone, Minas came forward: "He had even been afraid that he might have lost the job to Vahakn if he hadn't been fast enough." Driven to act by "a hostile urge," Minas takes a position intended for Vahakn, condemning Vahakn to his parasitic fate. If Vahakn had begun working at the hotel instead, he would have effectively been saved. Hortense would have taken charge of him, she would have turned him into a man, and "because only Hortense knew how to turn a boy into a man, Vahakn had remained a boy." This is what Minas thinks. "If he hadn't acted so imprudently that day, Vahakn would still be alive because of Hortense and her ways of preserving a man's dignity. He was the one responsible for Vahakn's death. . . . Here he was, upstairs in the big hall on the first floor where Vahakn should have been." It is clearly a question of exchange and interchangeability—one instead of the other. Here the idea of legacy appears for the second time in an overwhelming way: "This is how he became the heir to the poorest Armenian on earth, who left him an immeasurable legacy." For the moment, the inestimable legacy is life and the chance to become a man by taking possession of Hortense. But it is already clear that Vahakn is Minas's perfect inverse. He is the one who dies so that Minas can live. In the part of the novel after Vahakn's letter, we see in Minas's notes and comments (which may have been reworked by

Zareh) that he is trying to think in a new way about his relationship with Vahakn. His thoughts emerge out of immense weakness—not Vahakn's weakness as we might think, but his own weakness. The weakness forms the core of their friendship and relationship. In a certain way, Vahakn took pity on him. He wanted to protect him and take him under his wing. It was "a sense of fatherly affection [that stirred] in Vahakn's heart." In short, Vahakn sacrificed himself for Minas. He suppressed himself to help his "child" become a man, so that Minas could become what he himself could not. The son inherits his father's disappearance. But he must also rid himself of that encumbering legacy, which is the most difficult task of all. Minas begins by denying it and accepts, triumphantly, his own denial. "Every rejection is an act of construction." Fathers never understand why children "suddenly flee their dedication," says Minas (or Vorpouni). Or perhaps fathers know the reason all too well and offer the possibility of escape and denial. They quietly offer the strength to part with them.

All of this certainly occurs in Minas. Vahakn must die in him so that he can become the heir who denies his legacy. And the identity between them is clearly stated in a passage written by Minas about Vahakn, where he himself appears in the third person (although it is possible that this passage and other similar passages have been edited and rearranged by "Zareh"): "Now he tried to look, through his imagination, into the eyes of the absent Minas, but he only saw himself, as though he were standing in front of a mirror." And conversely, Minas "still saw [people] through Vahakn's eyes," but because of the denied legacy, he could become another man. He managed to make Vahakn fade. The Vahakn hidden in him is a survivor incapable of adapting to life—a survivor who is always waiting, who cannot erase the stain that has tarnished him, who continuously flees, who becomes a murderer, who is forced to suppress himself to suppress the dirty feeling that haunts him, and who will forever be a stranger. By inheriting Vahakn and his death, Minas can say the following about himself: "The foreigner had left him." It is certainly a dangerous legacy that Vahakn leaves. At the end of the novel, Minas returns to the idea one last time in his letter to Zareh. The immediate purpose was to discuss the idea of waiting, specifically waiting for Nicole, who would become his wife in the following volume and die in the throes of childbirth. "I've inherited the inclination to wait from Vahakn." Because he inherited everything from Vahakn and his essence, his very identity, is to be Vahakn's heir, he could have inherited that last habit as well. This observation, albeit written ironically, will prove dangerous: "When you read my manuscript, you might wonder how that kind of inheritance could have such an ending. Maybe it's not the same, but it's close." It could end with another suicide or culminate in a murder, be it direct or indirect, which is how Minas's love for Nicole ends in the next volume in the series.

The Author of a Testimony

In all regards, Minas is an heir par excellence. He is the heir to Vahakn's death and to the murder Vahakn commits, but he is also the heir to Vahakn's miserable life and his parasitic philosophy. The murder and suicide are precisely what will allow Minas to cope with the ordeal of life. He also inherits the testimony of the survivor and makes it into a book, or at least sends it to Zareh with all the necessary paraphernalia to make it into a book. Of course, everything said about Minas as an heir will remain incomplete as long as Vahakn's testimony is not examined (the topic of the next paragraph). In the meantime, if we still believe that the three-tier structure of transmission is inspired by formalism, we must recall The Agony of a People (*Zhoghovurdi më hogevark'ë*), the first extensive testimony based on the hell of the deportations. Zabel Essayan gathered the testimony from a survivor named Hayg Toroyan and signed it with her own name.[5] This testimony is written entirely in the first person in the voice of the survivor. Essayan, who was living in Baku at the time, had met Toroyan in the summer of 1916. Toroyan had already published narratives in the Armenian press in Baku that were based on his own ordeal. Buoyed by her skills as a writer, Essayan transcribed the story of this young Armenian who had traveled down the Euphrates with a German officer between November 1915 and January 1916 and had seen the concentration camps begin to form along the river. She conveyed his story in flawless Western Armenian and transformed it into a readable narrative, sprinkled with engaging scenes to sensitize others to the misery of the victims. The testimony ends with the suicide of the German officer, who could not bear to live with what he saw along the deportation route. Essayan's work was published in the February and March issues of the newspaper Գործ (Gorts) in Baku with her name in the byline—not Toroyan's name.

Essayan's work has the same structure as *The Candidate*. The survivor tells the story and the amanuensis collects the testimony. In The Agony of a People, the survivor's amanuensis signs the testimony, even though the narrative itself is entirely in the first person and only conveys the voice of the survivor (apart from the short preface in which Essayan explains her task). The act of signing is certainly justified: as the writer, she is the one who gives the narrative its style and, therefore, ultimately considers herself its author. But because there is reason to examine the author of a testimony, the act of signing is anything but insignificant. It puts the status, function, and meaning of testimony back into play all at once. There is "real" testimony in The Agony of a People, whereas Vahakn's testimony in *The Candidate* is "literary." However, it is only the novel that emphasizes the three-tier structure of testimony, of every testimony, as it is collected and as it is transmitted, and henceforth as it comes into being through the interplay between the spoken and the written. The Agony of a People does not problematize its own structure within itself and does not reflect on the interplay between the signatures that the very structure entails. It nevertheless recreates the three-tier structure in its own way, by producing a suicide scene. We can even go so far as to think that it is the German officer's suicide that gives meaning to the entire narrative and endows it with a distinctive literary quality. In this way, the three stages of testimony are recreated in secret, as it is spoken, collected, and conveyed.

The reader's hesitation is most pronounced when discussing the genre of this publication. Is it testimony or is it literature? The fact that Essayan signs the text seems to transform it into literature, but it obviously presents itself as testimony. The ambiguity regarding the nature of the object is part of the very issue. An important side note is that the German officer in The Agony of a People took photographs. If these photographs had been developed at the time, Essayan would have brought them to Paris and entrusted them to one of the two Armenian delegations at the Peace Conference in 1919. But the photos remained silent and the officer succumbed to suicide.

Here as well as in the novel, the injunction to write came out of the officer's suicide, but we see that the positions are not the same in real testimony and literary testimony. The injunction circulates differently. When Essayan signs The Agony of a People, is she in the position of the author (like Zareh in Vorpouni's novel) or in the position of the friend who receives the injunction (like Minas)? Two signatures are still required to make a testimony: one to validate the truth of the facts and the other to validate the truth of the transcription. The two signatures have two entirely different functions and are distinct from the author's signature. By presenting itself as a testimony, hiding the interplay between the signatures and not explicitly recording the injunction that stems from the officer's suicide, The Agony of a People does not state what makes it possible as a testimony. It does not lay bare the structure of testimony, leaving it to the readers to decipher. But Vorpouni deciphered it for us in *The Candidate*. In his hands, the novel became a tool to uncover what remains hidden in all testimonies.

We have only done half the work, however, without discussing the source of the injunction. It is written into Vahakn's testimony and, therefore, from the beginning, we know that here lays the essential difference between the "fictional" testimony and the "real" testimony. In the latter, the dead witness no longer speaks. His words and images are lost forever. His madness has been entirely erased, whereas in the novel, it is the dead witness who speaks. He is already dead as he speaks. As a dead witness, he has already written the injunction that his friend—his amanuensis and heir—will violently receive and internalize forever. This is what we are left to understand. This is where literature begins. It begins with the witness. It tells the truth of testimony. It says that we must be dead to bear witness—always. There is no exception. But if we are dead, dead as a witness, how can we bear witness? A similar question will arise with regard to forgiveness.

The Collapse

The temporality of writing is not the same as the temporality of events. Minas began to put Vahakn's notes, perhaps reviewed and corrected by Zareh, down on paper after Vahakn's suicide and after having read his letter. But since the letter does not appear until the middle of the novel, we know about Ziya's murder well before Vahakn explains his act. In fact, we know about the murder even before meeting Ziya and gaining insight into his ties to Vahakn. The murder is mentioned very early in the novel in a scene where Vahakn is sitting at an outdoor café and trying to make passersby stop to pay his bill:

> This bizarre pastime was not a sign of boredom in the least, nor was it a means of deception, as many supposed, even if he did rely on these games to make a living to a certain extent. Afterward he, like the others, was convinced that this way of life was a kind of obligation, dictated by some dark, internal forces that were suddenly revealed right after Ziya's murder, because at the very moment they were revealed, Vahakn retired from his pastime, despite the high cost of giving up his livelihood. In fact, he had already stopped thinking about living. He stopped caring altogether as soon as he escaped those dark, internal forces, as he called them, that mental state that he carried around—unpredictable, stubborn and obscure—until the moment that Vahakn vanished once and for all, surrendering his entire being to the anarchy of fate.

When this passage appears in the novel, the reader has no way of understanding it. Vahakn's mental organization collapses all at once as his wait comes to an end and his expectations of life suddenly become clear in the form of a revelation. He did not need to wait for the moment he committed murder to have this revelation. At the very moment he is face to face with Ziya, the Turkish student who becomes his friend, he knows that this will be his fate: to die by making another die. But then why call it a "collapse" or a "destruction"? Because it was Vahakn's pathological state—let's call it a schizophrenic state—that allowed him to resist and it is that very same state that shatters all at once when he meets Ziya. His own secret is suddenly revealed before his eyes. Later in the novel, in the pages of his testimony, Vahakn will describe with remarkable clarity the circumstances that created his terrifying mental state. These pages have no rival in Armenian literature or perhaps in any other literature. From this point, it becomes clear that "killing" is synonymous with "killing oneself" and that Vahakn is already a dead man when, after Ziya's murder, he starts writing his "testimony." And yet, until the very end of the novel, the equating of murder and suicide will remain an enigma.

The Gift of Death: Friendship and Redemption

Before examining the testimony, it is worthwhile to review a passage in which Vahakn's collapse already seems to be explained and the enigma solved. It happens when Vahakn utters a sentence in which "Minas suddenly discovered the secret of Vahakn's demise": "No, brother. It's impossible to separate ourselves from being Armenian. Even if we try, it won't let go of our collar. Being Armenian is a sickness, a sickness rooted in revenge, and the horrible thing is that it's revenge without hatred. We Armenians genuinely don't know how to hate." In Minas's eyes, the enigma of the suicide is fully explained by this strange comment. His notes will support this hypothesis and highlight the fact that Vahakn was not motivated by hatred: "Vahakn died because he couldn't hate. He couldn't hate Ziya. On the contrary, he loved him and killed him out of love." And when Vahakn is drawn to Ziya's neck, seemingly noticing a stain on his tie, Minas simply remarks that "Ziya couldn't possibly have sensed the hidden, stubborn, insidious chase inside him that would cost him his life." It is not clear in this remark if it was Vahakn or Ziya who was to pay with his life. In any case, Vahakn's obsession consumes him entirely. This is how the enigma of the simultaneity of murder and suicide is presented to the reader, who has no other way to solve it. But one more step is needed. For Vahakn, to write and to die are equivalent. He says it succinctly—and, once again, strangely—in the very beginning of his testimony: "So I decided to write this while I was standing in front of his body. If they hadn't called us in, I wouldn't have written anything, because I'd already decided to kill myself that day."

It is a strange comment because the two sentences seem to contradict each other. If he had decided to kill himself that day, how could he have written anything? He decided to write. He decided to get it over with. There is no space between writing and death; they are the same. And yet a space that enables testimony is created entirely by chance when Minas and Vahakn are called into the police station as Ziya's friends. From that point on, writing the testimony takes place in an eerie space in which Vahakn lives as his own ghost, existing beyond life like a dead person who continues to speak and move but is already a corpse, already his own image. And he writes to save Minas from the same fate and to make him the heir to his ghost: "For a month now, I've been struggling to decide whether or not to write. But I'll do it. Not for my sake, Minas, but for yours. Pay close attention to the words of this dead man. Yes, these are the words of a dead man, words from the dead. I was already dead when I stood in front of Ziya's body."

In this passage, the survivor is speaking, but the meaning of the word "survivor" has changed slightly. In this case, the survivor should not be understood in the ordinary sense as someone who has escaped certain death, who will always bear the mark of genocidal violence, or who has survived while everyone around him has died. Here Vahakn is speaking from beyond the dead. For the first time, we hear the voice of the dead witness. He is grateful to Minas for having known what friendship is and for having "lived with [him] for a month after [he] was already dead inside." The idea of legacy resonates even stronger once Vahakn addresses Minas as the poet he is supposed to be. He gives him a poetry lesson; he teaches him the nature of poetry. Minas would only have known it from afar, abstractly, had he not inherited Vahakn's legacy. In the case of Vahakn, the event that turns him into a survivor is the murder of his Turkish friend. The murder sends him directly to the realm of the dead, beyond the mirror; it turns him into a corpse while he is still alive. Relative to the current state of survival in which Vahakn is now situated, another theme—subtle, emotional, and hidden—develops over the course of the letter: friendship.

In the last section of *The Politics of Friendship*, Jacques Derrida comments on Maurice Blanchot's various formulations of friendship. Derrida cites lines dedicated to Michel Foucault after his death,[6] commenting on the moment when Blanchot himself recalls a phrase traditionally attributed to Diogenes Laertius—"Oh my friends, there is no friend"—and adding: "It is thanks to death that friendship can be declared. Never before, never otherwise. And never if not in recalling (while thanks to death, the friend recalls that there are no friends). And when friendship is declared during the lifetime of friends, it avows, fundamentally, the same thing: it avows the death thanks to which the chance to declare itself comes at last, never failing to come."[7]

Death is what a friend offers to a friend. But if the old tradition of friendship is best expressed in the genre of the eulogy, the opposite occurs in Vahakn's letter. The dead man writes his own eulogy and addresses it to his friend. In this way, he also describes the secret of friendship. A friend always speaks from beyond the dead. The experience of friendship is one of survival. It is an offering of one's death to a friend in one's lifetime. Friendship and survival are one and the same. This is why Vahakn writes, "our friendship over these past two years . . . has brought me to this point." It brought him to this "bliss." If they had not been friends, Vahakn would not have met Ziya; he would not have died through the murder he committed; and he would not have become the survivor that he is now. Beyond his name and his letter, he would not have been able to offer his death to his friend. His happiness is in his ability to express his friendship.

Reaching "this point," where friendship and survival can be said in the same breath, where he can give death as an offering and transmit it as his legacy, Vahakn can also save his friend, toss him into the ring of life, and make him a poet. Vahakn saves Minas from the need to take his own life through killing, from the necessity of the double gift of death. It has already been done. Here emerges the central moment in Vahakn's letter and testimony. To understand this moment is to delve deep into the experience of the survivor, where "a Turcocidal impulse has been planted in each one of us. A killer plotting in the dungeon of our souls is waiting for the chance to leap out of his hiding place." If a Turcocidal impulse has truly been planted in every Armenian, if it secretly commands, and if each one of us feeds a murderer deep within ourselves, then we are all unknowing murderers. Even if we have not committed any crime, we are potential murderers. The crime that we are prepared to commit will ultimately coincide with our own death. There is no escape. "And look, this is what happens. Murder, then suicide."[8] Sparing his friend from this fate is the most precious gift Vahakn could give: "If the same opportunity arises one day, I don't want you to go the way I have."

The Poison

On January 19, 2007, the Turkish Armenian journalist Hrant Dink was assassinated in front of the headquarters of *Agos*, the newspaper he founded and edited. The terrible paradox of the assassination was that Hrant Dink represented forgiveness and reconciliation par excellence. Throughout his life he worked for a rapprochement between the two peoples, for the word "Armenian" to cease to be used as an insult in Turkish, and for the presence of his community to be recognized and accepted in Turkey, but also for Armenians—in Turkey and abroad—to finally rid themselves of the poison that has been eating away at them, of that type of resentment that the victim feels when justice has not been served. The word "poison" prompted his assassination. The perpetrator lives in the victim like an eternal poison. But it so happens that the perpetrator does have a name for the victim. Hrant Dink had worked to free the word "Turk"—the name of the perpetrator—of its weight in the minds of victims and survivors. He considered this freedom the cost of reconciliation, but he was understood by extremists in Turkey and by the official government in exactly the opposite way he had intended. He was heard as having equated them with the perpetrator. He was dragged before the courts until his assassination, which he had practically foreseen. We must, therefore, endlessly restart the work of forgiveness and reconciliation.

In 2009, I gave a series of public lectures in Istanbul to reflect on the themes of forgiveness and reconciliation with my audience, who were also my interlocutors. These lectures were held precisely in the name of friendship. They were translated into Turkish and published in one volume.[9] My examination of Vorpouni's novels is a continuation of that project. Vorpouni's novels can be read as the novels of the survivor. In particular, we see in this extraordinary novel, *The Candidate*, how the survivor speaks as the living dead. He bequeaths his death to his friend while he is still alive. He bequeaths his death so that others can live. It is a novel about friendship, but it is also a novel about forgiveness and reconciliation. The act of bequeathing one's death to a friend is the act through which the friend will find an antidote to the poison of hatred and resentment. It is the act through which the word "Turk" will no longer be associated with the perpetrator in the minds of the descendants. Vorpouni has left his novel behind as his legacy to subsequent generations. Frankly, subsequent generations have not paid much attention. Perhaps they will pay more attention to the novel's lessons about friendship and forgiveness now that the book exists in translation.

My work on the connection between art and testimony asks for two things. First, it asks for sustained attention to be paid to what happens at the boundary between "literature" and that which we call "testimony." That boundary is recorded within literature. Today, it is the task of literature to explore and test the boundary, which is quite porous. We are either on one side or the other and sometimes we do not know which side we are on. This is an entirely contemporary phenomenon that did not exist a quarter century ago and should be studied in its own right. I have been devoted to this topic not only in my *Writers of Disaster* series, but also in more specific work on texts presented as testimonies.[10] In 2007, I edited Setrak Baghdoyan's testimony on his years of deportation and survival (one of the longest testimonies in Armenian), which he spent his entire life writing and rewriting.[11] It was in the same spirit that I published the French translation of The Agony of the People. In the afterword of that book, I reflected on the aporia of testimony, prompted by the uncertainty of the boundary that separates testimony from literature. In contrast, Zabel Essayan strove for "universal consciousness" and did not concern herself with the aporia that her literary endeavor laid bare. In all of these works, the intention was to make testimony speak against itself, to show how it can fold in on itself, and to describe how it can contradict itself in its aim and conclusions. Regardless, we continue to publish testimonies as texts and not as documents intended to shape history or enhance universal memory.

To understand what Vorpouni means, we must be aware of a second parallel in real life. Besides the parallel with real testimony, there is the parallel with real murder: the terrorist attacks against Turkish diplomats in the 1970s. These attacks and murders illustrate the climate and provide a powerful counterexample to Vorpouni's intentions with his novels. They were the result of several decades of *poisoned* education that Armenian youth received around the world, particularly in the Middle East. They were initiated and encouraged by the pseudopolitical

Armenian organizations of the diaspora, and they constitute a moment of *pure shame* in the recent history of the Armenian diaspora. Was the denialist Turkish state not complicit and not an heir to the crime committed in 1915–16? Certainly. From then on, were the officers and state officials not figuratively complicit in the same crime? Without a doubt. Nolens volens. What can we conclude? That these attacks, hostage-takings, and murders were acts of justice? What justice is there in killing? No, they were murders motivated by logical yet monstrous resentment, gross political powerlessness, and a vile drive for publicity. The instigators of these murders were criminals, and not the least of their misdeeds is the harm they have done to Armenians themselves, which to this day does not prevent them from sleeping at night, confident in the righteousness of their actions. "I don't want you to go the way I have," Vahakn said in the letter to Minas and, beyond Minas, to all those he hoped would listen. Clearly those who sent young men to kill themselves and others in Turkish embassies and elsewhere did not risk ending up like him: dying to offer their death to a friend.

Ziya's murder was set in 1927 in a novel written in 1965 and published in 1967 on the eve of these assassination campaigns and terrorist attacks. Was the novel prophetic? Did it predict crimes that I argue are detrimental to the memory of the victims of 1915–16? It was certainly prophetic, but as a warning, a means of prevention, and a hope of redemption for the victims and for a future without poison and resentment for their descendants. The real murders were exactly what Vorpouni had feared and wanted to denounce in advance. In the deranged act of killing the considerate young Ziya, Vorpouni's Vahakn also kills the perpetrator in himself, whom he harbors and who forms him, who lives and acts in his place, and for whom he dies. Here we are, all of us, without exception. But this message of Vorpouni's was never heard. *The Candidate* is one of the greatest novels in the diaspora, but it came too early and from too far away. It was never read by its presumed audience—the Armenians of the diaspora—and it is entirely unknown to Armenians in Armenia, who rarely address these kinds of issues. Future generations will only hear what is said in the novel about forgiveness and reconciliation from *this* translation, if they ever hear it at all.

The Rape

In Vahakn's testimony, he describes his memories of the deportations like any other survivor described them. The difference is that Vahakn is already dead when he begins to write; he is dead as a witness, which arguably alters the status of testimony in its entirety. What Vahakn will describe, then, is torture in the proper sense of the word. Do I need to explain that the most dreadful effect of torture is the suppression of the capacity to bear witness, to kill the witness forever?[12] And yet, Vahakn tells his story. Life continued for him. He continued to live until the moment he became a murderer, but at what cost? Will we ever understand what he wrote to Minas: "Would you understand if I told you that Ziya's killer is not the one writing this note? . . . Even when I took Ziya's neck between my fingers and pressed, it seemed as though I were a witness to a crime being committed by someone else." The word translated as "witness" here is **ականատես** (*akanates*), denoting someone watching from the outside. He committed the murder and was a witness to it. The murder was committed outside of him. This schizophrenic division becomes clear as Vahakn describes how he was tortured. The torture made him a "candidate." In becoming a murderer, he put an end to this postulation, but he also put an end to his own life. He let the dead within himself—the dead produced by torture—possess him entirely.

The torture takes the form of rape. On the deportation route, Vahakn's mother died (I do not comment here on the circumstances of her death, for which her son will consider himself forever responsible) and he was adopted by a Turkish woman named Fatma. Here the terrible rape scenes appear: "That night, Fatma sowed in me the seeds of a murderer." The description is practically clinical. First, the stiffening of his body: "The skin on my body was like a thick hide that nothing could penetrate." Then abandonment and retreat, fleeing outside his body, or deeper within it, to an impregnable inner fortress, before complete petrification: "I kept hugging myself tightly, so tightly that even the force of a knife would be powerless against my strength. . . . Closing my eyes to what she was doing, I thought of my mother's blood, which was still outside on the road." His orgasm was the result of pure violence done to a body stripped of its soul forever: "The silent shudder through my heart and thighs became the last tremors of death." The following morning, he found a way to bear this coercive violence.

> It seemed that I had spent a long time in the grips of death. I had found a way to make life bearable, to forget life by living in death. This led to my quest to find the moment that opened the door to nothingness, the door that I would pass through. Can you understand that state of mind in which you can no longer feel anything, where all thought is absent? A vegetative state. What am I saying? At least a vegetable has a drive to live. It knows how to veer its course to avoid an obstacle and mount quiet, stubborn resistance against all hindrances, until at last it emerges into the light. Let's say that I was like an object that was always subdued and never showed the slightest sign of life. You throw it, it lands where you want it to land. If you throw it into a corner, it stays there. . . . Never does it ever resist. Fatma did all of these things to me and I gave in to them . . . [when] she would come to me . . . I was like a piece of timber. On the inside, I was like a wooden plank.

There is something scandalous in this scene. It is not in the conventional style of a testimony. Everything here is dumbfounding—the descriptions of Vahakn's internal division, of his need to leave his body and take shelter in an impregnable inner refuge, of his petrification, and of his transformation into a corpse. Later on, when orphan collectors take Vahakn from Fatma, his mourning can begin. Until then, it is impossible. Only then does he see the beauty of the world for the first time: "I only knew that as I was crying, a mass of emotion was dislodged in my heart . . . my mother who had lost her mind and, with pleading hands, was still calling after me, and there I was, laying on the road, stubborn and deaf to her pleas. . . . I cried for my childhood, for my tarnished, violated childhood." Through writing, Vahakn is trying to find the exact moment, however tiny in the ocean of time, which led him to become what he is now. "What was the moment that passed through his senses and was recorded and captured on film? It was the one that would eventually turn Vahakn into an inept stepson of life. In other words, what would turn him into the candidate of his Turcocidal impulse?" Here is the source of the "filth," the dirt, the feeling of being irreparably dirtied, which fuels his recurring escapes, even on his wedding night: "In any case, the filth was what I always tried to escape. Wherever I was, the filthy feeling would engulf me." He must rid himself of the filth before all else. He tried using tears to purify himself as he was leaving the village, but they did not rid his soul of the filth: "It was the feeling of being forced to scrub away four years' worth of crusty sediment and filth that suddenly made me cry with all my heart that day. . . . But it wasn't the time that had come, it was the unexpected awareness that it was coming . . . because tears wouldn't be what would wash my soul. And I waited. I waited for the idea to come on its own."

We needed to go through all of this analysis and quote Vahakn's prose to prepare for what is coming now: the most difficult, most surprising, and most violent theme in his letter/testimony. The theme of *sacrifice*, which occupies the entire remainder of Vahakn's letter and offers a response to the double enigma: the enigma of the murder and the enigma of the simultaneous suicide. Does sacrifice help solve the enigma? This is what remains to be seen.

Sacrifice and Forgiveness

We need purification. We need to purify ourselves from the filth. We need to eliminate the perpetrator we harbor in ourselves because "one day a terrible storm splattered all the mud in our land, expelled us, and settled in the depths of our souls." As a consequence, "we want to be cleansed, Minas. We want to be cleansed, so we can live." The need for purification seems straightforward, but how should it be done? The ancients made sacrifices to their gods. They spilled blood to purify themselves from the same mud, from the same sediment, and from the same filth that they certainly felt themselves. "The ancients used to spill the blood of a rooster, a lamb, or a slave, and fathers used to sacrifice their own sons to cleanse their souls." Here we see the theme of sacrifice most explicitly. Through Vahakn, Vorpouni references "pagan" ritual sacrifice as well as the Old Testament and the Akedah, a father's interrupted sacrifice of his son by divine command. But Vahakn does not stop there. He also alludes to Christian sacrificial motifs, which he interprets for his own sake. He argues that

Christ's blood no longer fulfills its role; it has become too diluted. There is too much water in that wine. Now new blood is needed to cleanse the soul and eliminate the filth of childhood. Consequently, it is under the sign of sacrifice, in the constellation of sacrifice, that Vahakn will say everything he has left to say about Ziya's murder. It is hard to believe. Is he really going to interpret the murder he committed as a sacrifice? What Vahakn has left to say involves the moment when he put his finger on Ziya's tie to brush off some ash that he might have imagined and when he plugged his ears to what Ziya was saying. What Vahakn has left to say involves the long process of maturation on his frenzied walks through the streets of Paris, until he finally understands what had happened at that moment and what Ziya meant the following day by the short note he wrote to his two Armenian friends. "Please forgive me. . . . Love is so blind that it makes me forget how sensitive you are. Once again, I ask for your forgiveness and beg you not to see any ulterior motives in my words."

Ziya, then, asks for forgiveness. In Armenian, the word "forgiveness" comes in two forms: ներէք (*nerek'*) and ներողութիւն (*neroght'iun*). There is no one word for forgiveness. Կը խնդրեմ որ ինծի ներէք (*Kë khndrem vor intsi nerek'*) and ներողութիւն կը խնդրեմ (*neroghut'iun ke khndrem*) can mean either "I apologize" or "I ask for forgiveness." The only other word in Armenian for forgiveness is թողութիւն (*t'oghut'iun*), which has a purely Christian connotation and is used for the remission of sin. The problem is that we are reading a novel, not a theological treatise. Moreover, the novel never says which language Ziya uses with his Armenian friends. Is he speaking French or Turkish? In Turkish, he could have said *özür diliyorum*, like a group of Turkish intellectuals said in December 2008. Here is the Turkish version of the petition they put online: "*1915'te Osmanlı Ermenileri'nin maruz kaldığı Büyük Felâket'e duyarsız kalınmasını, bunun inkâr edilmesini vicdanım kabul etmiyor. Bu adaletsizliği reddediyor, kendi payıma Ermeni kardeşlerimin duygu ve acılarını paylaşıyor, onlardan özür diliyorum*" (My conscience does not accept the insensitivity showed to and the denial of the Great Catastrophe that the Ottoman Armenians were subjected to in 1915. I reject this injustice and for my share, I empathize with the feelings and pain of my Armenian brothers and sisters. I apologize to them). In English, they apologized. They apologized for something they were not at all responsible for, either individually or collectively. It was disturbing. They did not say in whose name they were apologizing or in whose name they were asking for forgiveness. Was it in the name of their fathers (who were no longer alive to ask for forgiveness)? Was it in the name of the state (which had never given the slightest hint of an apology)? Or was it in the name of humanity (which could not care less)? And if they asked for forgiveness (which is less than certain), they were not asking themselves if there was anyone in front of them to respond or to grant forgiveness in any way. Moreover, as previously discussed, wasn't the inability to grant forgiveness or even to think about it the most painful, unbearable, and distant consequence of the genocidal event?

But what does Ziya—a poor, Turkish student in Paris in 1927—have to do with all of these considerations? He asks for forgiveness for not having taken into account the particular sensitivities of his Armenian friends or their vulnerabilities. Why would he have to take their sensitivities or vulnerabilities into account? The secret of these three lines is revealed slowly over the course of the novel. It is not immediately apparent to the reader or to Vahakn himself. In fact, Vahakn had not listened to what Ziya was saying the night before at the café, but his ears had nevertheless registered the content of the conversation. Or perhaps Vahakn had interpreted the conversation through the note that Ziya sent the following day. In the following lines, the "truth" is suddenly revealed in Vahakn's eyes. It comes as a complete surprise and intervenes in the novel like an anamorphosis, never to be mentioned again:

> You're to blame. Do you know why? Because you think it's natural: since you can be in love with a French woman, Ziya can be in love with an Armenian woman. It all seems so natural to you. Perhaps it is natural, but tell me, is there anything natural in our lives? In the life of an Armenian? No, don't you think he told us so tenderly about the love he had for an Armenian woman to convince us of his sympathy for the Armenians? And to go on talking of ulterior motives, when it was his goal to make us feel that motive in the right way, so that—even though we may be far from them and released from them—we will continue to suffer on these distant shores.

There was no other mention of this Armenian woman in the novel. We learn that that night at the café in Paris, Ziya had confessed his love for an Armenian woman and that the following day, he had written a note to apologize for his indiscretion by explaining the circumstances and specifying that he had no particular motives. What kind of motives could he have had? To wound? In Vahakn's eyes, Ziya had written the note to make his motives known in case they had not been paying attention the night before. Ziya asked for forgiveness to make his "insult" even clearer. This is the reason why the novel says nothing about the Armenian woman. The essential component is not what Ziya says, but his motives, or what Vahakn interprets as his motives: an insult heightened by a plea for forgiveness. But is it truly an insult? During the forgiveness campaign in 2008, did the signers add insult to injury? Some people thought that the plea did not weigh heavily enough after a century of humiliation had been added to the initial will to annihilate.[13] But the signers had little to do with this humiliation. Eighty years later, Ziya could have been one of the signers. It is true that from the 1920s until 2005, there were not many voices in Turkey that spoke out against the denialist policies of the state. The questions I raised above could be posed to the Ziyas of today. In whose name are they asking for forgiveness? A desire for appeasement and reconciliation is obvious in their actions.

In 1965 as well as in 1927, it was too early to imagine appeasement and reconciliation and clearly too early to ask for forgiveness, even fifty years after the fact. Therefore, the *novelistic* murder emerges exactly at the site of forgiveness. It emphasizes the impossibility of the latter. Conversely, through the concomitance of murder and suicide, it also strives to begin the time of forgiveness, from which we had been barred forever as the most immediate and obvious consequence of the Catastrophe. If the word "catastrophe" indeed means anything at all, it should suggest this impossibility, this malediction over our heads, and this inability to forgive the unforgivable. Jacques Derrida has the most insightful remarks on the topic:

> We often return to the issue of sovereignty. And since we are talking about forgiveness, what makes the "I forgive you" sometimes unbearable, even obscene, is the assertion of sovereignty. It addresses everything,

> confirms its own freedom or usurps the power to forgive, even as the victim or in the name of the victim. Yet, we must also think of absolute victimization, that which deprives the victim of life or of the right to speech or of this freedom, this strength and this power that authorizes, that gives access to the means to say "I forgive you." Here the unforgivable consists of depriving the victim of this right to speech, to speech itself, of possibility in all its forms, of all accounts. The victim would still be a victim, moreover, stripped of the slightest, basic possibility of potentially considering to forgive the unforgivable.[14]

Beyond the novelistic murder (i.e., the sacrificial killing of the perpetrator whom I harbor in me), the capacity for forgiveness could, therefore, be recovered. This is at least what the novel suggests, which does not mean that the formula "I forgive you" is suddenly within reach. Who are we to forgive? In whose name would we do it? Forgiveness certainly does not depend on us. And yet, beyond the Catastrophe, that which is bequeathed to the survivor is the time of forgiveness: the time that was refused *before* the Catastrophe or *because* of the Catastrophe. There was no way to imagine anything like a "moral economy of time." But, once again, why must there be a murder in a novel for us to at least consider the possibility of recovering a time of forgiveness? The enigma of Vorpouni's novel revolves around this question. With the murder committed by Vahakn, the victim takes the task of purification upon himself. The victim—represented by the figure of Vahakn—quite explicitly considers himself a high priest of sacrifice in modern times, but a high priest of sacrifice for whom the victim is so similar to himself that the two become indistinguishable. Isn't this true of all sacrifices once the blood of the sacrificed is shed?

Consequently, it is clear that Vorpouni envisages the beginning of the time of forgiveness, which is essential for us to return to humanity, within the constellation of sacrifice. The opening up of the time of forgiveness requires a sacrificial act whereby the high priest of sacrifice and the sacrificed become one. At the moment when Vahakn, the absolute victim, thinks he understands Ziya's motives, he says: "Don't you think that he told us so tenderly about the love he had for an Armenian woman to convince us of his sympathy for the Armenians?" But then what were his motives? According to Vahakn, they were to make them feel the power of blood and to derive from it a particular jouissance, however subconscious it might be.[15] If we understand Vahakn correctly, that jouissance is the epitome of a system of sacrificial domination, again no matter how symbolic and subconscious the blood of the sacrifice might be. Let us admit that it was applied on a large scale in the Ottoman Empire, the empire of sacrifice. And because the empire was run on that basis, it was (and still is) a political jouissance. Vahakn's obsession is that it will never end, no matter how far we are from the sacrificial empire. We will always be subject to the same process. It inhabits us. We have no way of freeing ourselves from it. It is this obsession with the sacrificial jouissance of the dominant group that is at play when Vahakn interprets Ziya's note: "His goal [was] to make us feel that motive in the right way, so that—even though we may be far from them and released from them—we will continue to suffer on these distant shores." Because it is sacrificial jouissance, we can only counter it with a sacrificial act and the shedding of blood—animal or human.

The primary objection we can make against Vahakn's reasoning (which perhaps is Vorpouni's reasoning as well) is that it conflates the annihilation project with the unspoken violence that circulates in the system of the empire of sacrifice—the violence that deprives the victim of all ability to mourn, to forgive, and, above all, to sacrifice. In the process of sacrifice, if the murderer and the victim are as close as they can possibly be, their relationship is still not reciprocal. Sacrifice is what forbids any kind of reciprocity. Yet these two examples of violence—annihilation and sacrifice—are not only distinct a priori, they are also conflicting. One is the opposite of the other, since the annihilation of an oppressed people brings the sacrificial system to an end once and for all. As long as the sacrificial system is perpetuated, there clearly cannot be any question of annihilation. By putting an end to the empire of sacrifice, annihilation also deprives the victim of all possible reflection on his own situation and how to overcome it.[16] As a result, only the absolute victim can bear witness to it, and only within the confines of a novel. In this sense, the rape scenes that Vahakn describes are also scenes of sacrificial violence: "In those moments, I felt as if I were a lamb about to be slaughtered, as I had seen her do, holding the animal's snout in her left hand and slitting its throat with her right."

The murder in the novel thus appears in the context of this logic of sacrifice. By committing murder, the subject never stops submitting to this logic and obviously never comes close to sacrificial jouissance. He simply lays bare for himself that he was exploited to the core and that he was the passive object of jouissance for the dominant group. It is this link that he wants to sever. But because he is one passive end of this link, he can only suppress himself. Yet Vahakn cannot stop seeing a redemptive dimension in his act, and he expresses the dimension in religious terms: purification, cleansing, and redemption, if not of the self than of others. Someone must die after committing murder before people can find the ability to forgive and before they can be freed from the presence of the Turcocidal impulse in themselves, i.e., from the potential murderer living inside them. This is the most developed aspect of Vahakn's rhetoric. In this aspect, the time of forgiveness depends entirely on the logic of sacrifice. But there is another aspect to his rhetoric, a much cruder, more primitive, more outrageous, and even more ridiculous aspect: the "three million" argument. There are supposedly three million Armenians in the world. If each one followed his hidden compulsion to kill and thereby kill himself (this is a secondary but enigmatic premise of his reasoning: for the absolute victim, to kill and to kill oneself are equivalent), there would be no Armenians left on the face of the Earth. The argument was already crude and vulgar when Vahakn reasoned that murder and suicide were equivalent and simultaneous because Armenians do not know how to hate. If they knew how to hate, murder would not be equated with suicide. The argument becomes even cruder with the realization that killing the perpetrator harbored inside of oneself does not change the state of being an absolute victim. In that case, there is no sacrifice. The sacrificial offering of death is only beneficial to someone in a position to benefit from it. Every other supposedly sacrificial act is nothing but self-destruction. Yet don't these crude arguments demonstrate the opposite of what was previously mentioned? Vahakn strives forcefully to give an antisacrificial meaning to his act. To do so, he needs a friend to whom he can transmit the meaning of his act. He needs to make his insane and irrational act sane and rational through a friend.

All of Vahakn's madness—the madness of a murderer driven to suicide—comes from the fact that he was an instrument of jouissance. Originally, he was an instrument of jouissance for Fatma. The descriptions of rape serve no other purpose. He then became an instrument of a symbolic and abstract, but all the more telling, kind of jouissance for Ziya, which explains why he sees Fatma in Ziya's gaze. The distinct identities of the gazes, the fading of one into the other, and their sudden conflation in Vahakn's disturbed mind are the expression of sacrificial jouissance. They constitute the external dimension of the feeling of having been exploited to the core: "It was there whenever I looked sharply and intently, whenever it was supposed to be there, because the fluttering of his gaze suddenly seemed close and similar—not similar but identical—to Fatma's gaze, whenever we used to quietly sit cross-legged around the low, round, wooden table to eat. Fatma's eyes would be staring at me and watching me, transfixed. . . . I would contract and tighten to become smaller and more distant."

Do you understand now why Vahakn wanted to strangle Ziya to death? Here is the answer. Apparently, it was a direct consequence of the sacrificial murder. It was a reaction to sacrificial jouissance and a way to oppose it. Behind all real testimonies lies the impossible testimony of the absolute victim, who has been the passive object of sacrificial jouissance. In the madness of murder, the absolute witness bears witness to that disavowed jouissance and to the fact that he had once been its passive object. No real testimony can bear witness to it. It must be the testimony of the living dead, the absolute victim, who is now also the absolute survivor, situated in that improbable—and purely novelistic—space between murder and suicide. Although this space is novelistic, it is not imaginary or fictional—quite the contrary. It is novelistic because in reality, or in what we call reality, the world outside of the novel, there is no space or distance between killing and dying. Why not? Because this space supposes one specific condition. It supposes that the person who kills the perpetrator in himself, and thus destroys the unbreakable bond formed with the perpetrator, has already understood that he was and still is a passive object of sacrificial jouissance. Yet in so-called real life, this is utterly impossible.

I suggested earlier that the absolute victim, or the absolute survivor, is also the absolute witness. The absolute witness is the one who awakens, but he awakens in death. The absolute witness is the dead witness, which explains why real testimonies never speak of what has really happened. They describe murders, barbaric acts, massacres, rapes, and infinite misery, but they cannot speak in the voice of the dead witness. In the same way, there can never be a testimony of torture. And yet, we must bear witness to what cannot be witnessed. No real survivor has ever been able to do such a thing. No real survivor has ever been able to say: "I have awakened in death." No one has ever been able to say: "I am killing myself because I am already dead, and I am already dead because what drives me is the will of the perpetrator, his will to make him feel jouissance. This will annihilates me entirely. It kills all possibility in me to speak, to bear witness, and to forgive." Of course, it is not from the outside that the perpetrator speaks: Vahakn hears the injunction; he does not hear anything else. And he kills. Once the injunction appears to him clearly, intensely, and inevitably, he responds to it with murder. There is no escape. At the moment he commits the murder, Fatma appears in front of him: "Yes, Minas, Fatma was there, on the knot of [Ziya's] tie." The strength he uses to kill is "the very same clenched force that [he] once used to resist Fatma."

In this chapter we have undone the threads of testimony, forgiveness, and sacrifice that make up the *The Candidate*, and we have tried to weave them back together in our own way. However, it seems that something is missing in the reconstruction. Equating murder and suicide remains what it was: an enigma. Let us repeat, in question form, everything that has been said. 1) Vahakn's madness is a sacrificial madness. Let us admit that this is the survivor's madness. Here not only is the survivor the product of a system of sacrifice, and therefore without any form of reciprocity, and not only is the murder/suicide explained by the system of sacrifice to which he was subjected, but Vahakn himself interprets his double act in sacrificial terms, as if *redemption* were possible or even real. How can we understand this? Should we take his sacrificial interpretation seriously? Should we understand that Vahakn, with his only gesture, managed to destroy the entire sacrificial structure that establishes him as insane? And finally, is it this destruction that he bequeaths to his friend through his testimony and through his death? 2) Vorpouni (the author of the novel, not his characters, Vahakn, Minas, or "Zareh") wrote a novel in which he thoroughly questioned what we call testimony and at the same time showed, described, and denounced the sacrificial obsession of the survivor. For as long as we do not grasp the inner workings of testimony or participate in our own way in the destruction of the sacrificial structure, the time of forgiveness will not begin for us. That much is clear, at least. But in the end, what is it that will be forgiven? What is there to forgive? The fact that we have been forever caught in a vicious system of sacrifice? Or the final annihilation without recourse, which was also the annihilation of this sacrificial system? 3) The novel creates an unlikely space between murder and suicide. It widens the gap between them. It is this space, this gap, which seemingly makes writing about the event possible by bequeathing death to the amanuensis. The end of sacrifice is needed for writing to be possible. But writing the event *is* the end of sacrifice, and it will happen only if it has been written. One supposes the other. What should be done with this circularity? It is as if the event is always in the future as a past event. Perhaps with the past event—in a time to come, in which the event will truly belong to the past and will arrive as a past event—will also come the possibility for forgiveness. Will it really come? Forgiveness, says Walter Benjamin, but never reconciliation.

Major Works by Zareh Vorpouni

Notes

Biographical Notes

Major Works by Zareh Vorpouni

Փորձը (The Attempt).* Marseille: Takvor Khatchiguian, 1929

Վարձու սենեակ (Room for Rent). Paris: Atmadjian, 1939[1]

Դէպի երկիր (Ճամբորդութեան յուշեր) (Toward the Country: Travel Notes). Paris: Araxe, 1948

Անձրեւոտ օրեր (Rainy Days). Paris: Amsoreag, 1958

Եւ եղեւ մարդ (And There Was Man). Paris: Unknown publisher, 1964

Գոհարիկ եւ ուրիշ պատմուածքներ (Koharig and Other Stories). Beirut: Sevan, 1966

Թեկնածուն (*The Candidate*).* Beirut: Sevan, 1967

Ասֆալթը (The Asphalt).* Istanbul: Marmara, 1972

Սովորական օր մը (A Regular Day).* Beirut: Sevan, 1974

Մահազդ (Death Notice).* Գամ (Gam) 1 (1980): 15–74

Ձի քո է կարողութիւն (For Thine Is the Power).* Գամ (Gam) 6 (1982): 41–81

Վարձու սենեակ (Room for Rent).* Գայք (Gayk) 5 (1993): 45–61 (excerpts)

*indicates that the novel is part of the Հալածուածները (The Persecuted) series.[2]

Notes

Translator's Introduction

1. For a detailed study of Armenian diaspora literature in France, see Krikor Beledian, *Cinquante ans de littérature arménienne en France: du même à l'autre, 1922–1972* (Paris: Centre national de la recherche scientifique, 2001), and Talar Chahinian, "The Paris Attempt: Rearticulation of (National) Belonging and the Inscription of Aftermath Experience in French Armenian Literature between the Wars" (PhD dissertation, Univ. of California, Los Angeles, 2008).

2. In contrast to Western Armenian, Eastern Armenian was the standardized language of the Armenians of the Russian Empire (later the Soviet Union and the Republic of Armenia) and the Persian Empire (later Iran).

3. Only two book-length works from this period have been published in English translation: Nigoghos Sarafian, *The Bois de Vincennes*, trans. Christopher Atamian (Dearborn, MI: Armenian Research Center, 2011), and Shahan Shahnour, *Retreat without Song*, trans. Mischa Kudian (London: Mashtots Press, 1982).

4. Krikor Beledian and Haroutiun Kurkjian, "Avec 'un habitant de la diaspora': Zareh Vorpouni, écrivain," *Hayasdan Monthly* 388 (1978): 13.

The Candidate

1. In Armenian, աղուոր (*aghvor*) and աղուորիկ (*aghvorig*) mean pretty or nice. The latter is the diminutive.

2. "Les bourgeois, on les pendra" (We will hang the bourgeois) is one of the refrains of "Ah, ça ira ! Ça ira !" an anthem of the French Revolution.

3. In September 1922, the majority of the Greeks and Armenians of Smyrna fled the city after the burning and pillaging of their neighborhoods by Turkish nationalist forces.

4. This is the first line of the song Անդրանիկի քայլերգը (The March of Antranig), an Armenian revolutionary song. The *Tashnagtsioutioun*, or the Armenian Revolutionary Federation, is an Armenian political party that formed in the late nineteenth century to achieve national liberation for Armenians in the Ottoman Empire. Sassoun, a town in

Eastern Anatolia, was the site of two uprisings against the Ottoman authorities in 1894 and 1904.

5. Հեթանոս երգեր (Pagan Songs) is a collection of poems published in 1912 by Ottoman Armenian poet Taniel Varoujan.

6. Vahan Tekeyan (1878–1945) is a celebrated Armenian poet. He was one of the few intellectuals to survive the Armenian genocide and continue to write in the diaspora.

7. *Fasouliayi pilaki* is a cold white bean dish made with carrots and tomatoes. In the text, Vorpouni uses the Turkish name of the recipe, more familiar to Ottoman Armenians.

8. La Source was a café on Boulevard Saint-Michel frequented by Armenian writers and intellectuals in Paris in the 1920s and 1930s.

9. Ծնծղայ (*dzndzgha*) are cymbals used during the Divine Liturgy of the Armenian Apostolic Church.

10. Turkish: "my son, my son."

11. In the years following the Armenian genocide, Armenian organizations, with the help of the Allied powers, organized missions to recover Armenian orphans who had been living in Turkish homes and to reintegrate them into the Armenian community.

12. Harpagon is the title character in the play *L'Avare* (*The Miser*) by Molière. His name is associated with stinginess and selfishness.

13. From 1894 to 1936, Les Halles received nightly deliveries between 1:00 a.m. and 4:00 a.m. on a special railway called l'Arpajonnais, which brought merchandise from Arpajon, a town south of Paris.

14. François Villon (1431–63?) was a poet who lived in Paris and was accused of killing a priest and stealing money from the chapel of the Collège de Navarre. He was banished from Paris for his crimes and disappeared after 1463.

15. The "horned" church refers to L'Église Saint-Vincent-de-Paul, also known as Église des Réformés, in Marseille. Its nickname alludes to its two spires.

16. "Cry, my son. Cry so you may grow up" is an adaptation of the last line of Vahan Tekeyan's poem Կա՛նձրեւէ, տղաս (It's Raining, My Son).

17. Բամբ Որոտան (Pamp Vorodan) is an Armenian national march, considered the unofficial anthem of the Armenian diaspora in the 1920s and 1930s.

18. Monsieur Jourdain is the title character in the play *Le Bourgeois gentilhomme* (*The Bourgeois Gentleman*) by Molière. The character is known for his affectations and pretensions.

19. In this passage, Vorpouni plays with the word ապրիլ (*abril*), which means both "April" and "to live."

20. "*La Marquise sortit à cinq heures*" (The marquise left at five o'clock) is a phrase first coined by Paul Valéry to describe the potential for banality in the novel.

21. Marquise de Sévigné is a chocolate shop in Paris.

22. "Who knows how to read the heart" is the last line of Vahan Tekeyan's poem Ես սիրեցի (I Loved).

Afterword

1. The other published volumes in the series include Ասֆալթը (Asfaltë) and Սովորական օր մը (Sovorakan or më). The fifth volume remains to be published and the sixth volume was published in the second issue of the periodical Կամ (Gam) in 1982. Very little has been written about Vorpouni: a few articles after his first novel was published in 1929; an article by Haroutiun Kurkjian in the periodical Բագին (Pagin) in 1966 about Vorpouni's rediscovery after the publication of And There Was Man; and sections by Krikor Beledian in Armenian in Մարտ (Mart; Beirut: Catholicosate of the Holy See of Cilicia, 1998) and in French in *Cinquante ans de littérature arménienne en France: du même à l'autre, 1922–1972* (Paris: Centre national de la recherche scientifique, 2001). The newspaper Հորիզոն (Horizon) in Montreal also devoted a special issue to Vorpouni in its literary supplement in December 1985.

2. Zabel Essayan (1879–1943) was the most distinguished Armenian novelist at the beginning of the twentieth century. She was also the only woman on the black list of Armenian intellectuals rounded up on April 24, 1915. One of her greatest achievements, Աւերակներուն մէջ (Averaknerun mej), her testimony about the anti-Armenian pogroms in Adana and the surrounding region in 1909, was first published in 1911 and translated into English in 2015. See Zabel Yessayan (sic), *In the Ruins*, trans. G. M. Goshgarian (Boston: Armenian International Women's Association Press, 2015).

3. For more about the interdiction of mourning, see Marc Nichanian, "Zabel Essayan: The End of Testimony and the Catastrophic Turnabout," in *Writers of Disaster* (London: Gomidas Institute, 2002), a different version of which has been published in *Loss: The Politics of Mourning*, ed. David L. Eng and David Kazanjian (Berkeley: Univ. of California Press, 2003). For more on the manipulation of mourning in South Africa, see Marc Nichanian, "Mourning and Reconciliation" in *Living Together: Jacques Derrida's Communities of Violence and Peace*, ed. Elisabeth Weber (New York: Fordham Univ. Press, 2013). See also the remarkable essay by Mark Sanders, "Ambiguities of Mourning: Law, Custom, and Testimony of Women before South Africa's Truth and Reconciliation Commission," in *Loss: The Politics of Mourning*. For more about the same manipulation of mourning in Turkish Kurdistan, see Hişyar Özsoy, "Between Gift and Taboo: Death and the Negotiation of National Identity and Sovereignty in the Kurdish Conflict in Turkey" (PhD dissertation, Univ. of Texas at Austin, 2010), and Özsoy's article in Turkish, "Şeyh Said'in Kayıp Mezarı: Kürtlerin Egemenlik Mücadelesinde Hafıza-Mekan Diyalektiği," *Toplum ve Kuram* 9 (2014): 307–38.

4. Walter Benjamin, *Selected Writings, Volume I: 1913–1926*, eds. Marcus Bullock and Michael W. Jennings (Cambridge, MA: Harvard Univ. Press, 2004): 286–87.

5. Hayg Toroyan and Zabel Essayan, *L'Agonie d'un peuple* (The Agony of a People), trans. Marc Nichanian (Paris: Garnier, 2013).

6. Jacques Derrida, *The Politics of Friendship*, trans. George Collins (London: Verso, 2005): 300.

7. Ibid., 302.

8. In Armenian, the word for murder is սպանութիւն (*spanut'iun*) and the word for suicide is ինքնասպանութիւն (*ink'naspanut'iun*), the act of killing oneself. Vahakn here formulates the enigma of absolute equivalence, of the quasi simultaneity or the necessary relation of cause and effect between the murder and the suicide, without giving any explanation for that equivalence or necessity.

9. Marc Nichanian, *Edebiyat ve Felaket* (Literature and Catastrophe), trans. Ayşegül Sönmezay (Istanbul: Iletişim, 2011).

10. The three volumes in the series have been published in French under the general title *Entre l'art et le témoignage* (Geneva: MétisPresse, 2006 and 2008). Only volumes one and two are available in English translation: *Writers of Disaster, The National Revolution* (London: Gomidas Institute, 2002), and *Mourning Philology*, trans. G. M. Goshgarian and Jeff Fort (New York: Fordham Univ. Press, 2014).

11. Setrak Baghdoyan, Երբ դրախտը դարձաւ դժոխք (*Yerb drakhdë dardzav dzhokhk'*), ed. Marc Nichanian (Los Angeles: Abril, 2007).

12. See Marc Nichanian, "The Death of the Witness," in *History Unlimited: Probing the Ethics of Holocaust Culture*, eds. Claudio Fogu, Wulf Kansteiner, and Todd Presner (Cambridge, MA: Harvard Univ. Press, forthcoming). This chapter takes up a debate begun twenty years earlier in *Probing the Limits of Representation: Nazism and the "Final Solution,"* ed. Saul Friedländer (Cambridge, MA: Harvard Univ. Press, 1992) and at the conference of the same name. I evoke this debate in the third chapter of my book *Historiographic Perversion*, trans. Gil Anidjar (New York: Columbia Univ. Press, 2009). It concerns both the status of testimony and the nature of the catastrophic event. On the subject of the murder of the witness as the primary intent or supreme effect of torture, see Idelber Avilar, *The Letter of Violence: Essays on Narrative, Ethics, and Politics* (New York: Palgrave, 2004): 47–49.

13. One of the most radical reactions to the forgiveness campaign came from Ayda Erbal. See Ayda Erbal, "Mea Culpas, Negotiations, Apologies: Revisiting the 'Apology' of Turkish Intellectuals," in *Reconciliation, Civil Society, and the Politics of Memory: Transnational Initiatives in the 20th and 21st Century*, ed. Birgit Schwelling (New York: Columbia Univ. Press, 2012): 51–96. Erbal's question is precisely the one described in this chapter: What are these few words of apology when they come after a century of denigration and humiliation of the victim?

14. This excerpt is taken from Derrida's interview on *Le Monde des débats* in December 1999. See Jacques Derrida, *On Cosmopolitanism and Forgiveness*, trans. Mark Dooley and Michael Hughes (New York: Routledge, 2001): 58–59.

15. The term "jouissance" encompasses meanings not found in the English words "enjoyment," "pleasure," or "bliss." In this case, jouissance is used in the Lacanian sense and is connected not only to psychoanalysis and transgression, but to domination and sexual pleasure. Here the word is left untranslated and not italicized, as it is found in English translations of Lacan's work.

16. With regard to the "sacrificial system" in the empire, see my essay, "L'Empire du sacrifice," *L'Intranquille* 1 (1992): 61–120, and my studies on the work of Hagop Oshagan in *Le Roman de la Catastrophe* (Geneva: MétisPresse, 2008), in particular chapters three through six, which deal with the sacrificial exploitation of the voice. I have also written about these questions in Armenian: "Երգին գերին" (*Yergin gerin*), *Hask Armenological Review* 7–8 (1995–96): 283–308, and "Աղբիւրի ակին, վրէպը վէպին մէջ" (*Aghbiuri akin, vrêbë vêbin mej*), Յակոբ Օշական: Գիտաժողովի նիւթեր (*Hakob Oshakan: Gitazhoghovi niut'er*), ed. Lilit Galstyan (Yerevan: Yerevan State Univ. Press, 2011): 84–126.

Major Works by Zareh Vorpouni

1. Վարձու սենեակ (Room for Rent) was published in 1939, but the book was not released until 1945 because of the turmoil of World War II.

2. The seventh novel in Հալածուածները (The Persecuted) series, Տիգրանուշի եւ Նուարդ (Dikranoushie and Nvart), is unpublished.

Biographical Notes

Zareh Vorpouni

Zareh Vorpouni, ca. 1978. Courtesy of *Hayasdan Monthly*, Paris.

Zareh Vorpouni (né Euksuzian) was born in May 1902 in the Ottoman town of Ordu along the Black Sea. In 1915, his father was killed during the Armenian genocide and Vorpouni, along with his mother and siblings, found refuge with a Turkish family before escaping to Sebastopol, Crimea. In 1919, the family immigrated to Constantinople and Vorpouni resumed his education at the Berberian School with the few Western Armenian writers who survived the genocide. His first piece of writing—a poem entitled Գառնուկս (My Lamb)—was published during this period in the newspaper Ժողովուրդի ձայն (Voice of the People), which was edited at that time by his teacher, poet Vahan Tekeyan.

In August 1922, Vorpouni fled Constantinople in the months of turmoil before the founding of the Turkish Republic. In the 1920s, he lived in Marseille and Paris, joined the Communist Party, and worked a variety of odd jobs. During this time, Vorpouni edited two Armenian-language journals, Նոր Հաւատք (New Faith) and Երեւան (Yerevan), and he published his short stories and essays in the dozens of French Armenian literary reviews of the era, including Անահիտ (Anahid) and Անի (Ani). It was in Yerevan that a version of his first novel, The Attempt, appeared as a short story in 1927. For exact citations of his works in these journals, see Kevork B. Bardakjian, *A Reference Guide to Modern Armenian Literature, 1500–1920* (Detroit: Wayne State Univ. Press, 2000): 445.

In 1939, Vorpouni was drafted into the French army, captured by the German army, and lived as a prisoner of war in Magdeburg until the armistice in 1945. He returned to literature in 1958 while spending his days working at a restaurant in Paris. Vorpouni's crowning literary legacy is Հալածուածները (The Persecuted), a series of seven novels in which *The Candidate* is the second.

Vorpouni died in 1980 in Bagneux, a suburb of Paris.

Contributors

JENNIFER MANOUKIAN is a writer and translator of Western Armenian and French. She earned her master's degree from the Department of Middle East, South Asian, and African Studies at Columbia University and her bachelor's degree from the Departments of French and Middle Eastern Studies at Rutgers University. Her first translation—*The Gardens of Silihdar*, the memoir of Ottoman Armenian writer Zabel Yessayan—was published in 2014.

ISHKHAN JINBASHIAN is an author, art critic, and translator of literary works. Formerly an editor with *Armenian International Magazine* and *The Armenian Reporter*, he is the author of the Armenian-language novel Արխիւ հասնումի (Archive of Arrival). His more than twenty English translations include Aram Sahakian's *Our Cross*, Mikayel Shamtanchian's *The Fatal Night*, Yeghishe Charents's *The Nayirian Dauphin*, Vahan Totovents's *New York*, and Sebuh Aguni's *The Crime of the Ages*.

MARC NICHANIAN was professor of Armenian Studies at Columbia University until 2007, after which he began to teach regularly as a visiting professor at Sabancı University. His most recent publications are *Mourning Philology* in English, *Patker, patum, patmut'iun* (Image, Story, History) in Armenian, and *Le Sujet de l'histoire: Vers une phénoménologie du survivant* in French. He has also published Armenian translations of three novels by Maurice Blanchot.